Ancient Protector

Ancients Rising Series

KATIE REUS

Cover Art by Sweet 'N Spicy Designs
Editor: Julia Ganis
Author Website: https://katiereus.com

Ancient Protector/Katie Reus.—1st ed.

ISBN-13: 9781635561418

Thank you to Claire Robinson, Erin McRae, and Toni & Gary Anderson for helping me with the Scottish phrases and language.

PRAISE FOR THE NOVELS OF KATIE REUS

"Exciting in more ways than one, well-paced and smoothly written, I'd recommend *A Covert Affair* to any romantic suspense reader." —Harlequin Junkie

"Sexy military romantic suspense." —USA Today

"I could not put this book down. . . . Let me be clear that I am not saying that this was a good book *for* a paranormal genre; it was an excellent romance read, *period.*" —All About Romance

"Reus strikes just the right balance of steamy sexual tension and nail-biting action….This romantic thriller reliably hits every note that fans of the genre will expect." —*Publishers Weekly*

"Prepare yourself for the start of a great new series! . . . I'm excited about reading more about this great group of characters." —Fresh Fiction

"Wow! This powerful, passionate hero sizzles with sheer deliciousness. I loved every sexy twist of this fun & exhilarating tale. Katie Reus delivers!" —Carolyn Crane, RITA award winning author

"A sexy, well-crafted paranormal romance that succeeds with smart characters and creative world building."—Kirkus Reviews

"*Mating Instinct*'s romance is taut and passionate . . . Katie Reus's newest installment in her Moon Shifter series will leave readers breathless!" —Stephanie Tyler, *New York Times* bestselling author

Part I
Before The Fall

CHAPTER 1

Starling, better known as Star to her millions of fans, stepped out of the luxurious en suite into the bedroom she and her band were using before the big show in a few hours.

"Breathe," Bella snapped at her. Bella, her PR manager, and also one of her best friends, gave her a pointed look. She'd pulled her long, inky black hair into a tight chignon and done some sort of swooping thing with her eyeliner today, giving her eyes an even more dramatic look. And in typical Bella style, she'd worn an all-white pantsuit with a sheer red camisole peeking out from the V of the buttoned-up, fitted jacket. She looked like the boss she was. Yeah, Star was the Alpha of their misfit pack, but Bella kept them all in line and organized. "Breathe in and out, slowly."

Star pasted on a smile because at this point they weren't sure if they were being watched by the owner of this massive estate in Wales.

Star was a world-famous singer but she was also very private, and Oscar—aka Osgar, Alpha of the Rabec clan and the ancient dragon shifter who owned this place—liked mysteries. He also liked things that didn't belong to him. Something she knew firsthand because the monster had kidnapped Star's sister.

Star was here to get Aurora back. They all were.

For an entire year they'd been searching for Aurora, and now that they'd found her, they weren't leaving without her. Star would burn this entire place to the ground before she did that.

Bella's snapped orders were a reminder, however. Because as of now they had to assume they were being watched or listened to at all times. They'd scanned the suite for listening devices and hadn't found anything, but they weren't taking any chances. "I know, I'm just nervous about the show tonight." *Lies, lies, lies.* She didn't give a crap about the show. None of them did. Her only goal was to free her sister and escape.

They'd already accomplished step one of their plan—getting the invite to this exclusive estate. It had only taken a damn year. An entire year's worth of planning had finally culminated in this one night.

There was no room for error because her sister's life depended on it.

Hell, all their lives depended on it. Because if they were caught by Oscar or his clanmates, it would be a battle to the death. And she had no doubt that they would end up revealing themselves to the humans here at the manor.

Because Star wasn't walking away without her sister, even if she had to reveal to the entire world what she was. The humans would get a big surprise when they found out they weren't at the top of the food chain.

"You look fantastic so I hope you're ready for the first part of the evening." Bella pulled out her tablet and started tapping away on it even though Star knew the woman had their entire schedule memorized.

Star glanced over at Brielle, who was standing by one of the oversized, bullet-resistant windows. Gauzy cream-colored drapes were pulled over them, but Brielle was still peering outside at the fountain in the middle of the formal garden. Past that, a huge stage had been set up so that tonight's show would take place under a blanket of stars. The stage itself had been set up days ago, a huge monstrosity large enough to hold multiple bands and production people at a time.

"Why do I have to do this stupid auction?" Star grumbled. She wasn't acting now for potential cameras or listening devices; she really did hate this part of the evening. But she hadn't been able to say no to the celebrity auction. She had to appear agreeable and easy to work with because they hadn't wanted to risk getting cut from the band lineup—and losing their invite to the estate altogether.

She was only one of the headliners, and if Oscar decided on a whim to cut her out of the show, sure her fans would have been disappointed, but the show would go on without her. So Star was taking part in a stupid "celebrity auction." All she wanted to do was start the show because while she was singing and creating a distraction, part of her team would be breaking Aurora out of the underground dungeon they were ninety-nine percent sure she was being held in.

"Wah, wah," murmured Brielle, not looking away from the window. Her auburn hair was pulled back into a long braid, showing off sharp cheekbones. The tiger shifter was about five feet eleven and stunning both in human and tiger form. "Want some cheese with that whine?"

"Yes, please don't whine," Bella added. "It's not becoming."

"I never promised that," Star murmured, half-smiling even as the ball of tension curled tighter in her stomach. They'd come so far and were so close to their endgame.

"Come on." Bella sighed and linked her arm through Star's. "Time to get out there."

Bella was about five foot two, petite and graceful as almost all feline shifters were. Bella was a rare snow leopard shifter. Her great-grandparents had emigrated from the Sichuan Province in China soooo many years ago, given how long shifters lived. Bella spoke eight languages and was one of the smartest people Star knew.

Bella was also one of four snow leopards on Star's crew. Which was why the majority of supernaturals who knew that her band was in fact supernatural assumed that Star was a snow leopard as well. And she liked it that way. Snow leopards might be rare but they were shifters just the same as all the others across the planet. There was no reason to kidnap her for that alone. But if anyone knew what Star was... If Oscar figured out that Star was Aurora's big sister, they'd all become targets because he would want to kidnap Star too. Quickly she banished the thought.

As they headed for the door, Brielle peeled off from where she was standing near the window and reached the door first in a few long strides. Brielle's twin sister Harlow was waiting outside and they fell into a formation around Star and Bella as they headed down the long hallway. Both tigers had been allowed knives—which were discreetly hidden under their black jackets. But there were no guns allowed on the premises, which was more of a country law than anything.

Not that it mattered. None of them needed guns or knives. Not when they could use their claws or turn into animals. And Star didn't need anything but her fire and power.

"The announcer will call you up on stage and the bidding will start at ten thousand," Bella said.

"Ten thousand?" Brielle murmured from her position in front of Star. "Seems like too much for such a scrawny thing."

"Hey!" Star protested.

"I'm just saying, I've seen you in the morning with bed head before your coffee. You're scary."

Behind them Harlow simply snickered but didn't say anything, which was pretty standard for the twins. Brielle talked shit and Harlow laughed.

Star sniffed imperiously but was glad for the bit of levity. She needed to stay in control, and not focus on the fact that her sister was in this compound, so damn close and yet so far. Because if she focused too much on that, she would lose her mind and put everyone else in danger. So she understood what her friend was doing, understood that she was trying to keep her calm.

"As I was saying," Bella continued. "The bidding will start at ten thousand and from there it will go up. You know what an auction is like. Afterward, I'll introduce you to whoever the highest bidder is and promise to set up a date later."

Star simply snorted. She understood that it was for charity, but why not just give the money to charity instead of bidding on a date with her and a bunch of others?

"Sounds good," was all she said instead as they stepped into an oversized ballroom with a couple hundred people already there. These were the VIPs who'd been let into the estate early before the big show in an hour.

Now that she was out in the open, she kept her fake, "superstar" smile in place. It was go time.

Before she could move farther into the room, suddenly Oscar was there—huge and imposing. Star resisted the urge to suck in a breath. She could sense the power rolling off him and had a feeling that humans could even feel it too. They might not know what they were experiencing, but they would understand that this male was a predator. And right now as he looked at her with far too much curiosity, her heart rate increased.

"Mr. Rabec," she said, keeping her voice light and pleased even though she wanted to set his ten-thousand-dollar suit on fire with him still wearing it.

He smiled at her, all charm and grace dripping from him, but she saw past the thin, civilized veneer. His dark eyes had a vastness to them, a deadness. "Star, I've told you to call me Oscar." His voice was lightly accented, a weird British and maybe Norwegian mix. "I hope you're excited about the auction tonight."

"Oh, of course," she lied through her teeth.

He chuckled lightly, probably scenting her lie, but whatever. His sandy brown hair was thick and gorgeous, and again, she had the urge to just shave it all off. "I know it's a pain but it's for such a good cause. I'm sure you'll fetch a nice price."

Eww, gross. She kept her smile in place. "Well, it's all for a good cause." And that was the truth at least.

"You know, I must say you have the most unique colored eyes. I think I've only seen that shade on one or two others in my life." He watched her closely then.

She resisted the urge to squirm under his scrutiny and laughed lightly. "Well, I'll tell you a secret," she said, leaning in slightly. "I'm wearing contacts. Purple is all part of my branding." She *was* wearing contacts—clear, useless ones for this reason exactly. If a supernatural someone commented on her eye color—and boy, did they ever—she could say she was wearing contacts and not lie.

"Ah, of course!" Something inside him seemed to ease then and he turned away as one of his security goons murmured something to him. "Well," he said, turning back to her. "Good luck at the auction. I cannot wait to hear you perform tonight."

"Thanks." She might have murmured something else polite but her blood had chilled over as Bella started leading her through the room.

Despite the throng of people in the room, a chill rolled over her but she fought it off. For the charity auction she'd opted to wear a Band-Aid-sized sparkly, purple dress. Purple was her signature color—she hadn't been kidding about the branding thing. The color thing was Bella's idea and her friend was a freaking genius when it came to PR stuff. And if it hadn't been for her, Star wouldn't have shot to stardom as fast as she had.

Yeah, she could sing, but all that other stuff? She was clueless about. Thankfully Bella, and Lola, another member of their crew who was in charge of marketing and web stuff, knew what they were doing. Not to mention Lola had another skill: hacking.

Because of her friends, they were able to enact this rescue plan. It was something Star would never forget for as long as she lived. Blood didn't always make you family.

As they stepped farther into the ballroom, Bella moved a few feet away from Star as a couple photographers moved toward her. The picture takers were all corralled behind a set of ropes, even in the huge ballroom, which Star thought was a smart move on the organizers' part. Star was aware of the twins nearby, but ignored everyone as she put her hand on her hip, turned her left foot out and gave the cameras her left side. Which according to Bella was her best side.

"Is it true that you're dating Mason Brown?" one of the photographers yelled out.

She simply smiled and posed for another picture, ignoring the question. The name sounded vaguely familiar—maybe he was an actor. She certainly didn't know the guy, however.

Moments later, Bella swooped right back in and guided her toward a waiting area next to the stage. This area had also been roped off but there was a table set up with bottled water, flutes of champagne, caviar and a bunch of other stuff. Apparently this was only for the people being auctioned off. "Here you go. Auction starts in four minutes," Bella murmured. "You're the first one up." Then her friend disappeared back behind the ropes and started talking to the PR person of another individual involved in the auction.

Someone she recognized from a television show, though their name was escaping Star at the moment, had a microphone and notecards in hand as they prepped for the auction.

The whole room was a cacophony of noise with well-dressed people, mostly in formal dresses and dark suits. But she was taking in the exits, scanning for familiar faces. Axel, who was the only male in her security team, was off now doing recon with two of her backup vocalists. She trusted them to do their part in all of this, but was still nervous. She couldn't help it. Her sister's life depended on it.

Beyond the roped-off area near the stage, servers carrying trays of champagne flutes milled about, blending into the background incredibly well. Unlike the glittering dresses of so many of the women here, the servers wore all black and a few of them looked as if they doubled as security as well. She couldn't know for sure, but according to what her team had found out, Oscar had strictly locked down his entire estate and had private security—aka his own dragon clanmates. So if she had to guess, some or all of the servers were dragons. But about half of the guests had to be human.

"You look gorgeous." A familiar male voice made her turn and smile.

"Jaxtyn." Star had no idea if that was his real name or a stage name but it suited the human. Tonight he had on a slim-fitting suit jacket—a clearly custom-cut dark blue and gold sequin jacket, which should have looked ridiculous. But with a buff body like his, Jaxtyn pulled it off. The television personality always had a smile on his handsome face and there was a genuineness to him that couldn't be faked. Something she found to be rare in the industry. "You look incredible yourself. Do you just live in the gym now?" she asked.

Jaxtyn laughed lightly, revealing perfect white teeth. "I've been going a little overboard with the running lately. It seems to be the only peace I get. I wish someone had told me that fame came with such a price."

Star understood that. Where she was in her career now, she'd lost the right to privacy. As soon as she rescued her sister, however, she was done with all of this. No more touring. Nothing. She would do anything to keep her sister safe. And disappearing was the only way to do that. It would be hard, but supernaturals had been doing it for ages. "No kidding. So did I see that you're going to be on some sort of ballroom dancing show?"

"Yep. My manager just made the announcement—"

He stopped as a well-dressed man spoke into the microphone, smiling broadly at the crowd. "If everyone will please quiet down, it's time for the celebrity auction!"

"I hear you're up first," Jaxtyn murmured, whisper-quiet.

"Yep." Yay her.

"I saw some delicious-looking men in the audience. I just hope someone bids on me. Can you imagine if *no one* bids?" He shuddered and she scented a faint trickle of real worry from him, so she nudged him with her hip.

"You're going to have multiple bids. Like...a dozen at least. Come on, you're gorgeous."

He smiled and shrugged but she could still smell the fear. And considering she didn't have the scent capabilities of most shifters, the fact that she could scent it at all told her he was truly nervous about tonight. Which seemed crazy to her. The man was stunning and talented.

"...Star, step up on stage!"

She blinked and realized that she'd been announced. Jaxtyn gave her a winning smile, as did the other singers and celebrities she passed as she stepped up the stairs onto the dais. Flashes went off as she strode across the platform and she focused on a random spot near the back so she wouldn't get distracted. It made it easier to keep her smile in place as she did what she thought of as her "Miss Universe wave" to the audience.

There were a few wolf whistles and cheers as she stepped up to the announcer.

"I don't need to introduce this rising star!" He laughed at his own pun and she hid a wince. "Star is a first-timer at this auction so let's start tonight off right! The bidding usually starts at ten thousand but I think we should start at fifteen—"

"Fifteen!" A male voice shouted somewhere from her left before he'd even finished.

"Twenty!" a woman called out.

"Twenty-five!"

"Thirty-five!"

"I like the enthusiasm! Let's see if we can get it to—"

"One million dollars," a deep male voice called out from...somewhere.

Star blinked as a hush spilled over the crowd, men and women turning around, then turning to look at each other. Her heart rate kicked up as she digested the bid. A million dollars?

What. The. Hell.

CHAPTER 2

Star realized she was staring into the crowd with a shocked expression at the million-dollar bid. She quickly jerked back to reality and smiled as she leaned toward the microphone. "I think we're going to call it," she said, laughing. "Unless someone else wants to pony up another million?"

That earned a laugh from the crowd even as her heart raced out of control. She couldn't imagine anyone bidding that much on a date. For anyone. Seriously, it was just dinner and the screening of some movie, like two weeks before it was released. That was it. And it was going to be chaperoned. Bella had confirmed it with the other PR people in charge of this whole charity thing.

If the person who'd bid on her thought they were getting anything else from her, they were out of their damn mind. But she'd learned over the years that some people had more money than sense, and thought that entitled them to whatever they wanted.

The announcer closed the bidding even as she started walking off the stage on the opposite side. Just as quickly, he announced Jaxtyn's name as the next victim. As Star descended the stairs, she looked over her shoulder to see Jaxtyn sashaying onto the stage and waving at the crowd.

Someone shouted out a bid even before the announcer had started the first offer. *Good for him.*

Before she'd taken one step off the stairs, Brielle and Harlow surrounded her as Bella stepped up in front of her.

"A Scottish man named Lachlan bid on you," Bella said, her voice subvocal so that only Star could hear among this crowd filled with supernaturals.

"And?"

"And he's a reclusive billionaire. That's literally all I know. I already talked to Lola and she said she needs more time to dig." Lola was the reason they knew Aurora was here at all. Bella continued. "His name and a brief description are literally all I got from the organizer."

"I hope he doesn't think he's getting—"

A huge, broad-shouldered man stepped into her path and the twins moved lightning fast in front of her, their body language defensive.

He lifted a dark eyebrow as he glanced between the two of them before briefly dismissing them and focusing on Star, who stood behind them. There was more than enough room between Brielle and Harlow for her to get a good view of the man.

She blinked, startled at the arc of electricity she experienced as their gazes collided. She felt that dark, smoldering look all the way to her core. Smoldering? That was a thing, right? Because he had it in spades. His eyes were a dark, almost indigo blue and she wondered if in the right light they'd have a violet glint. Not that she cared. Good God, stop staring, she ordered herself. But she found herself mesmerized by those eyes as everything else around them fell away. The crowd. The annoying announcer. Even her packmates. There was a strange scent in the air…and it made her lightheaded. For some strange reason, she felt as if they'd met before—which made no sense. But deep in her core, she felt like she knew this man.

Until he gave her a slow, wicked smile. The smugness broke her free of whatever was going on in her head right now. She had no time for a smug male. Ever. But definitely not right now.

"My name is Lachlan," the male rumbled, his Scottish accent fainter than she'd heard from other Scotsmen. It was lovely all the same. And the male was most definitely a shifter of some kind.

He was too big not to be, and he had a very distinctive masculine—animalistic—scent that said he wasn't human. It reminded her of wide-open skies and springtime.

"Of course." Bella gently nudged the twins out of the way and held out a hand for him. "I'm Bella, Star's manager. The organizer let me know you were the winning bidder. Congratulations Mr., ah…"

"Lachlan is fine." He simply nodded, not taking his gaze off Star. "I saw you sing live last month. You were incredible." His complimentary words were blunt.

She wasn't great at scenting truth or lies, not like other shifters. Technically she was a shifter but she was...different from the others. Still, she didn't scent any lies rolling off him. And really, what would be the point of lying to her about that? Smiling politely at the compliment even as it warmed her from the inside out, she said, "Thank you. Where did you see me?"

"Denmark."

She nodded. She'd done a couple shows there before heading to London. "I'm glad you enjoyed the show."

"You have a real gift." Sincerity and a hint of something else laced his beautifully accented words. *Damn, that voice.*

And for the briefest moment she saw a flash of his animal in his eyes. It was so damn fast that if she hadn't been staring, or if she hadn't known about the existence of shifters, she'd have probably convinced herself it was a trick of the light. But she knew what she'd seen. This tall, sexy man was a dragon.

Haaaaaard pass.

Oh God, did he know what she was? No, she was so careful to keep her identity a secret. And she still wasn't sure how Oscar had discovered what Aurora was. And yeah, intellectually she knew that "not all dragons are bad," but damn. *No, no, no.*

"I would love to talk with you—"

"I'm so sorry Mr., ah, Lachlan," Bella said, cutting him off in that efficient way of hers. Petite she might be, but she was a force of nature. A tiny tornado, Brielle called her. She gently grasped Star's arm and started moving even as she continued. "We have a show to get ready for and less than an hour to do it. I'll be in contact with your assistant for—"

"Contact me personally. Any time of day or night. The organizer has all my information on file." He might have responded to Bella, but his penetrating gaze was still on Star.

Unnerved by that look, unnerved by his very presence, she managed to rip her gaze from his and fall in step with Bella. What...had that been? She felt... She wasn't even sure what she felt, but a worm of guilt wiggled its way inside her. She shouldn't be thinking about anything or anyone other than her sister right now.

"That man wants more than a date," Brielle murmured as they stepped out into a quiet hallway that would take them directly to where the rest of the band was getting set up. It was one of the employees-only hallways they'd been informed about and was blocked off for the majority of the guests.

"No kidding," Harlow murmured. "Did you smell those pheromones?" She made a gagging sound.

Star glanced between her friends who were on either side of her. "Seriously?" She hadn't been able to scent anything, but no surprise there.

"Oh yeah." Harlow tapped her nose as they maneuvered around one of the catering staff rolling a cart filled with little appetizers down the hallway. "He wants a very happy ending to your date."

"We need to find out more about him," Bella said quietly.

"I think he was a dragon," Star said, quiet enough for their ears only. And for some reason, that thought wasn't as revolting as it should be. Or not revolting at all.

The other two shifters sobered suddenly.

"I believe it," Brielle said. "I noticed three other males with him. They blended into the background but they had the same coloring and facial similarities. Definitely clanmates if they're dragons."

"And he's not with Oscar's clan. That much I know," Harlow added subvocally. "But that male was an Alpha so I'm surprised Oscar would even allow him here."

They'd researched the hell out of Oscar's clan once they'd discovered he'd taken Aurora. They knew most of the names and faces of the clan. Besides, Lachlan was Alpha to the bone. Whoever he was, he would have his own clan. Star would bet money on it.

Rolling her shoulders, Star let thoughts of the sexy Scottish dragon drop from her mind. She would worry about who the male was another time. Because Bella hadn't been lying. She had to get ready for the show.

The most important show of her life.

She was the opening act and it was going to be a huge production with fireworks. While she was singing, her team would make their move.

Energy hummed through her. Energy mixed with anxiety. But she squashed the fear down tight into a little box and threw away the key. She couldn't focus on it *and* do her job. And right now, her job was to make sure that everyone's eyes were on her, so her team could do their job and rescue Aurora.

Then they were getting the hell out of the country.

CHAPTER 3

"A million dollars? That's like eight hundred thousand pounds. Give or take." Cody, Lachlan's younger brother, came to stand next to him, hands shoved into his pants pockets. Without waiting for a response, he continued. "That seems reaaaally smart. Just throw a bunch of pounds away. On one date. Better yet, why not set it on fire, ya bawbag?"

"You are the one who told me to bid on her." Lachlan hadn't even known about the auction until an hour ago. His brother had told him that he should bid on Star.

And it had sounded like a grand idea.

"I was joking."

Lachlan simply grunted. "It's for charity."

This earned him a laugh not only from Cody, but from two of his clanmates standing a few feet behind them.

"Aye, right." His brother snorted. "Okay, then. What the hell were you thinking?" Cody muttered.

"Last time I checked I dinnae answer to you, lad." Lachlan cut a dark glance at his brother, who immediately straightened. Now was *not* the time to have a conversation about finances or his decision tonight. First of all, they were wealthy as fuck. Their finances were fine. More than.

His dragon clan had hoards stashed all over the world, as they were ancient. And in the thousands of years he'd been in Protective Hibernation, his people had done well for themselves, made investments. His younger brother was talking to him not as Alpha Laird, however, but as a sibling. He wasn't sure why Cody even cared.

Lachlan had only come tonight because one of his... Not exactly allies, but an ancient dragon he'd known thousands of years ago had invited him. As the Alpha Laird of a neighboring clan, it would have been rude not to attend Oscar's soiree. But the truth was, Lachlan had only made the final decision to actually attend when he'd been informed that the female Star was singing.

He'd discovered her half a year ago when one of his younger clanmates had been blasting her radio in their oversized castle kitchen. He'd been about to tell her to turn it down when Star's voice had punched through right to the heart of him, her sweet siren song playing out of the radio. A year after rising, he was still adjusting to this new world and all the technology, but once he'd heard her voice, he'd asked his cousin to download all of her music for him.

She sounded like nothing he'd ever heard before, as if she was singing only for him. Which he knew was daft. But it didn't alter the fact that her music spoke to him in a way nothing ever had. It made him think of a different time, of the only female he'd loved—and lost. Now to meet her in person? Fuck. He'd had to actually keep his dragon at bay because both halves of him wanted to know everything about the lass. He couldn't ever remember having to leash his dragon back like that. Not since he was a dragon bairn and that had been...too many thousands of years ago to count.

Her long hair was a dark indigo that looked natural to him, but he knew that humans and shifters could dye their hair. He assumed she'd dyed it, as indigo wasn't a natural hair color, but it looked good on her. Mainly because it matched the color of his dragon scales. Though in truth, everything looked good on her, including that tiny scrap of a dress, a dark purple that matched her eyes. And something told him that those weren't contacts either. They were too bright, too vivid, too...expressive. When she'd looked at him, she'd felt attraction. That much he was sure of. But it had disappeared so quickly, to be replaced by...he wasn't certain. But it hadn't been good, whatever it had been.

"I'm done here." Abruptly Lachlan turned away from the continuing auction. He had no interest in bidding on anything or anyone else. The only reason he'd come was to hear Star sing in person again. This growing obsession he had with her had to stop. At least that was what he'd tried to tell himself. But now that he'd met her in person, had scented her... His dragon clawed his insides, telling him they would not be walking away tonight. He would speak to her again at least.

"You know you're going to get hell from Rhona later," Cody grumbled as they walked away together.

Rhona was the clan's accountant and damn good at her job, but he didn't think she'd give him any grief. Not that he cared. He was Alpha Laird. "Aye. I'm sure once I remind her it's a tax write-off, it'll soothe her ruffled feathers." Things like taxes were something new he had also adjusted to in this era. There were so many things he was still learning.

Cody simply grunted then grabbed two flutes of champagne from a passing waiter, downing one after the other.

"Classy," Lachlan murmured as they moved through the crowd.

Grinning, Cody grabbed two more after setting his other two down on an empty high-top table. "That's my middle name. Now when can we get the hell out of here?" he asked so quietly that only Lachlan could hear him. It wouldn't do to offend any of Oscar's dragons milling about.

And they were *everywhere* on this compound. The place itself was so ostentatious, but apparently Oscar had been throwing parties like this for the last decade.

It was good to see that some things never changed. Even thousands of years ago, Oscar had been obnoxious and had always loved throwing a wild ceilidh—though back then his parties had been far more hedonistic. The other thing that had changed was that shifters were now interacting with humans and other supernatural beings. Even if humans had no idea that supernaturals even existed.

"Her PR manager Bella is quite bonnie," Cody continued, sipping his drink now as they stepped outside the ballroom into a much quieter hallway. "And so were her security lasses. She's simply surrounded by beauties."

His dragon breathed out a sigh, glad to be away from the crush of humans and supernaturals alike. Deep down, he was far more in touch with his wildness and wished he was in the skies right now. Flying high above everyone and everything.

Something inside him shifted in that moment as he realized what it was about Star's voice that affected him. When he heard her voice, everything faded away. He and his dragon were at peace, not worried about the future or wars he knew would eventually come. Because how could they not? He was not a fool and it was easy to see that humans would one day discover the existence of his kind. And when they did, the weaker species would lose their collective minds.

But when Star sang…he didn't think about flying or the politics of his people. He simply was. It was a refreshing change.

Lachlan shrugged as they stepped outside into the fresh air, realizing he'd never responded. "I suppose," he said as they made their way through the lush garden. Bright pops of color and wild scents surrounded them.

"You suppose? All those women are incredible. I would worship at the altar of their bodies for ages."

"Whatever. You're chatty tonight." He didn't want to talk about some other female, or females. Not when Star was all he could seem to think about—how it would feel to thread his fingers through her long hair as he raked his teeth over her neck. As he brought her pleasure. After his loss, he'd never thought he'd want another female again. He'd gone into Protective Hibernation while still grieving—and had woken still missing his love. It disturbed him to want another female so badly. Knowing he was letting his mind wander, he shut down that thought as much as he could.

But he was still consumed with the image of her—it was seared into his brain. She wasn't overly tall, but not petite like her manager either. Compared to him, she was fairly short at maybe five feet five, but her legs seemed to go on for days, giving her a taller appearance. Maybe it was because she was so lean…or maybe because she seemed to have a larger-than-life presence. Her big, expressive eyes and megawatt smile drew him, making it impossible to look away. Now, *she* was a bonnie lass.

Using the VIP pass that Oscar had given him and all the other Alphas in attendance, he flashed it at one of the security people where a roped-off section was near the stage.

About fifty feet away he could see all of the night's bands gathering, including Star's. He was aware of his brother saying something, but he ignored Cody, his gaze drawn to Star and her bandmates. They were on the edge of their roped-off area, all talking animatedly together.

He watched in curiosity as the two tiger females on her security team spoke quietly to her, then basically disappeared into the background. He frowned. They should be with her at all times. She was famous. And from what he'd learned about this new era, she would need protection. Even if she was a shifter. Because people could be unhinged.

He scanned the other three bands as well as the individual singers. They each had a team of security. Humans and shifters alike.

His frown deepened. No, he didn't like Star being unprotected at all. If he'd noticed that she had no security, surely someone else would as well. "Her security has left her," he said, interrupting whatever it was Cody had said.

Cody raised his eyebrows. "Aye?"

"Teague, Cian, keep an eye on her," he murmured to his two clanmates who were hovering on his periphery. He didn't need to specify who he was referring to.

Without a word, the two males broke off, heading into the throng of people as they made their way to where the bands were. His presence would stand out too much if Oscar had anyone watching him—and after that million-dollar bid, he'd already gained enough attention—but his people should be okay.

He wished he knew what kind of shifter Star was, and it bothered him that he couldn't place her scent. He'd heard gossip among his clan, and other packs and clans across the globe. Everyone assumed she was a snow leopard, but when he'd been close enough to scent her, his instinct had rejected the idea.

He wasn't sure *what* she was. The only thing he knew for certain was that her scent reminded him of the Highlands, crisp and wild and free.

And that his dragon wanted her with an intensity he'd only ever felt for one other woman.

CHAPTER 4

"You got this—as always," Brielle said pointedly to Star. She knew her Alpha was worried about not being part of this side of the operation but Star couldn't be. No way could Star blend in for a rescue mission when she was part of the pending show. Not to mention she was *Star*. She'd just been part of a huge auction and had worldwide recognition.

"Thanks." It looked as if Star wanted to say more but Brielle knew why she held back. Right now, it was all about appearances. "And…thank you."

Brielle only nodded, but come on. Like she needed any thanks for this. Aurora was her girl, part of their misfit pack of supernaturals who'd never fit in anywhere but together. Brielle loved her. They all did. Aurora was like a baby sister to all of them.

And no matter what happened, they were getting her out tonight. Still, she understood that Star would sacrifice anything for Aurora. They weren't twins like Brielle and Harlow, but they might as well have been for how bonded they were. And Star had practically raised Aurora from the time she was five, so it was more of a mother-daughter bond than anything. As two of the last remaining of their kind in the world, Star and Aurora had always been careful about not revealing what they were to strangers. But somehow Oscar had discovered what Aurora was.

Before leaving the stage area, Brielle subtly placed a tiny earpiece in Star's hand and nodded once as Star and Bella turned, meeting up with the rest of the band. Marley and Athena—drummer and guitarist—and Taya and Kartini, backup vocalists. The band had ten minutes until the first part of the show started. Which meant Brielle, Harlow, Lola and Axel had ten minutes to infiltrate where they thought Aurora was being held. So while the band was performing, they'd be getting Aurora the hell out of the compound.

"All right, guys, let's do this." Lola's voice came over the line. "You know the deal. Head to the kitchen. Currently it's skeleton staff."

Harlow nodded once as she looked at Brielle and jumped into action. They were Star's security now but for eight years they'd been in the Marines. They knew how to be stealthy on ops and now was no different.

It didn't take long to make it back to the mansion—which was thankfully starting to clear out since the show was about to begin.

Once they were in the industrial-sized kitchen, Brielle flashed her security badge to one of the caterers who was carefully stacking dirty champagne flutes into a bin. Brielle and Harlow needed to bypass the human and sneak into one of the staff-only corridors. Sure, they could just knock the human out, but someone would find the unconscious woman and send up an alert.

"Is there a staff bathroom nearby?" Brielle murmured to the human female, knowing full well there was one right through a nearby door. The one they needed to get through. "Don't feel like battling through the throng in the main ones."

The blonde flicked a glance at Brielle's badge that said she was part of Star's personal security and Brielle saw a flash of interest in her eyes.

Before the woman could answer, Brielle said, "Here, take this," as she pulled out an autographed picture of Star. She always kept half a dozen on her for random situations and she'd found that people were much more accommodating when she gave them one. "And if you're here after the show, I can introduce you to Star." A lie, but for a good cause.

The woman blinked. "Ah, thanks."

"Come on," Lola murmured through the comm line, her impatience clear. "Wrap this up."

The human glanced around first and then pointed at a side door that looked more like paneling. "Just go through there. You should be fine. Third door on the left before you hit the stairs. If you make it to the stairs, you've gone too far."

"Thanks, appreciate it."

"No problem... Listen, my name's Erin. I get off around midnight if you want to meet up later tonight. Ah, not to meet Star. I mean, if you want to meet up with me and grab a drink or something." She blushed as she said the words.

"Oh my God," Lola groaned through the comm line.

"Yeah, we'll set something up," Brielle said, already striding away from the pretty blonde toward the door. Another lie, but it didn't matter. "And thanks for this."

Once they ducked into the corridor, Harlow snorted. "How is it you get hit on everywhere we go?" her twin muttered. "I mean, we're twins and no one ever hits on me."

"Yeah, but I actually talk to people. You just stare at them as if you're deciding whether to kill them or not."

"Fair enough," Harlow murmured as they hurried down the hall—bypassing the bathroom and heading straight for the stairs.

"I'm officially into the mainframe," Lola said over the secure frequency. "You've got eight minutes. Maybe ten. Security is chaotic because of the show starting and they're going to assume this is due to interference from the pyrotechnics and other stuff. But your time is limited. The stairwell door is open...now."

"Copy," Brielle murmured even as the keypad by the door lit up and she heard a soft snicking sound. She eased open the door, Harlow right behind her, and stepped into the stairwell.

Unlike the lushly decorated and adorned hallways in the main part of the house, this one was narrower and utilitarian. And instead of going up, they headed down to where there were supposed to be two sets of elevators.

"Okay, I've got eyes on the security cameras and there are two guards four floors below. I can't find any other feeds connected to the underground area so there might not be any there."

Two guards? They could deal with that. It had cost a whole lot of money and some bloody knuckles, but they'd gotten the architectural plans to Oscar's place. The real ones. Oscar had added on to this place years ago, and while they didn't know with absolute certainty that Aurora was here, he'd developed what equated to a dungeon below his estate. Completely insulated, with prison cells. Considering the other info they'd dug up on the dragon Alpha, this had to be the place.

And if Aurora wasn't here, their pack was done trying to play nice. Star was barely holding on to her control. Brielle had no doubt they would go after him and his clan directly and beat him to death if he didn't tell them where Aurora was. Tonight, probably.

On instinct she shoved back the violent impulse, her tiger wanting to come out to fight as she and Harlow hurried down the stairs on quiet feet.

As they silently neared the landing above the final floor, she scented two individuals just as Lola had said.

She looked at her twin and gave the signal.

Harlow nodded and started to unleash her claws, but Brielle shook her head and began taking off her clothes quietly so as not to utter a sound.

Harlow frowned at her but Brielle continued to strip down until she was completely naked and motioned for Harlow to stay back. They'd done this move many times before in an op and it always worked. Men were so predictably stupid sometimes—and she was grateful for it.

Hurrying down the rest of the stairs on her bare feet, her tiger lurking right below the surface, she smiled at the two armed men in plain black suits standing in front of the set of elevators. Given their size and scent, she was guessing these security guys were dragons.

"Hello, gentlemen." She gave her most winning smile even though both their gazes dropped to her breasts. "I'm hoping you can help me as I'm lost," she said in a slightly pouty voice.

The dark-haired male on the left blinked once, still staring at her breasts while the other one stepped forward, his gaze right on her crotch.

Okay, so they deserved what was about to happen. They should be ashamed of themselves for getting distracted by a naked female. Maybe because they were dragons and used to being the apex predator in any room, they weren't being as smart as they should be. Either way, she was going to use this to her full advantage. Giggling lightly, she took another step forward, all feline grace and sensuality.

The one on the left finally dragged his eyes from her breasts to her face. Suddenly he shook his head. "Wait...what are you doing down here? How did you even get down here?"

"Someone sent me as a present for all your hard work."

That stopped them in their tracks, the scent of their lust sharp and cloying.

She dropped her voice an octave. "If you're really good, I'll let you have me at the same time."

Just underneath the aroma of lust, Brielle scented her twin even closer now and knew Harlow would have her back. She released her claws in milliseconds as she lunged at the male who hadn't gone for his weapon or even his radio—he hadn't done a damn thing to protect himself. Just stared at her breasts like a fool.

As she went straight for his jugular the other male reacted, but it was too late. She cut deep across his throat, the slicing arc hitting its mark perfectly.

Next to her, Harlow's blades sang through the air, embedding themselves right in the second male's throat.

The male Brielle had sliced up stumbled back, eyes wide, but he didn't fall.

Brielle was vaguely aware of her sister and the other impaled male fighting. She knew her twin could take care of herself so she focused on her prey.

She wrapped her legs around him tight so he couldn't pull away from her. He clutched at his throat with one hand to stop the blood flow even as he sliced at her with his other hand. He opened his mouth and she could scent and feel the heat of his dragon fire about to unleash. She had only seconds now.

Ignoring the slicing pain in her side, she shoved her claws straight through his chest and grabbed his heart. Killing a dragon was damn near impossible, especially if they shifted or blasted fire at you.

Which was why they'd had to take these warriors off guard. It was such a delicate balance, knowing the weakness of your enemy.

Grasping his beating heart, Brielle ripped it from his chest in a hard yank even as her sister finished off the other male. For good measure her twin not only ripped the other male's heart out, Harlow beheaded both of them with her blades in two quick strokes before the males had even hit the ground.

Ugh. There was so much damn blood.

"Use one of their palms on the scanner. I'm still trying to break through the encryption but it's taking too long." Lola's crisp voice came through their earpieces. She'd been watching them battle over the security cameras she'd hacked into, but ever the professional, Lola never interrupted when they were fighting someone. She understood that any sort of distraction could cost them their lives.

"Will do." Brielle grabbed the nearest dead body and flattened his palm against the bio scanner.

The elevator doors swished open and she shoved out a breath of relief. She tried to wipe off some of the blood on the guy's pants but it was pretty pointless.

"We might lose you now." Once they went deeper underground it was highly possible they'd lose their connection, but they'd prepared for that.

"I've got your back, ladies." Axel's voice came over the comm line. "If you're not up in six minutes, I'm coming down after you. As of now the coast is clear in the kitchen and hallway."

Axel was acting as their backup for this op, in case anyone realized what had happened and tried to come down after them. He would make sure no one got through those elevators. Because according to the architectural plans, there was only one way in and out of this dungeon. Which was good and bad.

She hated not having another escape route and knew her twin felt the same way.

"What a freaking mess," Lola muttered over the earpiece as they stepped into the elevators.

Yeah it was, and thankfully Lola had taken over the security cameras for now so no one would see the dead bodies and the growing pool of blood—that was turning into a lake.

Harlow silently handed Brielle her bundle of clothing.

She quickly pulled her clothes on even though she knew she might have to shift and fight down here. They weren't sure what kind of security they'd be facing on this subfloor. It could be anything or anyone.

Well get ready, motherfuckers. This dragon clan had taken one of their own.

She would have no mercy for anyone involved in taking Aurora. And neither would Harlow.

CHAPTER 5

Buzzing with anticipation, Star stepped out onto the stage, her heart rate skyrocketing. Normally she would have savored the huge crowd chanting her name, would have reveled in it and let it feed her energy for the show.

Not tonight.

The chants, the pulsing lights, the noise and smells…it was all too overwhelming. All she could think about was Aurora, about her crew. If anything happened to them—

"We've got her!" Brielle's excited voice came over the comm line. "Limited body count so the extraction was smooth. Heading for the extraction point. Do the song," she said before silencing communication.

Oh God. They had Aurora. And in the five minutes it would take Star and her band to perform this opening song, the others should be able to get Aurora fully out of the compound. Then Star and the others would leave instead of hanging out backstage and waiting for their next song. Her throat tightened as she tried to compartmentalize her emotions but they were shoving up hard and fast. Aurora had been saved. Now they just had to make sure she got out of here.

She straightened, forcing herself to stay calm. It was showtime. All her crew depended on her now.

The way tonight was set up, each band or individual singer performed one song at a time. By the time it cycled back to her crew, they would be long gone, hopefully on a plane over the ocean.

Wearing a skintight sheer purple bodysuit that basically looked like a sparkly monokini, she strode out onto the stage in her five-inch heels, a huge train of feathers trailing behind her. The outfit tonight was ridiculous but it went with her Star persona. And whatever, she liked it even if it was flamboyant.

The crowd went wild as she held up a hand, waving at everyone. She wasn't sure how she was doing this, how she was keeping her shit together.

Athena started on the guitar, one of the spotlights highlighting her, then Marley started on the drums, a soft tempo for now. Star focused on the lyrics as Athena hit the next note.

This was it. She grabbed the microphone off the stand and belted out the first words as a multitude of lights illuminated her. She danced across the stage, her energy upbeat as mini fireworks exploded behind the stage, bright purple starbursts.

The song was about freedom, about rising from the ashes and starting over, and she felt every single word in her soul. She'd promised her fans something new tonight, and even though her main—pretty much only—concern was saving Aurora, she still hoped the audience loved the music.

The tempo changed and her hips swayed in tune with the new, wild beat that had a mix of eighties and modern feel to it as she sang her heart out, word after word.

All for her sister.

Aurora was the only reason Star was able to keep her fear under lockdown right now.

As she shimmied across the stage she felt eyes on her—and she knew they were dark indigo eyes, a color so shockingly beautiful. She wanted to write songs about that dragon, about his arresting face and scent. Even his damn voice gave her the shivers. The good kind.

But she ignored the strange feelings growing inside her. She absolutely ignored the knowledge that the dragon shifter was sexually attracted to her—and the fact that she *might* be interested in him as well.

Because sexual attraction was nothing right now. Nothing at all.

She raced to the other side of the stage as Marley started a short drum solo. The crowd had already picked up on the chorus and started singing along as Star belted out the chorus again.

The words and music hummed through her and she had to fight back the fire inside her, the fire that wanted to be free, to show off to the whole world exactly how bright Star could shine. It was always a struggle to contain her fire, but especially now when her emotions were riding a razor wire.

As the song came to an end, she stood in the middle of the stage, her purple feathers flaring out as she took an exaggerated bow. As she stood again, a kaleidoscope of fireworks exploded behind and over them, making the crowd go wild. They screamed for more, chanting her name over and over.

She smiled at their demands even though now panic had set in as she wondered if the others had gotten out of the compound with Aurora. If they hadn't... Things were about to get ugly.

As if Brielle read her mind, her voice came through the comm line. "We're officially home free and past the gate heading to the airport." Brielle's voice was clipped. "Axel is waiting for you guys in the getaway vehicle. I give it three minutes before they notice the bodies or the fact that someone hasn't checked in. Get out of the compound before then."

"Cameras are back online now," Lola added over the line. "With the exception of the route you'll be taking. Don't deviate from it."

Star glanced at the others as they strode off the stage, their movements purposeful. They'd gone over this plan a hundred times and knew exactly how to get from here to the garage unseen by cameras. If no one on security saw Star and her band leaving during the middle of the show—it was the only thing that might give them enough time to get past the gates.

Star waved at her fans one more time before hurrying off the stage as the next band strode forward.

Marcus, the lead singer for one of the other bands, gave her a high-five and congratulated her on the new song as he hurried past her.

"Thanks!" she said as she strode after her bandmates, her heels clicking away.

Bella waited at the edge of the stage, her expression pinched even as she tried to keep a smile in place. "This way."

"Hey, where are you guys going?" one of the production crew asked as Star and the others left the backstage area.

"Wardrobe change." Star said it dismissively, as if surprised he'd even asked her.

"Then do it here," the human male snapped.

Star snorted. "And risk some pervert getting me on camera? No way. I'll change in the house and be back with plenty of time for our next piece." Without waiting for a response, she flounced away with her entourage as if she was every ounce the diva. The waving feathers helped sell it.

By the time they'd made it back to the mansion, she could practically feel the figurative fire of their enemies breathing down her neck. She knew she was just letting her imagination get away from her, but they had to get out of here now.

Once security realized Aurora was missing, a silent alarm would be set off and Oscar would lock his estate down. And if Star was questioned, Oscar's security team would scent a lie from her or one of her crew. It was only a matter of time.

She figured he'd lie to the humans and tell them some sort of terrorist threat was going on to keep them locked down.

It was eerie how quiet the mansion was as they hurried through the service corridors toward the six-car garage where Axel was waiting. As they rounded one corridor, they nearly ran into two female waitresses, both human.

Star smiled politely and ignored the surprised looks as they continued on their way. No one questioned them but they might say something to their boss which was why they needed to hurry. Star picked up her pace, her heels clicking loudly on the tile. She was desperate to see her sister.

As they burst into the garage, an SUV roared to life as the headlights flashed once, then twice. That was the signal.

The six of them raced for the vehicle and piled in, finding seats as Axel tore out of the garage.

"All the valet parking went into an overflow lot next door," Axel said, his words clipped. "We've got a straight shot out of here."

Even though she wanted to tell him to get on with it, they drove the standard fifteen miles an hour along the long, winding driveway so as not to draw attention to themselves.

She felt like dozens of eyes were on them. Maybe they were.

By the time they'd made it to the exit gates, Star had changed out of her purple costume and into black pants and a black sweater. She'd also managed to tame her wild hair and tuck it up into a dark cap. Not exactly a great disguise, but she wasn't standing out now. And she didn't imagine that security was going to search cars as they left.

The gates automatically opened as they approached but as they pulled halfway through, the guard from the gate shouted, "Hey, hold on," as he jogged toward them.

Axel gripped the steering wheel, the leather crackling under his fingers.

"See what he wants," she said quietly. They were through the gate already. Halfway, anyway. That was something.

He rolled down his window. "Everything okay?" Axel asked, his voice casual as could be.

The man approached, paused, then held up a finger as he shone the flashlight into the front seat then in the back seat. It was clear he was listening to an earpiece because he nodded once.

"I'm going to need to get a good look at everyone. Everyone out of the vehicle."

Damn it, but at least Aurora was gone.

"What the hell is this?" Axel snapped in the most indignant tone she'd ever heard from the laid-back lion shifter. "Is this how you treat your guests?"

The man's expression didn't change and his dragon flashed in his eyes once, briefly. "Someone stole something very priceless." His tone was flat, uncompromising. "It's just standard procedure. Now everyone out—Wait a minute, aren't you Star? And you're...Taya." Frowning, he looked at the rest of the bandmates who'd all changed into plain clothes. "What the hell are you guys doing? Your show is still—"

Axel floored it, nearly running over the guard as he tore away from the gate.

The man cursed behind them, but his voice quickly faded as they raced away into the night.

* * *

"I don't like this," Star said into the quiet of the SUV as she turned in her seat to look behind them. They'd been driving for seven minutes exactly and there weren't any vehicles following them. No gunshots pinging off the vehicle. No firebombs.

Nothing. It felt totally wrong.

"I don't either." Kartini broke her silence as well as she looked out the window, her gaze tilting upward. "They have to be in the sky."

That was what Star's gut instinct was telling her too. She pulled out her phone and dialed Brielle.

"We're in the plane ready to go. Engine is running," Brielle said upon greeting.

"Leave without us. They know something's up and I'm pretty sure they're tailing us from the air. They've got to be. Get out of here now. We'll meet up in the States. Tell Aurora I'm coming but I need her to be safe."

There was a rustling sound and then her sister's tired voice came over the phone. Fire licked over her whole body for a brief moment when she heard Aurora's voice before she got her emotions under control.

"I'm not leaving without you," Aurora said quietly. "He wants me alive. He won't attack the plane. Get here now."

The line went dead, and when Star tried calling back neither Brielle nor Harlow answered their phones. She cursed. Damn it, she needed Aurora gone, safe! It was hard to think knowing that her sister could be flying off to safety but instead was waiting for them.

Axel continued winding through random little neighborhoods as they made their way to the private airport.

"We're not going to lose the dragons." She knew that in her gut. "We'll fight them off at the airport if we have to, but Aurora is right. They don't want her dead." And Star's power was at full capacity right now. After that show, her adrenaline was wild and out of control. If she had to battle a dragon... Or more than one. *Bring it on.*

She looked around at the rest of her band, her friends, her *family*. "No matter what happens, get Aurora out of here. That's an order." She rarely gave them true orders, but she needed them to understand that she was serious. That she was in Alpha mode.

"We get out together," Axel said.

"Always have to have the last word," she murmured as he pulled onto a two-lane highway.

"I can't help it. It's my lion nature."

As they reached the back gate to the private airport, Axel slowed, pulling through the open gates cautiously.

"It's just like Brielle said." She'd told them that they would be open.

Considering how much they'd bribed nearly everyone on the night shift at this airport, they'd better not have a problem getting out of here. Their next stop from here was France. Then they would be hopping all across the globe until they finally ended up in New Orleans. But they would only go there once they were certain they'd lost their tail.

Oh shit! A dragon appeared out of nowhere, letting its camouflage fall as it blasted fire at the front of the SUV.

Her heart jumped in her throat even as Axel swerved to the left, his expert driving the only reason they didn't roll.

"Taya, Kartini, shift when we open the doors!" Star gripped the handle of her door. "Now!"

As one, they all threw open the doors and rolled out with Taya and Kartini taking to their avian forms. The Eurasian eagle-owl shifters banked to the left away from the dragon flames as Star called on all her power and sent a burst of brilliant purple flames skyward.

The dragons attacking them were camouflaged but she could see where their fire was coming from. They couldn't avoid her fire. Her *power.*

"Get to the plane!" she screamed.

Bella shouted at the others, mirroring Star's order.

She understood their need to stay and fight but right now this was up to her. She was a goddamn warrior. They were all fighters but she was more powerful—it was why she was Alpha.

As her packmates ran toward the waiting plane, she raised her hands high in the air and sent out another pulse of flames, sparking high and wide.

There!

The camouflage fell as her fire made contact with a brilliant violet and gold dragon.

The beast screeched, his underbelly raw and bleeding from the blast of her fire. *That's right.* She was one of the few beings who could take on a dragon's fire and survive.

A pure golden dragon came out of nowhere, swooping toward her in a bomb dive as she started running toward the plane.

Raising her hands above her head, she blasted this one too, the fire rolling from her fingertips and slamming into his snout.

The dragon veered off course, stunned midflight. As it began to free-fall, she picked up speed, her leg muscles straining as she raced after her packmates.

They were all racing up the stairs to the plane now. They were so damn close. *Yes!*

The gold and violet dragon swooped down in front of her suddenly and blasted fire at her, completely engulfing her body.

She felt the heat as it licked around her, burning her clothes to ash, but she pushed back with her own fire, securing a bubble to protect herself as she continued running. It required a whole lot of power, but with enough concentration she could withstand another attack if necessary. Knowing Aurora was so close gave her added strength.

When the dragon finally stopped his onslaught, she swore the giant beast looked surprised, his head tilted to the side, his giant wings flapping as he stared down at her.

She gave him double middle fingers before calling on her internal fire once again. But before she could blast him, a dragon bigger than she'd ever seen swooped out of nowhere, and slammed its jaws around the gold dragon's throat in a vicious, powerful display.

Hooooolllly shitballs.

She stared for only a moment before she turned and ran the last fifty yards to the plane.

She wasn't sure who the dragon was or why he was helping her, but she wasn't sticking around to find out. Aurora and her packmates were her priority.

Bella was waiting at the top of the stairs, her expression tense as Star dove through the plane's door.

Before she'd even pushed to her feet, Bella and Axel had the door shut and closed.

"Go!" she shouted, though it wasn't necessary.

The pilot, an avian shifter they'd paid a lot of money, had already started forward.

The plane rumbled under them, but Star kept her balance as she hurried through the interior, not caring that she was naked.

Aurora was slumped over in one of the plush seats, a blanket wrapped around her shoulders, but her beautiful violet eyes lit up when she saw Star.

A sob rose in Star's throat.

"I knew you would come for me," Aurora whispered, her words raspy.

Star was vaguely aware of someone draping a blanket around her shoulders before she sat down next to her sister and pulled her into her arms.

Aurora hugged her back, her grip weak.

"I will always come for you." As she hugged Aurora, through the little window of the plane she stared as four full-grown dragon shifters battled each other on the tarmac, their fire and carnage wild and out of control. One had the most beautiful indigo scales, glinting under the moonlight.

In that moment, she knew that if any humans caught this on video, supernaturals had just been outed to the world.

And she couldn't find it in her to care.

She had her sister back. And all her family was safe. That was all that mattered.

Part II
After The Fall

CHAPTER 6

Star jogged up the driveway of the three-story mansion in the lower Garden District where she and her crew were now living. Since they'd ping-ponged across the world in an effort to lose any potential tails from Oscar, it had taken them weeks to make it to New Orleans. And during that time the entire world had gone mad.

Absolutely, bat-shit-eating, banana crackers *mad*.

A bunch of villainous dragons had outed themselves to humans, and though the dragon fight and fire show she'd taken part in at the small Wales airport six weeks ago probably hadn't helped, it hadn't been the precursor to the current insanity. Or maybe it had, she had no idea.

All she knew was that a sect of dragons had tried to take over the world—yep, take over the world like dumbass super villains—and instead had decimated a good portion of it, killing billions of people, human and supernaturals alike.

Asshole was too soft a word for them. Maybe they hadn't cared about the fallout, maybe they'd wanted so many people to die—there was a lot she was still learning. She'd gotten tidbits from the now supernatural-run news, but things were coming out in bits and pieces.

New Orleans was one of the cities in the US still doing well enough. They were currently rebuilding, and Star knew that King, the designated Alpha of the city, would be working together with witches and other supernaturals as they helped to rebuild here and in surrounding areas.

A lot of supernaturals wouldn't like the idea of working with witches, but she'd always thought witches got a bad rap. People were so negative about them but she didn't understand why. Yeah, witches had done some messed-up stuff, but guess what? Dragons had almost destroyed the freaking world. No one better be throwing stones right now, as far as she was concerned.

Shelving those thoughts for now, she waved once at Axel, who was doing perimeter patrol along the wall. Until the threat from Oscar and his clan was eliminated, they would always be a danger to Aurora. And now Star, if they'd figured out what she was. After that fire show she'd put on at the airport it was possible, but she wasn't sure what the dragons knew at this point.

As far as she knew, that sexy Lachlan and his clanmates had been the victors. Somehow she ordered her mind off Lachlan. No good would come of thinking—aka obsessing—about him.

Axel waved back and gave the signal that everything was okay.

As she stepped into the foyer of the mansion, she found Harlow coming down the front set of stairs, a half-eaten apple in one hand. "She's still in bed," Harlow said neutrally. "I tried getting her to come downstairs. So did Lola. She tried to bribe her with chocolate, but no go."

Aurora. Her sister had been cooped up in her room as if she was still a prisoner. She'd recovered from having her blood drained over and over, had regained her strength. She was no doubt very emotionally stressed, but Aurora couldn't hide away forever. It wasn't healthy and she needed to talk to someone.

"Clear out the house," she said quietly as she headed upstairs. Star had tried to cajole her into coming downstairs every single day, tried to appeal to her sense of family. She'd listened every day to anything and everything Aurora wanted to talk about. But mainly Aurora had just been quiet, wanting to sleep.

Star had tried to find a therapist for Aurora to talk to, but was coming up short on that end. She'd encouraged her to start sculpting again, to just see her family—to eat without being convinced. She'd been so soft with her sister, but maybe Aurora needed tough love. It was impossible to know and she hadn't tried it yet. Though it went against her nature, she was going to try anything at this point.

Crunching on her apple, Harlow simply nodded.

"We'll meet you out in the garden soon." They'd started their own garden and she might have used a teeny bit of her own magic to get it kick-started. Maybe that was one reason Star liked witches. Her kind and witches both used natural, earth magic. In different ways of course, but the core magic was the same.

She raced up the stairs until she reached the third floor.

Seriously, Aurora had chosen the third floor and farthest bedroom from everyone. Before, she would have been right in the thick of things. Her sister was a social butterfly, and cutting herself off like this wasn't going to help her healing.

Star didn't bother knocking, simply opened the door and strode inside.

"Hey! Knock much?" Aurora grumbled, not moving from the bed where she had the covers pulled up to her neck. The room was dark, but it was clear her sister was wide awake. She wasn't reading or doing anything to entertain herself. Nope, she was just lying in bed staring off into space or drowning in her thoughts.

Star simply snorted and headed for one of the three huge windows. She pulled back the thick white silk drapes over one, letting in rays of sunlight. Then she moved to the next. Then the last one, blasting the room with natural light even as Aurora shoved the covers off and jumped out of bed.

"What the hell are you doing?" She yanked one of the curtains closed again.

"You're coming outside with me. We're going to tend to the veggie and herb garden. If you don't want to help, fine. You can sit and watch us and hang out with your family for ten minutes. Maybe get some vitamin D."

"You're not my Alpha," Aurora snapped as she stalked toward another window.

"Yeah, well, I *am* your big sister. And I swear to the goddess that if you close the other curtains I'll set them on fire." Star knew she should dial it back, but nothing had worked with Aurora so far, certainly not patience.

Okay yeah, maybe it hadn't been that long since she'd been freed, but Star couldn't let her sister hide away from her family. She risked going into a depression spiral that would just get worse and worse the longer she hid away like this.

Aurora turned to stare at her, wearing the same damn clothes she'd had on for a week.

"And take a shower before you meet us downstairs. You stink." It wasn't true but she knew her sister, and her sister needed a little tough love right now.

Aurora glared even harder but subtly sniffed her armpit. Then she winced and wrapped her arms around herself. "I'm still adjusting," she muttered.

Sighing, Star sat on the side of the bed. "I know. I've been trying to give you time. Maybe six weeks isn't long enough. But...you were in prison for a year. You're acting like you're still there. I just...miss you. We *all* miss you. People all over the world have lost their whole families. You're still alive. I...I'm an asshole. I shouldn't be pushing this hard." She sure as hell shouldn't be telling Aurora to shape up because other people were hurting too. That was a garbage thing to do. "Oh my God, I'm sorry. Seriously. I'm going into crazy big-sister mode or something." The truth was, she'd been running on raw fear for a year straight before they'd saved Aurora and she hadn't adjusted to this new reality either. She couldn't quite believe Aurora was here with them, free. And maybe Star was having a hard time getting used to this Aurora.

Aurora closed her eyes and scrubbed her hands over her face. As she let her head drop forward, her long, dark braid fell over her shoulder. "You're not an asshole," she muttered, dropping her hands and looking at Star. "I've tried about a dozen times to make it downstairs. But I keep chickening out. I feel...off and overwhelmed. And I'm not sure how to get back to who I was before."

"It's going to take a while to get back to your normal, I'm sure. But he didn't take your life. You're still a fighter, still powerful," she reminded her sister. They both were. Oscar and his clan had caught Aurora off guard—it had taken a dozen of his warriors to bring her down when she'd been alone. No one could have withstood that kind of attack. And then he'd kept her in an iron cage, unable to escape.

"I know. I...I feel like I could sleep for an eternity."

Star hated everything Aurora had been through and wished there was someone other than Star she could talk to. Someone impartial, like a therapist maybe. Someone with training. But with the city rebuilding she wasn't even sure if that kind of service was available anywhere, much less to supernaturals. And Star felt out of her depth. "Maybe just take a shower. You don't have to come downstairs if you don't want. I'm sorry I was being pushy. I'm just worried about you, and this is new territory."

Aurora smiled and reached her hand out, grasping Star's. "I can do a shower. And...I'll try to make it outside. Just give me time, okay?"

Star nodded and stood. "I will. And I would hug you but not until you take that shower." Her lips twitched slightly as Aurora stepped back.

"I am kind of ripe," her sister muttered. "And I'm pretty grossed out with myself right now." She disappeared into the bathroom but Star didn't leave.

Instead she opened the windows, letting in fresh air before stripping the sheets. Then she hung up some of her sister's discarded clothes. She wanted Aurora to come out and see the bed cleared off so she couldn't get back into it without putting on new sheets. When she was done, she looked around the prettily decorated room. There were bright pops of color everywhere. The comforter was a simple pin-tucked white, but a purple and red throw blanket from Morocco had been tossed onto the end of it. And colorful pillows were on the chaise by the window. The furniture was all upcycled stuff from Aurora's place back in Saint Augustine. The art itself was from local artists in New Orleans, some oil paintings and others simple sketches. Star had chosen every single piece specific to her sister's tastes. And she'd also brought everything that had once mattered to Aurora from where she'd lived before.

She'd bought this house sight unseen nearly six months ago, knowing that it was going to be a landing point for all of them once they found Aurora. New Orleans was a friend to magical creatures and King was a strong Alpha. He embraced diversity among his pack, which was one of the main reasons they'd chosen the city in the first place.

Though there was another reason. Someone close to Star and Aurora lived nearby and they'd needed to find her—needed to discuss borrowing a weapon that should help them against Oscar if he came after them. But they hadn't been able to find her just yet. She'd moved in the last year, and

Star was still working on figuring out her exact address. But she had no doubt she was in the city or on the outskirts. She would never leave New Orleans.

The shower was still running so she headed downstairs. To her surprise, Harlow was waiting by the front door.

"How'd it go?" she asked, eying the bundle of dirty sheets.

Shifters had exceptional hearing, but they'd been three stories up and Harlow clearly hadn't been trying to eavesdrop if she was asking. "She's getting in the shower at least."

Harlow grabbed the sheets as they headed to the kitchen. "That's progress. And I'll start this for you."

"You don't have to do that. And that's what I'm trying to tell myself about progress. One day at a time."

Even as she did try to tell herself that it was good her sister was taking these steps, guilt still gnawed away at her. She should have been with her sister; Aurora *never* should have been taken. If they'd been together, they might have been able to take on a clan of dragons. Maybe they wouldn't have survived, but at least they would've killed a whole bunch of them.

"You hungry?" Harlow asked as they reached the kitchen.

"This will do." She grabbed a bright red apple from the aqua-colored bowl on the island countertop.

Harlow nodded and veered off toward the laundry room, which was attached to the kitchen.

Gardening had never been her thing, but everyone was trying to be more resourceful, to be more independent and grow their own food. King was working with different farmers in the surrounding areas and she'd heard that there were greenhouse vegetable and fruit gardens going up everywhere—they planned to build one in the yard here as well, in addition to the garden they'd already started. And Bella was talking about getting chickens and goats.

King was also working to set up warehouses for temperature-controlled storage for all sorts of food. He'd basically taken over any abandoned warehouse and was turning them all into places that manufactured anything the people of New Orleans might need. It was damn smart and she was impressed with how he was rebuilding, even if it was in the early stages.

Luckily it wasn't like they were starting from scratch. There was limited internet and communication between various cities across the world. And many Alphas were already in alliances with each other, which made things a whole lot easier as they restructured the power balance in general.

Supernaturals were adjusting better than humans, that was for sure. Because now supernaturals were out to the world and in charge of law enforcement and all governments. That had been a huge shock for humans everywhere. Right now Star knew that Kyoto, Edinburgh—and most of Scotland and the UK in general—Rio de Janeiro, Mauritius, parts of India, South Australia, parts of New Zealand, and many island nations around the world had come through largely unscathed compared to other areas that had been razed to the ground. There were so many areas that had simply ceased to exist—including big cities along the eastern seaboard in the United States. Washington DC was gone as well as other capitals around the world like Moscow and Cairo.

So even if there was some infighting in New Orleans among supernaturals, that was for King to worry about for now. She was just trying to keep her own family safe at this point.

* * *

"I'm about done with this gardening for the day," Taya said as she stood and tugged off her gardening gloves. In typical Taya fashion, she wore jeans and a T-shirt with no adornment, and her long, bronze, naturally caramel-highlighted hair was pulled up into a ponytail.

The sun was an hour away from setting and Star was done too. But not for the day. She had a meeting in less than an hour and needed to at least rinse all the dirt off first. Since they'd arrived in New Orleans, she'd been go-go-go, trying to make sure they had strong allies and that she could keep her sister safe. And if she was busy working, then she didn't have time to sleep.

Didn't have time to dream. The bizarre dreams she'd been having for the last year were getting more frequent, more intense. And she was over them.

"Hope you guys aren't headed back inside," a familiar voice said from the lanai.

All of them turned at once as if it had been choreographed.

Aurora stood there, her brunette hair pulled up in a ponytail, her face freshly scrubbed. She wore a pair of Star's leggings and one of Axel's oversized sweaters, which engulfed her.

"Nope, not going anywhere." Grinning, Taya tossed her gloves next to the bean plant she'd just potted.

"Are you hungry? Thirsty?" Star asked, striding toward the lanai.

Aurora stood next to the wrought iron patio table that once upon a time had been spray painted a pretty blue. Now the paint was flaking off. "I'm good. But it's nice getting fresh air." Aurora eased down on one of the paint-chipped chairs and smiled at everyone. "The garden looks incredible. And I see you started on the greenhouse building today too."

The others crowded around the table and chairs, basically staring at Aurora.

"Oh my God, you guys. I'm going to go back to my room if you sit there and stare at me like I'm an animal at the zoo."

Brielle snorted and kissed the top of Aurora's head. "I'm going to grab a bottle of wine from the cellar. I'll also bring out some food. You might not be hungry but I'm starving."

"You're always starving," Aurora murmured and dispelled the tension in the air.

The others sat and started talking all at once.

Star pulled out her cell phone, ready to cancel her appointment.

Aurora stopped her as if she'd read her mind. "I know you have that meeting with Cynara tonight. Don't cancel it because of me. I'm not going anywhere. Promise."

Star wanted to ask her sister if she was sure, but also didn't want to insult her or spook Aurora into running back upstairs. She needed to treat Aurora like normal, and the fact that her sister was downstairs with all of them, relaxing? Yeah, Star had to play this right. She shoved her phone into her back pocket. "It's kinda creepy that you knew I was going to call her."

"Sister power."

She laughed at that.

As Brielle stepped back outside with a huge charcuterie tray, Axel bled out of the shadows, likely called by the food. Freaking lions and their stomachs.

"Something smells good… My favorite sweater!" he said laughingly as he approached the table.

"It's mine now." Aurora pulled the turtleneck up over her face and inhaled. "Even if it does stink like lion."

"I smell great. And I have it on good authority that my natural scent is like Calvin Klein cologne."

"Is that what your last girlfriend told you?" Aurora asked, snickering. "Because she lied, lion. She lied."

Star snagged some cheese as she listened to the banter continue between everyone.

She wasn't naïve enough to think that Aurora was magically all better, but the fact that her sister was down here was a huge step in the right direction.

Not wanting to make a big deal about leaving, she excused herself so she could wash up and change out of her dirt-stained clothes. The sound of laughter trailing behind her warmed her from the inside out. Aurora was going to come through this.

Of that, Star had no doubt. Her sister was strong.

That monster had kept her in prison for a year, draining her blood for his own sick uses. One day Star was going to kill him for what he'd done.

For now, they were safe and had regrouped. Regaining strength and allies mattered. Hell, it was almost paramount if they wanted to come out alive after a battle with his clan. But one day…Star would end him.

One day she would make him sorry he'd ever been born. Star was playing the long game with this. Oscar would die eventually.

Slowly and painfully. He wouldn't be the first dragon she'd killed either—and something told her he wouldn't be the last.

CHAPTER 7

Showered and dressed, Star met Axel by the front gate. "You look nice tonight," she said, surprised.

He lifted a dark eyebrow as they stepped out onto the sidewalk. "Surprised, really?" Tonight he'd worn slacks and a dark green button-down shirt that looked good against his bronze skin. He'd pulled his longish hair back into what humans were calling a man-bun. For Axel, it wasn't like he could help it. No matter how much the male cut his hair, it just grew and grew in thick, luscious dark waves. If she didn't love him so much, she might be jealous.

She laughed lightly. "Sorry. I'm so used to seeing you in your tactical gear patrolling. Just weird is all."

"As weird as those wolf shifters walking down the street? Because I'm pretty sure one of them is wearing a blue headband."

She blinked once as they strode along the uneven sidewalk. Axel hadn't been kidding. Two gray and white wolves were trotting down the middle of the road as if it was no big deal. And yep, one of them had a sparkly blue headband, which somehow looked adorable.

Freaking wolves, was all she could think. Because that was such a wolf thing to do.

This would take getting used to—for her and definitely for humans. Now that supernaturals were out to the world, they weren't hiding what they were anymore. Well, not *all* of them. She was, but that was a different case. And she had a feeling some people would keep their identities secret unless they trusted others completely as well.

She and Axel fell in step with each other, and they both waved at the wolves who barked in response.

Yeah, that was pretty surreal.

"So what's this meeting about?" Axel asked as they reached a four-way stop.

The walk to the French Quarter was about twenty minutes from where they were and she liked stretching her legs. She wasn't the only one because there were a decent amount of joggers out this evening. Two jogged across the street in front of them as they made their way to the other side.

She'd studied a detailed map of the city but she also liked getting a layout for where everything was. There was so much beyond the city limits as well but she would explore that later. "Cynara wanted to talk to me about putting on a few shows around the city."

"I think that's a good idea."

She shot him a sideways glance as they crossed the street. Mardi Gras beads still dangled from the trees above them, something she learned was a typical sight around here. Even in the aftermath of The Fall, the beads were still clinging everywhere. Though she'd heard that King's pack had decided to do away with the plastic beads in general since the plastic caused such a litter problem.

"Agreed. We need all the goodwill we can get from people. We need allies everywhere if Oscar decides to come after Aurora again." And probably her, if he'd figured out Star was the same, which was a real possibility considering she'd shown off some of her powers at that airport.

"You're right."

"I kind of expected pushback from you." Axel could be such a mother hen sometimes. Which she appreciated.

He lifted a shoulder as they passed a teal house with yellow trim and a group of shifters and humans building a greenhouse in the corner of the yard. A couple waved at them, but mostly continued what they were doing.

"I don't like you putting yourself out in the open. I don't like any of the band doing that. Because it's going to let Oscar know where you are if he doesn't already. But my money is on him figuring it out sooner than later regardless. You're *Star*. And..." He shrugged his broad shoulders, constantly scanning for danger even as they walked. "We can't operate as an island. We need friends and we need to be seen. It'll be a hell of a lot harder for Oscar to come after you or Aurora if we have public favor. I hate that it matters, but it does."

"Yep." And Star's friend Cynara, a half-demon, half-vampire, was powerful in her own right and had four very powerful brothers. Not to mention an old-as-hell mate who'd once been a Roman general and was a badass, if what Star had heard was anything to go on. "I'm glad you're on board."

"Hey! Stop!" a female voice cried out from somewhere nearby.

Axel shared a glance with Star and they bolted into action, her boots pounding against the concrete in tune with his as they raced down the sidewalk.

"Stop that now, you jackass thief!"

They rounded the corner to find a woman yelling at a male who was walking off with her generator. The male didn't even glance at the human, just picked the generator up as if it weighed nothing. Okay, so he was a shifter. And Star was pretty sure the woman was human since (a) she wasn't attacking the thief and (b) she had a distinctive human scent.

Star motioned for Axel to stay back. She raced across the neighboring front yard to confront the thief at the edge of the lawn. "What the hell are you doing?"

The male looked her up and down, a sneer on his face. He was a shifter of some kind, but she wasn't sure what type. Jaguar maybe. Feline for sure, given the beast that flickered in his eyes for a moment.

"He's taking my generator. It belongs to King's pack." Star couldn't scent any lies rolling off the human woman. She didn't scent fear from her either, just anger.

"You're dumb enough to take one of King's belongings?" Star didn't make a move toward him yet, but she was ready to rush him if necessary.

A casual shrug. "He's not my Alpha."

"He is your Alpha if you're living in New Orleans. Or the surrounding area." And really, she wasn't going to argue semantics with some random stranger who was stealing. King was the Alpha. Period.

The male set the generator down and stalked toward her, his face twisted into a snarl. He let his claws release and his cat show in his eyes. Okay then, definitely jaguar. And it looked like this fool wanted to fight.

Star started forward, her fingertips tingling with fire. Right now she needed to let out her repressed anger, but before she could take another step Axel raced past her, a snarl in his throat even as he shifted to full lion, his clothes shredding as he moved.

Damn it. She'd wanted to take care of this herself, but apparently Axel had the same idea. He tossed the jaguar to the grass in a full-body slam.

"Are you okay?" She turned to look at the human, quickly assessing her from head to foot. Her curly hair—which was chocolate brown with a riot of auburn streaked through it—was secured into a thick ponytail that looked as if it was straining against the band, and her T-shirt and ancient-looking jeans were paint-splattered with a variety of colors. But Star didn't scent any blood or see any physical injuries.

"I'm fine," she murmured, wrapping her arms around herself. She actually did seem shockingly fine with the savage fight going on a few feet away. "I'm in charge of the reconstruction of these few blocks and a big part of Uptown. Normally my dragons are with me or King leaves a couple wolves with me, but I just stopped by to assess the work my crew did today. I hadn't even planned to be here this evening."

Star looked over as the jaguar howled in pain, Axel pinning him to the ground with a giant lion paw.

"So this guy has never hassled you before?"

The woman shook her head. "No—holy crap, are you Star?" The woman dropped her arms, her eyes widening as she seemed to fully see Star for the first time.

She nodded. "Yeah."

The woman blinked once. Then twice. "My name is Avery. I'm a huge fan. I didn't know you were supernatural too. That's so cool. I didn't recognize you at first because your hair isn't indigo."

Star half-smiled even as she kept an eye on the males, both of whom had shifted back to human form. They were also buck naked right now and Axel had ruined his clothes. "Thanks. Hey…did you say 'your dragons' earlier?"

"Ah, yeah, I live with a bunch of dragons and my younger brothers, who are human. They're all basically a bunch of adolescents—not literally, it just feels like it most days—and they're great at construction." She shrugged.

Now it was Star's turn to blink. This human female lived with dragons?

The woman smiled at her. "It's a long story... So I'm not supposed to ask what you are, right?"

Star grinned. "That's right. It's considered offensive by some. But the really old ones, the ancients, don't care. They'll ask you what you are in a heartbeat. And they'll comment on your smell, whether it's good or bad. And they might even lean in to your personal space and just sniff. So...yeah." The ancients had very little civility in them.

Avery snorted. "Oh, I know all about some of the ancients. The smelling thing took me off guard at first, but whatever. Look, I need to call King because—"

Two wolves raced down the street, heading toward them like missiles. It didn't matter that they were in human form, the dark-skinned male and bronze-skinned female had that whole rangy, lean wolf look about them. And they were dressed in simple fatigues that seemed to be the uniform of King's pack.

The wolves took one look at Axel and the jaguar, then headed straight for Avery. "What happened?" the female asked in a way that made it clear she knew Avery. "Either of them hurt you?" The wolf's eyes said that if Avery had been hurt, someone was going to die.

Star stepped back as Avery started talking to the wolves. Before Avery had even finished, the male had the jaguar trussed up in cuffs that were very likely spelled. Or something of the equivalent, she guessed, because the male was struggling and couldn't break them even with his supernatural strength.

Axel shifted back to human and strode up to Star, his arms crossed over his chest as he eyed the cuffed jaguar with annoyance.

"Thanks for stopping this asshole," the female wolf said as she turned from Avery. "We've got him from here. But are you guys good?"

Star nodded. "Yep."

"All right, then. We've got this covered. Oh, if you're headed that way, there's a yellow house on the left. Stop in and ask for extra clothes if you need them," she said, looking pointedly at a naked Axel. "Tell them Maria sent you."

"Thanks," Axel said. Then he looked at Star. "I'm just going to go full lion for the rest of the night."

She nodded as he shifted to his animal form, not surprised he'd decided to shift again. He hadn't gotten to run in a while. Then she turned back to the adorable human. "Hey Avery, I live in the purple and yellow mansion on Harmony Street. Stop by tomorrow any time after ten if you want. You can meet the whole band."

The human's eyes widened and she nodded enthusiastically, the dark curls of her ponytail bouncing wildly. "I will totally be there."

Half-smiling at the woman's enthusiasm, Star headed off with Axel. She was glad the human hadn't recognized her at first. It gave her hope that she'd be able to blend in a bit better. Star hadn't used magic to change her hair color now that they'd settled down here, but she probably would for any future shows.

She had a feeling the lack of recognition also might be because people had a whole shitload on their minds now that half the world had been decimated. Things like fame weren't that important anymore. At least not to everyone.

The rest of the walk was brisk and uneventful. As they reached the back door to Cynara's nightclub, one of the security guys raised an eyebrow as he looked at Axel, who was still rocking his lion form.

"Look man, sometimes it's okay to come inside in animal form, but not tonight."

"We're here to meet with Cynara, not go into the club," she said. "And he doesn't have any clothes with him."

The guy rubbed a hand over his bald head, then spoke quietly into what must be an invisible earpiece. Then he nodded once. "All right. Through here, up the stairs, first door on your left. You're free to hit the club—afterward, obviously, but shift to human form if you do."

"Will do," Star promised.

The guy nodded as he opened the door for them. "By the way, I saw you live a couple times before... Before The Fall. You're fucking awesome. Any time you come to the club, don't wait in line, all right?"

She nodded once and held out a hand. "Thanks."

Axel made a sort of snuffling sound and trotted by the guy, his tail swishing in the air as if he was actually king of the jungle. When he shook his mane, letting all his fur fluff out, she didn't bother stifling her laugh.

"You are so far beyond ridiculous sometimes," she muttered as Axel raced up the stairs ahead of her. The walls were a deep purple, the railings all black, and there was fun, funky art dotting the walls.

Axel turned around and looked at her from the top landing, then simply licked his paw once before racing on. When she found him, he was sitting perfectly still in front of the door the bouncer had indicated.

The door had a simple sign in black and white that said *OFFICE*. And the color of the door was indigo. Seriously, what was up with that color popping up so often lately? Yeah she'd dyed her hair indigo for ages, but now when she thought of the color, she thought of Lachlan's eyes.

She wasn't sure why she couldn't stop thinking about that sexy, smoldering dragon with his delicious Scottish accent. Okay, she'd literally just answered her own question. She knew *exactly* why she was thinking of that male. And she was almost positive he was the dragon who had saved her and her band as they'd made their escape from the airport in Wales.

The dragon's scales had been the same beautiful indigo color as Lachlan's eyes. So yeah, it had to have been him. Gah, she needed to stop thinking about him. AKA fantasizing about him.

Before she could knock, the door swung open and Cynara smiled at the two of them. Of Asian descent, she had bright purple hair that definitely wasn't a dye job. And her matching bright purple eyes weren't contacts either, though Star was sure humans had always assumed they were. Petite and lean, she had on a black and gold bandage dress that hugged every inch of her body. It was like slashes of material simply covered the important bits but everything else was all skin. And the spiked black heels she wore were killer.

"Star! I'm so happy to see you." The half-demon, half-vampire flashed her fangs as she stepped out, raising an eyebrow at Axel's huge lion form. "I don't know if you're going to fit in here comfortably."

"You got any clothing?" Star asked as she pulled Cynara into a tight hug.

"Yeah," she said as she stepped back. "A couple of my brothers leave stashes here." Turning on her heel, she went to a closet and rummaged around before pulling out a pair of cargo pants and a huge T-shirt that looked like it would definitely fit Axel.

She tossed them to the lion. "Change outside. Justus gets annoyed when I see other men naked."

Star snickered and shut the door behind her so Axel had privacy. "Are you serious?"

Cynara nodded. "Oh yeah. Mated males are so bizarre sometimes. I mean, I work at a club with shifters who are constantly in a state of undress."

"Do you like him to see naked females other than you?"

The woman laughed, throwing her head back. "Fair point. Hell no. Look, thanks for stopping by," she said as Axel stepped inside as well. She gave him a nod as she continued talking to Star. "As you know, I wanted to talk to you about doing a few charity shows. The city is rebuilding but people have lost so much. Especially humans. Not only did they lose a lot, and in many cases entire families, but their whole reality has shifted to this new one where they're not at the top of the food chain. It's a lot for anyone to deal with. I was talking with King and another Alpha, Finn, who is the Alpha of—"

"Girl, I *know* who he is." Star had performed at Cynara's brother's club in Biloxi, where Finn was a powerful Alpha who ran a huge swath of the Gulf Coast area. He'd also mated with a bloodborn vamp.

Cynara nodded once. "That's right. My brain is running on like two cylinders right now so I forgot. Anyway, I talked to him and a couple other dragon clans spread around the United States. Everyone is rebuilding as quick as they can, but it's the same thing everywhere. Humans really are struggling. I think it would be pretty awesome if we could do a few charity shows for morale. One in Jackson Square, one near Tulane. Obviously it's a lot to ask, but—"

"Of course I'll do it! It's not a lot to ask. I would be more than happy to." Star actually missed singing. "I know it hasn't been that long since we performed, but...I thought it might be frivolous to put on shows now."

Cynara snorted. "Art and entertainment are never frivolous. We need it now more than ever."

"Agreed." Axel nodded in approval as he scanned the shelves of her tiny office. The male was always curious—typical feline.

ANCIENT PROTECTOR | 67

"Great. I thought I'd have to convince you more. But if you're on board then I'd love to sit down and talk about an actual schedule with you. I'd also like to ask you to do a show here at the club. I'll pay you for that one of course. We'll figure out something. I can pay you in favors or whatever."

Star shook her head. "No way. It's on the house." Ever since The Fall, the powers that be hadn't worked out a monetary system yet. Right now people were basically dealing in favors, and King had made sure that no one in the city was going without food or shelter or healthcare as they got a structure set back in place. In her opinion, some things actually worked out better in this new world since nobody had to worry about going bankrupt because they broke a leg or needed emergency surgery. They just got what they needed taken care of at a human hospital—and supernaturals went to see a healer.

There was a sharp bang on the door, followed by a male voice. "Cynara, you're needed on the floor."

Star smiled at the female. "Look, you know where I live so if you want to sit down and go over anything, feel free to stop by tomorrow. We'll figure everything out."

"I will. I'm gonna go take care of whatever's going on downstairs, but I'll call you later."

"I kind of can't believe how busy you seem to stay."

She lifted a shoulder. "People need to blow off steam and this is the place to do it."

"How are you even getting things like alcohol?"

Cynara grinned, flashing her fangs again as she headed for the door. "I struck up a deal with a local witch. She's hooking me up with some prime magic. Not to mention a couple local breweries survived the carnage and are going full steam with production. People are freaking crazy—the world's upended, but they've got their beer." She rolled her eyes with a laugh.

"I think a lot of supernaturals are going to be surprised by how much we have to depend on witches and half-demons to rebuild this world."

Cynara grinned then. "I agree."

"It'll be good for their egos." Witches and half-demons had been looked down upon for far too long.

Her grin grew even wider. "You're preaching to the choir."

They talked for a few more minutes before someone banged on the door again. As Cynara ran off, they let themselves out. Once they were in the fresh night air, Star inhaled deeply. "You were pretty quiet back there."

"Nothing to say," Axel said. "And when have I ever questioned you in front of outsiders anyway? You're my Alpha." He looked almost affronted.

Reaching out, she patted his forearm once. "I know." She and Axel and all the others had been friends literally since childhood. Each of their parents had belonged to an artists' commune. Or more like a co-op, in supernatural terms—but humans had called them a commune.

So they'd grown up surrounded by artists, sculptors and writers. Their commune had been a great cover in the human world—just a bunch of "fucking hippies" living in a giant mansion when in reality they'd all been various types of shifters who hadn't fit into packs, clans, covens or prides. Their parents had just lived the life they wanted and taught all of them to do the same. Their parents had wanted them to grow up free to be who they wanted.

But from the time they'd been little, Star had more or less been the Alpha of their group. With the exception of her sister, because Aurora had been born later and they had a different relationship anyway. She wasn't even sure what it was that drove them to have a leader, some sort of animal instinct, but shifters always looked for someone to lead them. And her crew had always trusted her role. Probably because she'd never given them a reason to doubt her and she would die for all of them.

As they turned onto Chartres Street, Star paused as she inhaled a deep, familiar masculine scent.

"What is it?" Axel asked, clearly sensing a shift in her.

She swallowed hard and forced herself to keep walking, to remain casual. "Just ready to get back home."

He nodded but straightened slightly, scanning every face on the street as they walked.

For her part, Star scanned too. But for a different reason. She scented him, the male who fueled her fantasies.

Lachlan.

CHAPTER 8

Star inhaled again and the scent was gone. Just like that.

It was impossible anyway. Lachlan wouldn't be *here*. From the little research she'd done into him—aka stalking, according to Lola who'd been more than happy to help her dig into his life—he was the Alpha of the Donnachaidh clan in northern Scotland. She had no idea how to even pronounce that or if it was his actual last name. He was apparently ancient so it stood to reason he had a different, ancient name. Oh, and the male owned a couple castles. Which was…okay, pretty awesome. But it wasn't like she'd checked on him because she cared. She'd just wanted to know more about a potential ally.

Okay, stop lying to yourself. He'd very likely helped her and the others escape Wales, so she did care. And he was quite literally the sexiest male she'd ever met so there was that too.

"Why don't you head on home by yourself?" she murmured to Axel, but she wasn't really asking. She was telling him to go.

He shot her a sideways glance as they stepped around a human couple walking a little Pekingese dog. The human woman looked at Star with a hint of curiosity, possibly recognizing her or simply thinking she looked familiar.

"I'm your backup." Axel's tone was mild.

"I'm good, I promise. I'm just going to get some *me* time." Which was code for when she needed to expel some of her natural energy.

At that he nodded and continued heading down the street. Star, on the other hand, took a left at the next alleyway and picked up her pace as she passed the rear loading entrance of a hotel that was now being used as lodging for displaced people.

Leaving the Quarter, she headed to Uptown in record time where she ducked into a small local park. Once she was sure she was alone, Star was silent as she climbed up a huge live oak tree. The branches sprawled out in abandon, Spanish moss and beads dangling from each branch.

She heard some humans nearby, and maybe a wolf or two, all walking along the sidewalk lining the park.

Maybe she was being crazy now, trying to get a bead on Lachlan. Because…why on earth would he be in New Orleans when he had a clan to lead half a world away? Still, for a brief moment she'd sworn that rich, dark scent that reminded her of waves crashing against jagged rocks had been right in front of her. But then it had disappeared.

Maybe she was being crazy, wishing for something that wasn't there. *No!* She didn't wish for him to be here at all. Did she? She didn't even know the male.

And she had no business being interested in a dragon anyway. Her sister was still healing after being in captivity for a year because of a dragon clan, and the world was rebuilding. She should not be thinking about some random male. Even if he was incredibly sexy.

Dammit, she really shouldn't have asked Lola to search for information on him, because late at night she'd been poring over the info Lola had given her. Even though she'd told herself it had been to find out exactly who he was, since he'd helped them escape, she'd known the truth. She'd just wanted more info on him for her own purposes. Sadly, she was pretty sure Lola had known as well.

Once she was sure she was relatively alone, Star called on her magic to guide her. Diving off the tree branch, she soared high above the treetops until the city grew smaller below. The mostly unused cars were little dots, not much smaller than the houses.

Her tendons and muscles strained as she arced upward. Unlike dragons, she couldn't camouflage herself, but the night was a good backdrop for her in this form. With the moon hiding behind clouds and the stars just as hidden, it was easy to blend with the shadows.

As she soared, she searched the skies for Lachlan, but no surprise, didn't see him. She did see clusters of dragons flying over Lake Pontchartrain, however. But…no big, beautiful indigo-colored dragon.

Sighing, she turned westward and headed back to the mansion. Not just the mansion, but home. At least for now. For her, home meant wherever she was with her family.

CHAPTER 9

Star raced through the lush, green field, her gaze catching on the edge of the cliff ahead. Heart pounding, she glanced behind her. She sensed him, but couldn't see him.

He was so good at blending in. Draoidheachd, she knew. Everything about him was magic. They played this game often. She ran, but he always caught her. He'd told her he always would and she believed him.

When he caught her, he picked her up, sometimes throwing her over his shoulder and taking her back to his cave. Sometimes he simply took her right in the grass. She liked it either way, liked the things he did to her body.

Well, like was too simple of a word. She loved everything about him even if she hadn't said the words. She was too afraid to. They were from different worlds.

"Got you," a deep, male voice murmured, scooping her up from behind.

Laughing, she curled up against him, burying her face against his neck. She never saw his face in these dreams, as if he was too beautiful to look upon. To even imagine.

But she could smell him, that rich, earthy scent that reminded her of the cold sea, clover and wildflowers in spring. "I like when you chase me."

"Have you talked to your family yet?" His words were quiet as he headed to the cliff's edge. He surprised her, not immediately pouncing and tasting between her legs like he loved to do.

She hadn't even realized males and females did that, but he'd told her he wanted to. So she tasted him too and loved the reaction she got. "Not yet."

Sighing, he sat down far enough away from the cliff that she couldn't dangle her feet over. This was one of her favorite spots, overlooking the wild ocean that never seemed to tire. Before him, she'd freely run along the cliff's edge, stretching out under the sun on the rare days the gray clouds didn't cover everything. But he worried about her, he said. He didn't like her too close to the edge. And since she didn't like to worry this strong, wonderful male, she kept a safe distance from the edge even when she wasn't with him.

"Have I not proved my love?" he murmured against the top of her head.

"No, yes, I mean...I know you love me." She wasn't sure why or how it was possible. This magic male who brought her wildflowers. "And I love you. I just need time." She was scared, if she was being honest with herself. She was scared his people wouldn't accept her.

As if he read her mind, he spoke softly into her hair, "You've already met my brother. My people will accept you."

Maybe. A rumble started in the distance, telling of a storm moving in. Shivering against the wind that kicked up, she burrowed against him, savoring his natural heat. She would need to return to her village soon or else her family would worry if she wasn't home by the time the skies opened up.

But when his callused hand slid up her thigh, pushing her skirt up, she knew they had a bit more time...

Star opened her eyes with a start, her heart rate out of control. A new dream.

Always with the same, faceless man. And she always woke up aroused or grieving. *Gah.*

Turning to her pillow she punched it with force. What the hell was it about these bizarre dreams that simply wouldn't leave her alone? They felt real, but she knew they weren't. They weren't from this age, no, but from a time long past.

And nothing made sense if she tried to dwell on the blasted dreams. So she closed her eyes and collapsed back against her pillow. It wasn't time to get up yet and she needed a couple more hours of sleep if she was going to function at all.

Unfortunately she was pretty sure sleep was going to be elusive for her tonight.

CHAPTER 10

"This would be a great place to build a small studio for Aurora." Star stood in the west side of their yard, pointing to an open area as she spoke to Bella. She was still feeling a bit off about her dream last night and finding it hard to concentrate on anything.

"I bet that human Avery will help you with plans."

Star nodded. Avery had stopped by earlier in the morning, coffee in hand and a smile on her face. She'd been a little starstruck at meeting the whole band, but pretty cool. Not like some humans could be. And she'd been really respectful, not asking what anybody was.

It was clear that she really did live with a bunch of dragons—male ones—and she'd said she'd loved hanging out with a bunch of women instead of "dudes who smell like sweaty socks half the time." Though she had gasped in surprise when Marley had stripped down naked, turned into a snow leopard and started prancing around the yard like a freaking show cat. Snow leopards could be just as silly as wolves.

"I just want to get Aurora out of the house, get her focused on something," Star said. Because Aurora was a gifted artist. Her real talent lay in sculptures, but she was also incredible with faces. Ink was her medium, and somehow she captured what people were thinking, their emotions. The detail was in the eyes and Aurora had a real gift.

Star hadn't gotten *any* of that talent. The only thing she could do was sing. Well, and she could play the guitar and piano. But Aurora was a savant, in a whole category by herself. And she hadn't showed an ounce of interest in returning to her art since they'd freed her. Not that Star blamed her. No, she blamed Oscar and wanted to rip his head off for what he'd done to her sister.

One day. One day, she reminded herself. She'd have that dragon's head on a pike.

She turned at the sound of wings flapping before a giant indigo-colored dragon suddenly swooped down in the middle of the yard. One moment the yard had been empty, and then *he* was there.

Her hair flew back under the waving of his wings, her heart rate jumping in a mix of fear and…was that excitement? *Yep.*

His scales glittered wildly underneath the sunlight, his matching eyes pinning Star in place even from twenty-five yards away.

"Shit." Bella jumped into action even as Star strode forward toward the big beast.

Her whole crew raced out of the mansion, claws out and ready for battle, but Star held up a hand, silently ordering them back. If this dragon was a threat, then they would deal with him.

"Shift to human," she ordered as she boldly came to stand in front of Lachlan.

Moments later, Lachlan, Mr. Too Sexy For His Own Naked Ass dragon, stood in front of her, completely and utterly gorgeous. Without his clothing on, she saw everything he'd been hiding under the custom suit. Her gaze trailed over his broad shoulders and the perfectly cut lines of his chest and abs—

Harlow cleared her throat.

Star blinked, her gaze narrowing on the sharp planes of his face. "What the hell are you doing here?" she snapped, putting her hands on her hips as she faced off with him. She forced her gaze to remain upward even though she really, really wanted to check out the rest of him. Maybe just a peek…

"I'm ready for our date." He said the words so simply, that rich voice wrapping around her, practically drugging her into a sense of security.

Of all the things he could have said to her, she was not expecting that. Her hands dropped to her sides as she stared into those intoxicating eyes. "What?"

"Our date," he said slowly. "It's been a month and a half. I shall have my date now."

She started laughing, probably a little bit maniacally, as she stared at him. "You came all the way from Scotland for a date when half the world has been destroyed?"

He lifted a broad shoulder and stared at her as if to say "duh."

She shook her head at him. "What is wrong with you?"

"Not a damn thing, lass."

What the hell? "Does King even know you're in his territory?"

He continued watching her. "I am free tonight."

Okay, that wasn't an answer, and he was also frustrating her, which she was fairly certain he knew. "I'm not going on a freaking date with you."

"So your word doesnae mean anything?" He lifted a dark eyebrow, challenging her.

She let out a growl of frustration, struggling to focus on the conversation when he was standing in front of her in all his naked glory. *Don't look lower!* she ordered herself. "This is insane. You show up out of nowhere, on private property, in *dragon* form, and demand a date."

"I'm not demanding anything. I'm simply honoring the terms of our agreement. I would like to take you out this evening. Or tomorrow. Lass's choice."

How magnanimous of him, letting her choose. She nearly rolled her eyes even though her other half wanted to come out and play—to show off for the male. *Horny bitch.* Somehow Star kept her gaze pinned to his.

Before she could respond Bella stepped forward, a tight smile in place. "Star will reach out to you about the date. Do you have a form of communication?"

"My mobile number is still the same."

"Great. She'll call you."

He kept his gaze on Star even as he spoke to Bella, his tone measured and even. "Will she talk for herself on our date? Or will you be there as well?"

Star gasped. "There will not be—"

Bella cut Star off. "It will just be the two of you, of course. Now leave before we all attack you. Go." Bella literally made a shooing motion, trying to make him leave as if he was a stray alley cat instead of a powerful, deadly dragon.

Lachlan glanced around, taking in Star's crew as well as Aurora, who had come downstairs and was watching him warily. Some had weapons out, others simply revealed their claws. Athena actually had her guitar in hand and was wielding it like a baseball bat. Considering the thing was spelled to be indestructible, Star wasn't surprised.

"You were there the night at the airport," Aurora said quietly.

He nodded. "Aye, I was."

"Why did you help us get away?"

Lachlan simply looked back at Star, staring at her long and hard—as if the answer was obvious. Apparently it didn't matter that she was a virtual stranger to him.

Star felt her cheeks flush and she inwardly cursed. She wasn't some teenager so easily affected by a male. Especially an obnoxious, smug one like this who'd shown up on their property, naked, demanding a date as if it was his due.

But...he had helped all of them escape. And the truth was she wanted to know why. It couldn't just be for sex. That was kind of crazy. But he *had* bid a million dollars on her. So maybe he was crazy after all.

"I called King." Brielle stepped forward, giving Lachlan a challenging look, as if daring him to make one wrong move. Her twin was right next to her.

Lachlan looked back at Star.

Star lifted an eyebrow. "Unless you've announced to the other Alpha that you're in his territory, I suggest you get out of here."

His jaw tightened, the male looking as if he wanted to argue. "I'll expect your call." Sharp, clipped words from the very naked dragon who was unabashed in his nudity.

Of course he had every right to be, with a body like that. He looked as if he'd been carved straight from marble.

As soon as he'd shifted and taken to the skies, they all let out a collective sigh of relief. Her other nature was disappointed the male was gone, but she shushed her right up.

She turned to Brielle once he was out of sight, trying to control her chaotic emotions. Something about that male called to her, and that was deeply disturbing. Her other nature had never reacted to a male before, never cared at all. "What did you say to King?"

"Nothing. I didn't really call him."

Star blinked in surprise. "You're very convincing."

Her friend shrugged. "The dragon helped us get away. I figure we owe him for that at least. And I'm kind of curious what he's doing here. I mean, it's clear he wants to bang you, but I'm guessing there's another reason."

"He's a male, and a dragon. Banging me is reason enough," she said, despite the tension in her shoulders and her belly. "I am made of awesomeness, after all."

Brielle raised an eyebrow. "I'm just saying, sex is a dumb reason to come halfway across the world. There's gotta be another reason."

"I feel like you're giving males too much credit," Aurora murmured.

"I'm afraid to say, Aurora is probably right." Axel's voice was dry. "Sex is a great reason to fly halfway across the world. It's probably the best one."

Star simply snorted even as Aurora and the others giggled.

That sound was music to Star's ears. She loved her sister's laugh and was glad that she was slowly coming back to herself. Even making a little joke was a big deal. She was finally starting to come out of her shell again.

"You probably do need to call King," Bella said on a sigh. "Even if we owe the dragon."

Star knew she was right. Still, somehow it felt like a betrayal of sorts to call the wolf Alpha on Lachlan and she wasn't sure why. They were in King's territory and she couldn't afford to spit in the face of one of her allies. Not one who had gone out of his way to make her and her family feel safe. Because if it came down to it, she had no doubt that his pack would step up and help them face down the threat of Oscar's clan.

Or at least she really hoped they would.

* * *

Star opened the front door after the first knock, not surprised to find King on the other side since she'd called him a couple hours ago. She smiled at him then stepped back as he and two of his wolves stepped into the foyer.

Security, she guessed. She knew there were all sorts of designations for wolf packs and dragon clans. Maybe they were called sentries, or warriors? She wasn't really sure of all the technical stuff though. Her crew didn't really have designations since they were from all walks of life. Except that she was their Alpha and most of them were of the warrior class.

She realized she hadn't said anything and cleared her throat. "Thanks for coming by," she said, shutting the door behind them. "You want to talk in the kitchen?"

He nodded and glanced around the interior even though he'd been here before when they'd first arrived for a brief introduction in person. Today he wore simple black pants, a black T-shirt that molded to his fit body and a leather jacket. She was also pretty sure that he had a sword tucked against his back, if the rumors she'd heard were true that he wielded one despite being a wolf. "What kind of emergency is this?" he asked, glancing at her now. His ice-blue eyes seemed more vivid against his brown skin as he watched her.

"It's not really an emergency, I guess," she said as they entered the kitchen. She felt weird telling King about Lachlan even though she wasn't doing anything wrong. But some part of her *almost* felt like she was betraying the big dragon. That was stupid though—he was an Alpha and he should've announced himself in this territory. That was like Alpha rules 101.

King nodded at the male and female wolf once and they headed out the back door. Loud rambunctious laughter from her own people trailed inside as the door opened then shut.

She sat at the countertop. "A dragon named Lachlan is in New Orleans. I don't know much about him except that he's Scottish and he helped us escape from Wales six weeks ago." Oh, and that he was sexy as fuck. But she kept that little tidbit to herself.

"How do you know he's here?"

"He came to see me a couple hours ago. He's said he's here to see me, but...I know I needed to let you know that another Alpha is in your territory. And he's not an Alpha like me. He is a full-on Alpha dragon who runs a huge territory in Scotland."

King simply nodded, his expression not betraying anything. For all she knew he was already aware of Lachlan's presence. "I know the name.

We have allies in common. I'll find him."

"I have his phone number."

King gave her a ghost of a smile. "All right, just text it to me. I'll reach out to him and see what's going on." He'd started to say something else when she heard the side door to the kitchen open and shut. Turning, she smiled to see her sister walking inside.

Aurora's long, dark hair was down today and she had on a loose, Grecian-style dress. At least she'd moved on from paint-splattered yoga pants and T-shirts that needed to be burned.

Star turned back to King, ready to introduce them, and paused when she realized that King was staring at Aurora. His expression had fully relaxed, his eyes a little bit wider than normal and his lips parted ever so slightly.

She'd never seen the Alpha looking so intent. He almost looked younger in that moment, as if he was inadvertently showing a different side of himself. It was impossible to tell how old supernaturals were just by the way they looked, but King wore a whole lot of years of battle and cynicism around him like a cloak. If she had to guess, he was a couple hundred years old. He'd have to be, to hold on to a territory like this. But right now as he stared at Aurora, he looked like a young man in his twenties.

She turned back to her sister to find Aurora watching him guardedly, her violet eyes slightly narrowed.

"Aurora, this is King. Officially." Star had already told her sister about the Alpha, obviously.

King moved around the island in a few quick steps. "It's nice to meet you." He held out his hand, all civility and politeness.

Okay, Star had never actually seen him act like this either.

Aurora tentatively took his hand and shook it once before wrapping her arms back around herself. Then she looked at Star. "I'm feeling kind of tired. Too much stimulation outside." Again with the half-smile. "I'm going to head upstairs, maybe work on some drawings."

Star hoped she was serious about the drawings. "If we're too loud, let me know."

She laughed lightly and shot another quick, curious look at King. "I can't hear anything up there. It's fine."

King watched her sister leave, staring blatantly before Star cleared her throat.

The wolf met her gaze and once again he was the hard-faced, cynical Alpha.

"The dragon, Lachlan, helped us get away in Wales. He killed a couple of the dragons who held my sister captive." Star wasn't sure why she was telling King that—okay, more lies. She knew exactly why she was telling this wolf.

King's eyes flashed pure wolf for a long moment. Then he blinked once, as if clearing his head. "You never told me why she was held captive."

"No, I didn't." And she sure as hell wasn't going to tell him now. It hadn't been a sexual thing, the only silver lining. At least that's what Aurora had said. And Star believed her. No, that monster had wanted her blood, practically draining her over and over until she was near death. And he'd made it impossible for her to escape the iron-lined room.

Star bit down hard, trying not to let the rage swell up inside her. If she did, her beast would take over and she would forget all about her promise of control and head back to the UK and burn Oscar's entire compound to the ground. And she wouldn't stop there. She would destroy any of his clanmates involved in taking her sister, any who had known about it and condoned it.

"Send me the details you have on the Alpha who took her." His growled words surprised Star.

She blinked. "Okay. Why?"

"If he comes after her again, I need to know more about anyone intentionally invading my territory."

"Of course." She'd given him some details about Oscar already, but only the basics, including his picture. But her whole crew had compiled a lot of info on the asshole over the last year. "Thanks for stopping by tonight."

"I appreciate the heads-up about the dragon. Oh, I talked to Cynara earlier. She said you were going to do a few charity shows. I think that's great."

"She seems to think it's a good idea, and I trust her judgment."

"The people in the city need entertainment. They need something else in their lives right now other than just rebuilding."

"Is there anything else we can do to help?" They'd all pitched in, in various areas around the city, but she wanted to offer up more assistance anyway. "I met a human named Avery who said she's in charge of an area close to here. If she needs anything, all of us will pitch in."

"I'm going to take you up on your offer of help soon. Right now we're working on the most crucial areas and getting the most vulnerable set up. I've got trained construction crews handling that and I trust them. I'm also currently in meetings with a coven of witches about more rebuilding efforts as well."

"That sounds like a whole lot of logistics to figure out." And it had only been six weeks since The Fall. She thought he seemed to be doing a pretty damn good job. At least from what she could see. But she knew there would be infighting because that was just the way things went.

"It really is." For just a moment, the male looked positively exhausted, but then his strong mask fell back in place.

"Hey, I appreciate the running water." Thankfully not everything had been destroyed, and they had things like electricity and water and functioning grocery stores. Those were the kinds of things that would keep humans from rioting. Unfortunately so many people had been displaced, so they were currently rebuilding homes that had been destroyed and figuring out living situations for people who had been visiting during The Fall and were unable to go home—because theirs had been destroyed.

"You and me both." He gave her a ghost of a smile.

CHAPTER 11

Cody leaned against the giant oak tree in human form, his ball cap pulled low.

"What are you doing here?" Lachlan asked from his perch high above his younger brother. In human form, Lachlan was naked and camouflaged a few stories up in the tree.

Cody started peeling a mandarin orange, the bright, citrusy scent carrying on the evening air. "Just wondering how long you're going to hang out here stalking Star."

As long as he damn well pleased. And he wasn't stalking. "Away wi' ye."

"King just stopped by her mansion," Cody said conversationally.

No shite. He had a perfect visual of the entrance to Star's mansion. Though the only reason his visual was so good was because of his dragon eyesight and the tree's height.

"What are you doing watching her place like a fucking weirdo?"

Lachlan didn't respond.

"You're acting irrational," his brother continued. "The fact that we're here at all is daft. We should be home looking after our own."

"I didnae ask you to come." In fact he'd ordered his brother to stay at the castle, helping watch over their people as they adjusted to the new world.

Of course, for his people it wasn't very hard. His home hadn't been damaged and his lands were already self-sufficient. But the humans and the surrounding towns were struggling, so of course his clan had reached out and were helping humans get on their feet as they restructured all facets of their new lives. Besides, he had to establish his dominion over his territory. So yes, his brother was correct. The truth was, he should not be here.

But at the crux of it, he couldn't stay away from Star. When she'd left the UK, he'd planned to follow her immediately, but the world had descended into chaos and fire. And on top of that, it had taken five long weeks for him to discover where she was. And that had only happened by chance, through a conversation with an old warrior friend who lived in New Orleans.

It had taken almost another entire week to get things ready before he could come here. And he wasn't leaving without his mate.

"I just dinnae understand why you're acting this way over pussy." There was a hint of challenge in his brother's tone.

Lachlan's fingers clenched around a branch above him, severing it completely. It fell to the ground, nearly hitting Cody in the head. Lachlan was only sorry that it didn't. "Speak of her like that again and I'll shove that branch through your chest." His words were a savage growl.

"Come on, just admit why you're really here." It was impossible to see his brother's expression, but his tone was smug.

"Go fuck yerself." His brother knew why he was here, he wasn't going to spell it out. His whole being chafed at the idea of answering to anyone, let alone his youngest brother.

"She's not a dragon." Cody's tone shifted ever so slightly, sounding serious for the first time in ages.

"I'm well aware." Why were they continuing this incessant conversation?

"The clan might not accept an outsider as an Alpha Laird's mate."

There it was. He'd been waiting on the pushback, and in truth was surprised it had taken Cody so long. "Then the clan will have to live without me." When he'd come out of Hibernation, the male who had been Alpha for far too long had immediately descended into Hibernation, glad to be able to go to sleep. His people had been more than happy to see him again, ready for his rising. But he would leave if they did not accept his female.

There was a long moment of silence, then Cody shoved away from the tree. "I'm going to scout out the city. I have my mobile on me."

Lachlan didn't bother responding. Instead he scanned the yard where

Star's bandmates and friends roamed freely in animal form. Two snow leopards were out getting exercise and the tiger twins were patrolling the wall. The lone male of the group, a lion, was licking his paws. Times had certainly changed, according to Cody who'd been awake for a solid decade.

Lachlan hadn't been awake long enough for the outing of supernaturals to seem odd to him. Before he'd gone into Hibernation thousands of years ago, supernaturals and humans had lived together. Apparently that had been forgotten long ago and not recorded in history. Which didn't surprise him, considering how garbled the history books and texts seemed to be today.

As he watched the patrolling tigers, he frowned at the small gaps in their security. They needed to tighten things up, especially if Oscar decided to hunt them down. From his own research after the battle at the airport, Lachlan had discovered that Oscar had taken someone from Star's crew—though Oscar hadn't realized it, or he'd never have let her and her band into his territory.

Yesterday when Lachlan had seen the interaction between Star and the one named Aurora, he'd realized they were sisters even though none of his research had revealed that. It had been in the subtle way Star had placed her body in front of Aurora's. And there was a clear familial resemblance—now that Star's hair wasn't colored, it was easy to see that her natural, chestnut brown was the same shade as Aurora's.

Aurora looked undernourished. If she'd been in captivity, that was no surprise. Whereas Star's body was toned and lean, making her appear taller than what he guessed was five feet, six inches. Their eyes had a similar hue as well, with Star's violet ones a shade paler than Aurora's. They were definitely sisters.

If things had not been so chaotic since The Fall, he would have gone to war with Oscar. And he still would for what the male had done—taking a female and holding her against her will? Sending his clanmates to the airport and almost killing Star? That was a crime punishable by death. He didn't even care why the male had done it. There was no reason good enough.

But Lachlan would not strike at Oscar until the time was right. And his only focus now was keeping Star safe—and convincing her that he was a worthy dragon. To be fair, Oscar might come after him, regardless, since Lachlan had killed three of his dragons at that airport.

When his mobile phone buzzed on the branch next to him, he glanced at it. He didn't recognize the phone number. He thought of ignoring it but answered on the chance that it was Star. "Yes."

"Is this Lachlan?"

He frowned at the unfamiliar male voice. "Who is this?"

"This is King, and you're in my territory. I should *not* be calling you. You should have come to me first."

Yes, he was well aware of that. What he'd done was disrespectful. "I'm after my mate." That was pretty much the only exception for which another Alpha would accept his rudeness.

A long sigh followed. "Be at my compound in one hour. Don't be late." The line ended and Lachlan realized the male hadn't told him where he lived.

Of course Lachlan already knew King's main compound, something the other Alpha clearly assumed.

Gathering his clothes from their cache, he quickly dressed then let his camouflage fall before he climbed down the tree. He sent off a text to Cody and his other warriors and headed to King's compound.

The last thing he wanted was strife with someone who could definitely be a powerful ally. And the male had given Star and her people a place of solace. For that, Lachlan found that he liked the powerful wolf.

* * *

Lachlan strode through the open gates into a lush courtyard full of colorful flowers and plants. The fountain in the middle depicted two naked women entwined together holding a jug as water poured from it into the basin.

"Your man will stay here," the petite female wolf told Lachlan, no room for argument in her voice.

He simply nodded at Teague—the warrior he'd brought with him for this meeting. He was in another Alpha's domain, and he would respect the rules. Besides, it was not as if he couldn't take care of himself. If he needed backup for this meeting, he didn't deserve to be Alpha Laird.

Quietly he followed the female, striding across the courtyard where two wolves were lounging.

One lifted her head to look at him and the other didn't bother to see who the new company was.

On the other side of the courtyard, the female pushed open an ornately carved, Mediterranean-style door. Inside, King was sitting in a cafeteria of sorts—Lachlan thought that was the right word.

But the big space was empty save for King and a male Lachlan recognized immediately.

"Reaper!" Surprise and another emotion filled him at the sight of the other ancient. It was good to see someone from long past.

King remained sitting where he was, his gaze on Lachlan. "So, this *is* the Lachlan you know," he said mildly to Reaper.

"Indeed it is." Reaper stood to meet him and pulled him into a tight hug, slamming his meaty fist into Lachlan's back once. Lachlan did the same.

"It has been a long time, my friend. I'm surprised to see you here." Reaper was a formidable and ancient warrior—to find him living in a wolf's territory was interesting.

"My mate is here."

He lifted an eyebrow. "The Dragon of War has mated?"

"The Dragon of War?" There was the slightest hint of amusement in King's voice as he stood.

Lachlan held out a hand for the wolf. He'd done enough research on the other Alpha to know that he was a good leader who only wanted the best for his city. Lachlan approved. For so long humans had put their weakest and greediest in power. It was time the world was run by those who actually cared about all beings—who cared about the greater good, not their own selfish interests.

"Indeed. I once saw Reaper destroy an entire army of Akkadian demons and then use their charred bones to—"

"That's enough of that," Reaper said, clearing his throat.

"I'm sure I would like to hear more later." King's tone was mild, but Lachlan saw the interest in the other male's expression.

"Now, tell me exactly why you didn't announce your presence before arriving in my city." The wolf was in the male's eyes, the deadly predator making himself known.

"Like I said, I am after my mate." And the truth was, if he'd announced himself, and King had refused him entrance, he would have come anyway. As Cody said, it was better to ask for forgiveness than permission.

"And who exactly is your mate?" There was a bite to King's words now as he watched Lachlan very carefully. A predator watching prey.

Lachlan was no one's prey. His dragon rippled under the surface as he stepped forward, forcing down the growl in his throat. "Her name is Star."

Just like that, all the tension in the other male's body eased, as if he'd been expecting a different answer and was glad of this one. "Does she know she's your mate?"

"Gods, no." That wasn't the kind of thing you just came out and told a female who was not a dragon. Dragons recognized their other half—not always, but he was listening to his dragon on this. Once, so very long ago, he'd met a female he was convinced was his other half. An ache in his chest flared up and he absently rubbed it. Thinking of the long-dead human who had stolen his heart would do him no good now and he needed to accept it. He also needed to know more about Star, more about why her sister had landed on Oscar's radar. And he had a feeling it had to do with whatever species the females were.

He'd been running over various options in his mind, especially given the show of power she'd displayed at the airport. He couldn't help but think maybe she was a witch. But...she didn't smell like one. She had a distinct, underlying animal sent. He just couldn't figure out what sort. Maybe she was a hybrid. A half-demon and half-shifter? Many of their kind controlled fire so it was possible, and it made sense, given the animal scent. "I willnae interfere in anything in your territory while I'm here. Unless someone attacks me. Then I will defend myself."

"How long do you plan to be here?"

"I cannae answer that." That was up to Star, of course.

"You have one week." There was no give in King's words as his wolf remained at the forefront.

Lachlan's dragon rippled again, not liking the challenging tone. "Or what?" he growled out.

"One week. If you're still here after that, I kick you out."

"I'm not challenging your territory." Surely the male could see that. Though if he wanted it, he would take it. He was a dragon after all.

"I am aware of that. But you are an Alpha."

And the unspoken words were that King could not allow another Alpha who owned a huge territory like himself to remain in the area for long. It threw off the balance of everything. Lachlan understood that. Reaper was technically an Alpha in nature. Well, no technically about it— he was an Alpha to the bone—but he wasn't an Alpha looking to expand his territory. No, he was a general used to leading armies. Used to war.

"Two weeks," Lachlan said.

King lifted an eyebrow. "I wasn't negotiating with you."

"Have some pity on me. I am but a simple male chasing after his female." He intentionally lightened his tone, knowing he sounded daft.

King let out a startled burst of laughter, and it took years off the wolf's hard face. "That's a new one. I'll give you a week and a half."

"Deal." He held out his hand and shook the other male's once to agree.

"What happens if she doesn't agree to go with you?" King asked.

"Then in a week and a half, I shall kidnap her."

King's eyes narrowed. "You will not," he rasped out, his wolf pushing hard now.

Lachlan had started to respond when Reaper loudly cleared his throat. King nodded once at Reaper, who immediately grabbed Lachlan's arm and led him out.

Lachlan lifted an eyebrow at his friend. "Are you babysitting me now?"

Reaper simply grinned. "Something like that. I've been tasked with keeping an eye on your annoying ass while you're in town."

"My annoying ass?" He scowled. "You sound like a human."

Reaper lifted a broad shoulder. "If you're lucky, I will allow you to meet my mate as well."

"I can only assume she is far too good for you."

Reaper laughed loudly, and the relaxing wolves lifted their heads to look over as they strode across the courtyard. "You assume right, old friend. She is much too good for me—she's a brilliant healer."

Lachlan gave him a surprised look. The Dragon of War and a healer? Times had definitely changed.

"And guess who else is awake now?"

He simply looked at him. Lachlan wasn't going to guess.

"Prima and Mira. And Arthur."

Lachlan snorted. "I knew Arthur was awake. He left Scotland a while ago. Not sure why."

"To chase down Prima."

Lachlan laughed now until tears nearly streamed down his face. Arthur was finally chasing down Prima? "Oh, that bloody fool."

"Maybe, maybe not."

"They're mated?" he asked as they strode down the street, avoiding the dripping water from an above balcony. Someone must have just watered their plants because the water overflowed in abundance.

"Of course not. Prima would not make it easy on him."

He simply grunted. Arthur had wanted Prima even thousands of years ago. But Lachlan didn't think either she or her twin would ever mate. They liked their freedom too much. Those two females were more in touch with their animal side than most dragons he'd ever known.

Of course, he'd never thought to mate either. Not after he'd lost his first love. Then six months ago he'd heard a siren's song and he'd been hooked.

Now he had to hook his female.

CHAPTER 12

Star inwardly cursed herself even as she stepped into the dimly lit restaurant off Chartres Street. She was pretty sure this street had been damaged—the sign to a boutique hotel was missing and some of the brick looked as if it had been stripped right off one of the walls, or burned off—but for the most part there had been a lot of rebuilding here. Rebuilding with supernatural power, if what she'd heard was any indication. So even though there was a faint charred scent that lingered in the air from all the fire damage, most of the structural stuff seemed to be taken care of. At least here. She hadn't seen the whole city yet.

Glancing around the L-shaped interior, she scented mostly supernaturals sitting at the square-top tables, but there were a handful of humans as well. From the looks of the place, once upon a time it had been a four- or five-star restaurant. But now it appeared as if they were serving basic burgers and fried chicken sandwiches. And the sign on the wall declared gumbo the special of the day. She could get on board with that.

The atmosphere was relaxed, with a low murmur of voices carrying across the room. Flickering candles were set on each table, giving the place an even more intimate atmosphere.

She wasn't even sure how going to a restaurant worked at this point. Would they pay or…what? And what would they pay with? She still had a bunch of cash but it was basically useless at this point. Or she assumed it was. King was restructuring everything at the moment and making sure people had their necessities met in exchange for nothing. He'd told her they would restructure financially eventually but she wasn't sure how that was going to work. Their house had been stocked up before they'd arrived so she hadn't even thought about what they'd do if they needed to replenish stuff. She knew there were grocery stores and bodegas across the city providing but she hadn't personally been to any of them.

Caught up in her own thoughts, she almost didn't see the hostess approach, a petite woman with dark curly hair and light brown skin. A wolf, if she had to guess.

The woman smiled at her. "Are you meeting people here, or alone?"

"I'm meeting—"

"Me." Sexy, indigo-eyed Lachlan appeared as if out of nowhere beside her, which of course was impossible given how huge he was. For just a moment, that strange déjà vu sensation punched through her, but she shoved it away. *Again.* Lachlan wasn't the kind of male she would forget. If she'd met him before the concert in Wales, she would have remembered. Still, when she looked at him, she felt—*things.* Far too many things that made no sense.

The hostess looked up at him and smiled. "I'll let you take her to your table, then. Your server will be with you in a moment. Enjoy." She turned from them and started organizing menus by the hostess stand.

"Am I late?" Star asked, fighting that buzzing sensation in her middle.

"No, I was early." He watched her with an intensity that was unnerving, his gaze dipping to her mouth for a brief moment. Sometimes when he looked at her, she felt like he was trying to see into her soul.

"I know this isn't the million-dollar date you paid for," she murmured, feeling nervous and more than out of sorts. The fact that he was in New Orleans at all was so weird.

She knew Axel was nearby keeping an eye on the restaurant just in case things went south, but she didn't actually think Lachlan was going to try anything dangerous. At least not in public—and she didn't think he wanted to hurt her.

"Getting to spend time with you is worth anything." His tone was deadly serious as he pulled out a chair for her.

Oh, damn. His sincerity—and his accent—were doing strange things to her insides. As she sat, she received a few curious looks and wondered if she'd been recognized—and hoped she hadn't been.

She also wasn't sure how to respond to Lachlan, so she simply cleared her throat and said, "Thank you. I mean for the chair thing. For...pulling out my chair." Oh sweet goddess, she was stumbling over her words like someone who'd never talked to another person before.

Thankfully he ignored her weirdness as he sat across from her. She wasn't sure how he sat in the chair with his huge frame. "How is your sister?"

She stilled in her seat, her eyes narrowing.

"What?" He paused, watching her carefully. "What did I say?"

"How do you know about my sister?"

"Well I know Oscar of the Rabec clan kidnapped her." His words were quiet, for her ears only. "The lass you rescued, that *was* your sister, right?"

"How do you know we're sisters?"

"Just an educated guess. I looked into your background and didnae see a link. But...when I saw the two of you together, it's clear there's a familial connection. I'd guess that you're her older sister."

She lifted an eyebrow. Had he gotten all that from seeing them together once? "Have you been watching me? Are you *stalking* me?"

"I dinnae ken if that's the word I would use."

Her temper simmered. "Okay, are you watching me from afar without my knowledge?"

"Maybe."

Despite herself, she let out a startled laugh at his tone and bluntness. "So you're just a weirdo and have no problem admitting it."

He lifted a shoulder and she found her gaze following the movement, then trailing along the length of his big, covered bicep. The man was huge. Even if she hadn't seen him in shifted form, she would have guessed he was a dragon. Somehow she forced her gaze up to his eyes.

"I dinnae ken that I would use the word weirdo either," he murmured.

"Well to answer your question, yes she is my sister, and she is fine."

"Why did he take her?"

"You don't know?"

He shook his head. "I'm not exactly on speaking terms with him after I killed three of his warriors." There was a savage note of satisfaction in his tone.

Oh yeah, she liked that too because she was glad those males were dead and was just sorry she hadn't been the one to kill them. She shrugged again. "He's a psycho, that's why he took her." And that was all she was going to say about that.

"He's currently dealing with the fallout of everything in his territory. I have my people keeping an eye on him and his land. If he makes a move to leave, I'll let you know."

"Why would you do that?" And why was he looking at her as if he knew her? It was unsettling.

He frowned at her. "Why wouldn't I?"

"Well, we're strangers, for starters. Look, what do you want from me?" It was driving her crazy trying to guess at his motives.

"I think that should be obvious." His voice dropped an octave.

She stilled again. Did he know what she was? Did he want her for her blood too? She tensed, ready to bolt.

But he continued, his indigo eyes going all molten. *Oh, damn.* "I just want the chance tae get to know you."

There was a whole lot of truth in his words and in his expression. She forced herself to take a breath. She was used to people wanting something from her—access to parties, the notoriety of being her friend, money. And while it was pretty clear he wanted something, she kinda figured it was in the realm of the whole male-female type of want, not anything else. Not sure how to respond, she cleared her throat and glanced away. And that was when she realized they were being watched.

"Ah, that couple over there is watching us," she murmured quietly. It wasn't overt but she knew when someone was spying on her. She'd gotten really good at sensing it.

He sighed, then turned and nodded once at the tall, striking couple. Oh, he knew them.

The female had long, copper-colored hair, bright green eyes, and wore jeans and a long-sleeved T-shirt. With those cheekbones and that height—she had to be six feet tall—she could have been a supermodel. In fact, Star wondered if she should know her.

The male was even taller than the female and had the typical, huge dragon build. His buzz cut gave him a military bearing but she guessed he hadn't been in any contemporary military force. No, he was probably some ancient general from thousands of years ago. It was impossible to gauge supernaturals' ages, but just looking in this guy's eyes—he was old and deadly.

Just like Lachlan.

Star's breath caught in her throat as she realized why she recognized the couple. They'd been shown in various news feeds in the aftermath of The Fall. There were videos of them in dragon form battling those who wanted to destroy the city and they'd been savage and beautiful. Afterward, there had been feeds of them shifting to human form and the big male kissing her as if he would die without her. It had been quite memorable.

She stood as Lachlan grabbed two chairs for the couple. Part of her was disappointed, but having a buffer between them was probably a good thing.

"This is Greer and Reaper," Lachlan said immediately. "She's a healer and runs one of the local healing centers. He is a former general and warrior currently working with King to rebuild the city. And you two already know who Star is so I willnae tell you that she's the most talented singer in the world."

It was standard for supernaturals to give a rundown of someone's history, but her cheeks flamed at his words and she fought the stupid smile that wanted to pop up at his ridiculous compliment. "It's nice to meet you," she said to both of them, then focused on Greer as they all sat back down. The couple murmured back similar niceties before Star asked, "Which healing center do you run?"

She rattled off an address, then said, "It's the one in the Irish Channel district. And I'm just going to say up front that I am a huge fan of yours. Like, incredibly huge. I'd heard rumors that you were supernatural." The female's expression was so open and kind, it was easy to see that she was a healer.

Star smiled politely and found her tension easing a bit. "I'm a fan of yours too—I saw what you did on those news feeds."

The woman's cheeks flushed red. "Ugh, those stupid videos," she muttered.

Star laughed lightly. "You were impressive. It was like watching superheroes on the big screen."

The female waved away her compliment.

"Can I ask you something?" Star said as the two males murmured something to each other. Something about witches and vampires and...something.

"Of course."

"I feel kind of weird asking since we just met, but since you're a healer..." She cleared her throat. "What should supernaturals do now if they need to talk to someone. Like a therapist or...something along those lines. I'm not asking for myself, but a friend." She wasn't going to tell Greer that she was asking for Aurora.

"I personally do sessions, but I work with other supernaturals who do as well. And the rules are the same as the humans have. Privacy is valued and respected. After everything that happened, the human therapists and psychologists haven't had a break either. They're really coming out in full force to help. Your friend can call me anytime if they need to set up an appointment. Or they can come see me. Or...you can too."

"Okay, thanks. I'll pass on the information." She turned to look at Lachlan when she realized the males had stopped talking. And Lachlan was watching her with that sexy intensity that threw her off-kilter. "So how do you guys know each other?" she asked, looking between them.

"We're both warriors." Reaper answered, as if that should explain everything. "Before he was Alpha and had a fancy castle, he and I fought in a few battles together." The other male glanced at Lachlan with respect.

She lifted an eyebrow. "A fancy castle?" Star actually knew he had one. You know, because she'd been stalking him a bit too. But she hadn't been able to find pictures online and her super-stalker Lola had only found one grainy aerial photo that gave her nothing.

"Technically I have two." That wicked mouth curved up ever so slightly.

Of course he did. She found herself laughing even as their server came up and took the order. Everyone got burgers, which made it super simple.

After a few minutes of talking, Greer said, "So, a little birdie told me you're going to be putting on a few shows in the city in the coming weeks."

ANCIENT PROTECTOR | 101

"You heard right. I'm assuming that little birdie is actually a demon-vampire badass who runs a club?"

Greer laughed as she nodded. "Yes. And I couldn't believe Cynara knew you. I was so mad she hadn't told me before."

Reaper snorted and reached across the table to take his mate's hand in a sweet, gentle gesture so at odds with the big male. "My mate might have offered up our future firstborn for the chance to meet you."

"Hey! I did not. Also, play it cool, mate," she playfully admonished him.

Star felt her cheeks flush slightly even as something strange settled in her belly. Longing. She glanced at Lachlan and found him watching her in that not so subtle way of his. And for a moment, she swore she saw longing in his gaze too. Hunger for something long gone—which made no sense.

With herculean effort, she tore her gaze from his. "It feels weird to be performing and singing, but I've been assured that it's needed right now. And my band is ready to get out there. Athena always gets antsy if she doesn't get to play enough."

"She's killer on the guitar," Greer said. "And you're right about the performing. King has things under control right now, but things are definitely tense in the city." Greer shared a look with Reaper that left a whole lot unsaid.

Star had questions but didn't know the couple well enough to ask—and she didn't think they'd tell her anyway. Still... "Is there anything I should be worried about?"

Greer cleared her throat. Then she glanced around the restaurant and shrugged slightly. "I'm not sure. I just know that the vampires won't fully accept King as Alpha. Not right now anyway. If he mates with one of their own that would change, but..." She shrugged. "It's just a feeling in the air, a sort of tension, I guess. That's on top of everything else as we rebuild. People are scared about the future, worried how things will take shape."

Star nodded, not exactly surprised. It was her understanding that King ran the city with the help of a handful of others—different species other than wolves, including vampires—but vamps and shifters were notorious for butting heads. Or more specifically, getting into full-on brawls or wars.

They'd actually had an awful war centuries ago—and probably millennia before as well. She was too young to know everything, but her aunt Cliona had told her stories. That was way before her time, however. She was a fairly modern girl, especially compared to these three, she was pretty sure. At forty-two, she was practically a baby—and most humans assumed she was in her twenties.

"Does your clan miss you?" Star asked Lachlan, wanting to know more about him, even as she told herself to keep her mouth shut. She had this rabid curiosity about him that was growing every day.

"My clan is a well-oiled machine. For now, they are doing fine." That delicious voice wrapped around her.

"How long are you in town?" she asked, pushing. She knew she shouldn't but she couldn't help it. She needed to know when this madness inside her would end—when he would be gone and she could put thoughts of him behind her.

He gave her a long, dark look, the kind of look that made her toes curl in her boots. A look he shouldn't be giving her in public with others sitting mere feet away. "I'll stay here as long as it takes."

She wanted to ask what he meant by that but bit back the question. Because she wasn't sure she wanted the answer. Or maybe she did. Her mind was kind of screwed up right now.

Their server chose that moment to arrive to refill drinks and deliver an appetizer that Greer and Reaper must have ordered before.

Dinner ended up being incredibly pleasant, nothing like the awkward date she'd been imagining. Lachlan was quite charming and good at deflecting any sort of compliment Reaper tossed his way. It was kind of weird—Reaper seemed to be trying to talk Lachlan up. And even though Reaper was rough around the edges she could tell he was completely smitten by his mate, and she was such a sucker to see couples in love.

Deep down she was a romantic. Even though she knew the chances of her ever finding a mate were slim. It was such a narrow margin for her kind in general. Her kind were nearly extinct anyway, something she really didn't want to think about.

As dinner wrapped up, she found out that they didn't pay with money right now, but both Reaper and Lachlan promised the owner of the place they'd come back and help out with some things of the handyman variety.

After saying goodbye to the others, she and Lachlan set out on foot since he wanted to walk her home. A cool breeze rolled over her, and in that moment, she wanted to pretend she was just a woman out on a date with a sexy man. But underneath the surface, a strange sensation buzzed, making her edgy. She never got like this, not really. But Lachlan was bringing out a different side to her.

There was a decent amount of people on the streets as Lachlan and Star slowly strolled along the uneven sidewalk. When they turned onto St. Peters Street—which appeared to have either missed the destruction completely, or was already rebuilt—she said, "I think your friends are following us. Am I off base?" she said quietly.

Lachlan sighed. "It's because Reaper has been tasked with keeping an eye on me."

She blinked in surprise. "Wait, like he's your babysitter?"

Lachlan shot her a dry look now. "No. But I'm an Alpha in another Alpha's territory."

"So them being at the restaurant wasn't a coincidence?"

"No. I only invited them over because Greer is such a fan of yours, and it's hard to say no to a lass as sweet as that." He seemed a little sheepish as he said the last part.

Star smiled at his words, realizing he might be a bit of a marshmallow inside after all. Which...was far too hot. Damn it. She needed to be keeping her distance from this dragon.

It was interesting that King was allowing the male to stay in his territory. And something told Star that if it came down to King versus Lachlan, it would be a very savage battle. She knew King was strong and had heard the rumors of him killing dragons. But Lachlan was ancient and she could feel the raw power rolling off him, caressing her skin in waves, as if he couldn't contain the power completely. Maybe he wasn't even aware of it.

"We lost our tail," he murmured. "Reaper must trust me enough to walk you home."

She knew that they likely had another tail—Axel was her backup tonight but he was doing a good job blending in because she hadn't seen him once. "Look, what do you want from me?" she asked as they turned left onto a quiet street away from the people out walking or jogging.

"You." Such a simple word but with too much meaning injected into it.

She sucked in a breath. "Lachlan, my home is here, and you live in Scotland. I'm not going to Scotland." Even though some part of her she couldn't even admit existed wanted to go there. Had always wanted to. It was this strange, driving need she'd felt for decades, and if she was honest, it scared her. There was no reason for the driving force, nothing she could figure out anyway.

He was quiet for a long moment. She could hear jazz music playing up ahead, streaming out from a little hole-in-the-wall bar. A few tables were outside and various groups of people sat, drinking and smiling. All human, from what she could tell as they passed by.

"I would like the chance tae court you while I am in New Orleans," he said once they'd passed the humans.

There was something more in his tone. His words were simple enough but the word *court* meant something else entirely, especially for a dragon his age.

She didn't want to say yes or no, because the thought of telling him no ripped open something inside her. And she wasn't sure why. "I don't know what to say to that," she finally settled on. That felt honest enough.

"Why did you choose New Orleans to run to?" he asked. "I know you had a home in New York before."

"That place was never home." Her words had more passion than she'd intended.

He nodded, as if he understood everything she didn't say. And maybe he did.

She cleared her throat, driven to tell him more even if she didn't understand why. "New York was a base of operations for us. It took a long time to find my sister. And that's where we lived while we figured out how to get to her."

"If I'd known you then, I would have ripped apart his territory to get your sister back."

She blinked at the savagery of his words because they were essentially strangers—even if it didn't feel like it—but she completely believed that he would have done exactly that. That he would have gone to war with this other dragon for her. That was disturbing on a couple levels. Mainly because she liked it so very much.

"Lachlan," she murmured, the feel of his name on her tongue familiar.

"I like it when you say my name." His Scottish accent got just a little bit deeper, and a whole lot sexier.

She fought off a shudder as something echoed inside her. Damn it, she needed to shut this down now. "Look, tonight was pleasant—"

"Pleasant? Already giving me the brush-off, lass?"

"Not the brush-off. Lachlan—"

He groaned. "I told you I love it when you say my name. Are you just trying to drive me mad now?"

His Scottish brogue was so crazy sexy and damn did she feel that all the way to her toes. "Fine, I won't say your name again."

"Oh, I want you to say my name. Particularly while my head is between your legs—"

"Lachlan!" She turned to stare at him. No one ever talked to her like that. People usually kissed up to her, and on the occasion a man or male worked up the courage to ask her out, they were usually douchey frat bro types. Or mega-rich assholes who assumed she would say yes. This... She had not expected this boldness.

He shrugged his broad shoulders, looking more delicious than she could handle. "I believe in honesty."

"I don't care," she spluttered. "You can't just say stuff like that."

"Why not? I know you want me."

"You're a very maddening, arrogant dragon," she muttered. "What?" she asked when he gave her a strange look and stopped. "That can't be the first time someone's said that to you. I feel like you probably drive people crazy all the time with your 'honesty.'"

"No...it's not the first time." Still, the look he gave her was almost guarded.

She looked away for a moment as they stood in the alley that ran behind shops and restaurants. It was quiet, though she could hear people in the distance—laughter, little strings of music coming from somewhere. But here in this moonlit alleyway, there was only the two of them. The knowledge that it was just the two of them here heated her blood.

She wanted to say his name but didn't want him to drop another sensual statement on her. Instead she pressed her palm to his chest, intending to... She wasn't sure what her intentions were. But the instant her fingers curled against his shirt, he let out another groan and dipped his head toward hers. He didn't pause, didn't wait as he brushed his lips over hers.

As if he had every right to.

She was the one who deepened the kiss, grabbing onto his shirt and tugging him closer. As she did, it felt like a dance they'd done a thousand times before, like coming home. Something inside her broke free as she sank into this teasing, the sweep of his tongue against hers.

Immediately he took over, a low rumble emanating from his chest as he hoisted her up, as if he couldn't get close enough to her. She wrapped her legs around him as if it was the most natural thing in the world. She had the feeling he wanted to pin her to the brick wall, but instead he simply wrapped his arms around her, cupping her ass and pulling her tight to him as he delved his tongue into her mouth.

Teasing, tasting, tantalizing. Triple Ts, and the man was making her crazy.

Heat flooded between her legs as he kneaded her ass, again in a way that felt so damn familiar. She didn't question it but grinded up against him instead, rolling her hips against him as they made out like teenagers. Even as they kissed, she hated that there were clothes in the way. Her nipples tightened against her bra cups, the friction sending another rush of heat through her. God, she couldn't remember the last time she'd simply made out with someone and it was invigorating and—

"Holy shit," she heard someone mutter from nearby and pulled back.

That was when she realized she was glowing. Well, her purple fire was flickering all across her body and her hair. And her skin had a soft, violet glow to it. *Oh goddess, no.* No, she hadn't felt the change come on at all.

"Get the fuck out of here," Lachlan snarled to the male staring at them.

She had no idea if the guy was human or not but he turned and ran like hellhounds were after him. At least he hadn't been carrying a cell phone and recording them.

She unwound her legs from Lachlan and dropped as ice flooded her veins. The fire died as panic punched through her and that soft glow dimmed as well. This time when she pressed her hand to the middle of his chest and pushed, she put distance between them before dropping her hand.

"Are you a dragon hybrid?" he asked her carefully as he looked at her dying fire.

"What I am is none of your business," she snapped out. She hadn't meant to be so harsh but... This had never happened before. She'd never lost control like this. Fire was always underneath the surface since it was a part of her, part of her soul. When she performed, when thousands of screaming fans fed her natural energy, her fire wanted to burst free but she always managed to keep it under control. Always.

Now, however, when the sexiest man she'd ever met had his tongue in her mouth, she decided to lose control? Just great.

"I've gotta go. I..." *Nope.* She couldn't stay here another moment. So she turned and ran.

Yep, actually bolted down the alleyway to get away from him because she was not dealing with this right now. *Nope, nope, nope.*

"Shite, Star! Hold on!"

Her boots pounded against the pavement and she put distance between them. Without looking behind her, she made a sharp left onto a main street and wove her way in and out of the walking humans and supernaturals. She didn't care if she was acting crazy or like a coward, she had to get away from him.

And fast. Before she did something crazy or stupid. Or both.

CHAPTER 13

Lachlan took off after Star, wondering what the hell had happened. For a moment he'd thought that might have been her mating manifestation, that she was a hybrid dragon—there were enough hybrids in existence that he knew it was possible. But she'd been so horrified by the sight of her flames. If it was her mating manifestation and she was disgusted by them—by *him*—she might as well have reached into his chest and ripped out his heart.

As he rounded the corner, a big male jumped down from a balcony right in front of him. The lion, Axel. Lachlan thought he'd scented the cat lurking around.

"Where do you think you're going?" the lion asked.

He simply growled at the male. He'd better move or get his head lopped off.

Axel stepped to the side when Lachlan would have gone around him. Sure he could have gotten into a brawl with him and beaten the hell out of the lion—and probably taken a few licks of his own—but he forced himself to think rationally. He wouldn't earn any points for attacking one of Star's people.

Calling on a diplomacy he didn't know he had, he gritted his teeth. "Move or I'll cut aff yer heid, ya bawbag." Okay, so maybe he wasn't very diplomatic after all.

"When a female runs from you, I don't suggest chasing after her."

"I always heard lions were lazy," he snarled, keeping his gaze on Star who was still sprinting down the street. When he saw a shadow peel off a wall in a dark alleyway and start after her, he stiffened.

"Lazy? You motherf—"

"Someone else is following Star."

The male turned, and as one unit they ran down the street.

"I'm not lazy," Axel muttered. "Lions always get a bad rap because we like to nap."

"I've met male lions." Seriously, why was he having this conversation at all?

He watched as Star made a left about fifty feet ahead onto another street.

The male in the hoodie followed suit, his movements clipped and determined. He was definitely following her.

Even while sprinting, Lachlan easily dodged humans walking along the sidewalk. Any supernaturals simply moved out of the way. Axel was right with him, keeping pace.

Though he'd lost sight of her, all he had to do was follow Star's scent. But he hated not having her within eyesight. He'd lost a female before. Lost a woman who smelled so damn similar to Star. They even kissed the same. And when Star told him he was maddening and arrogant, she'd said it with the same tone of exasperation.

They weren't the same though; it was impossible. He knew that in his heart, but when he'd tasted Star tonight, it had been like coming home. It had been like kissing his long-dead mate. A human female he'd never gotten to mate because the fates had taken her from him far too soon.

Panic punched into him and all he could focus on was getting to Star, stopping whoever that male was. As they rounded another corner, he followed her scent trail to the exterior wall of a cemetery. Finally slowing, Lachlan tapped his nose and pointed at the wall.

Axel nodded in agreement.

He gave hand motions that he was going over the wall. Without pause, the agile lion jumped onto a nearby oak tree and crawled up it.

Lachlan jumped up in one swift move and grabbed the top of the wall before propelling himself over.

His boots landed with a thud on the gravel below. *There!* He spotted the shadowy figure ducking behind an oversized gravestone. It looked as if this cemetery had seen battle recently as rubble was strewn everywhere and crypts were busted open and toppled over.

Not bothering to cover up his scent, he followed Star instead of the male. She was in here somewhere. Hiding.

Hurrying in between the fallen statues and crypts and jumping over any that got in his way, Lachlan paused when he heard a male voice snarl out, "Got you, you little bitch."

Lachlan went full dragon, his clothes shredding as he shifted in one sharp burst of pain and bright, sparking magic. He launched into the air so his wings wouldn't get trapped between the row of crypts.

As he rose higher, he immediately spotted the male running away and Star sprawled on the ground. *No!* He let out a raging stream of fire, fueled by years of pain and agony.

The male screamed as the flames enveloped him but the screams died as quickly as they'd come. The male must be human or vampire since he burst into flames in moments before quickly disintegrating before Lachlan's eyes.

Dismissing the waste of space, he quickly shifted back to human in seconds, turning to find Star standing there, her pale violet eyes that were so hauntingly familiar wide with...not fear exactly.

"Are you okay?" He scanned her from head to toe, looking for any injuries. His dragon settled when he didn't scent any blood.

"I'm fine. I don't know what he wanted. I think he was vampire though—he flashed his fangs and he had supernatural strength. I could have taken him," she said, almost admonishingly.

He didn't care. She was his to protect.

"That is definitely too overcooked." Axel came to stand next to them as he eyed the charred lump of remains. "Did you recognize him before jackass here went all Firestarter?"

Lachlan narrowed his gaze but didn't bother looking at the lion.

Star still watched Lachlan too even as she responded to Axel. "Maybe he recognized me. It could have been just a weirdo fan. He didn't say much before...poof."

"God knows you get enough fan mail from psychos," Axel muttered.

Lachlan frowned, this knowledge unsettling. "You do? What kind? Who sends you—"

"Dude, you're starting to heat up again." Axel took a step back and Lachlan realized that he was indeed starting to breathe out smoke.

Shite. He ordered his dragon to calm down so he could talk rationally to his female. The idea of psychos sending her messages or...anything, made him want to hunt them all down. Hunt, kill, then raze their homes to the ground.

"Look, people have sent me a lot of strange messages over the years. Mostly harmless. Weird, but harmless. We have had a couple real threats. Or they would have been real if I was human. We've taken care of all of them." There was a bite to her words that eased his dragon back a bit.

"Well since we can't do an ID on the guy or even check to see if he had a freaking wallet on him, we have no idea who he was or if he was working with Oscar," Axel said, giving Lachlan a sharp look of disapproval.

Yeah, Lachlan really should have thought that through better. But he'd simply reacted, which wasn't like him. He was an Alpha and he was ancient. He had control over himself. Or he had until Star—until a woman who reminded him so much of his long-dead mate—had walked into his life.

"There's not much we can do here," Star said quietly before giving him a pointed look. "And you can't very well run around the streets naked."

Oh, hell. He'd completely shredded his clothes and shoes in his shift, and she was right. "Fine. Let's head back to your place. I'll shift and follow after you."

"That's not necessary." Her words were stiff.

"And yet it's happening."

It sounded like Axel stifled a laugh as Star glared at him. Without looking at Lachlan again, she shrugged, then spun around and gave him a view of her very perfect backside. "The skies are free. If you want to follow after me, be my guest."

"I will." His dragon would follow her to the ends of the earth.

CHAPTER 14

 King used the shadows across the street from the abandoned warehouse to blend in as he approached it. Supposedly this was where a pack of rogue wolves had taken up residence. And according to rumors, they'd been harassing a local vampire coven.

Right now he was trying to keep the peace between a multitude of species, all mourning, while simultaneously rebuilding the city back up and making sure they came through this tragedy stronger. And if a bunch of wolves were harassing vampires or even targeting them, it could easily destroy the fragile trust he'd started to build with the majority of vamps here.

Vampires, just like wolves, were under his protection, and he would destroy anyone who sought to sow discord. This was his territory and he owed it to his people to keep the peace. It was the only way life would get back to a semblance of normal. He looked over at his packmate Delphine and motioned for her to go around back.

She simply nodded and disappeared into the darkness.

He stuck to the shadows, and remained in his human form as he made his way across the street. There were more than a few warehouses down here that he had plans for, but as he was currently rebuilding other parts of the city and making sure everybody had basic necessities like shelter and food, the building of this area would have to come later.

Hell, he wished he didn't have to sleep or that there were more hours a day for all that he wanted to do. It was too much and there wasn't enough time in the damn day.

As he neared one of the boarded-up windows, he could hear low murmuring inside. Multiple voices. Male and female. This was definitely the place. Their stink was all over the exterior.

King's wolf was just underneath the surface, his eyes definitely glowing, so he kept his gaze down as he climbed the exterior wall of the warehouse. There were a few open windows high above and he was going to use them to enter. They would realize he was here soon enough, but until then he wanted a small element of surprise. Other than Delphine and him, the rest of the crew were going to remain outside until he needed them. And they would know if he did. But he was an Alpha; if he couldn't handle a bunch of rogue wolves on his own, he didn't deserve to run his own pack, much less an entire city.

At this point in his life, every decision he made had to be calculated, to an extent. He had to be strong. Always. If anyone sensed any sort of weakness, it could destroy everything he and his people were working to build.

Once inside, he silently walked along the rafters until he found a ladder along the wall. He could have easily jumped down, but this way was quieter.

"I don't like the idea of using bombs," a male voice rumbled. "It's such a human thing to do." Disgust laced his words.

"True enough, but it will have maximum impact. We need people scared. Humans are already terrified and we need to create more fear."

King's wolf pushed at the surface. *Bombs?* No doubt about it. These fuckers were going to die tonight.

"We'll blame it on the Cheval coven. Make it clear they were behind everything. Then the humans will go after the vampires during the day and the vamps will retaliate."

King listened for a few more moments as the fools argued with each other about which act of terror was better before casually stepping out of the shadows. "So you foolish little pups want to cause strife in my city, to take over my territory." He didn't bother to raise his voice—he didn't need to.

The interior went quiet, the cluster of about a dozen wolves turning to face him.

The leader stepped up immediately, making it easy to identify him. Good. King would make sure he lived. For now, anyway.

"And targeting vampires?" King sighed, as if bored already. "It's a little prosaic." He took another step forward, his movements casual. His leather jacket hid his short sword, though he didn't need the damn thing to take out *these* shifters. He might use it though because he didn't relish the idea of ruining his new jacket. And his wolf was not in the mood to come out and deal with these weaklings.

"You're not fit to be Alpha," the dark-haired male with dreads snarled.

"Is that right? And you are?"

"You're working with dragons and vampires. And witches," he spat. *"Witches."*

"Not that I owe you an explanation, and not that any of you are going to survive the night, regardless, but I'm looking at the bigger picture. Something your peon brains can't comprehend. You want the city to devolve into what, anarchy? You're a pup with no concept of the world, of how bad that will be for everyone. Yourselves included. Or maybe you're just so goddamn selfish you don't care. Witches will help us rebuild. It's all for the greater good. And this new world has no room for your bigotry and foolishness."

"You think you can take us on?" Now the other wolf laughed, the sound bouncing off the walls.

King snarled low in his throat. "I know I can." And now it was time to stop talking.

The other male stepped forward, his hands curling into fists, showing off a bunch of gaudy rings. "You're not even a hundred years old."

He was over a hundred, actually. But King had gotten that his whole life. He wasn't strong enough because he was too young. He was a bastard who didn't even know who his father was. And what kind of wolf abandoned his own pup? He must have been a weak, unworthy pup. Or his skin was too dark. *Yeah, yeah.* He'd heard it all. Same shit from a different fool.

King drew out his sword, the swishing sound making a soft, singing echo throughout the warehouse. God, he loved that sound.

The male in front of him sneered as he looked at the sword. "You can't even shift?"

King didn't respond. His wolf only came out to play for real threats and these morons weren't worth its time. But no more talking. Lightning fast, he lunged, slicing the guy across the chest hard and fast and deep.

The guy stared in horror, in pure surprise at how fast King had moved. The neurons of his tiny brain were finally catching up to the pain as blood started rushing out of him.

By now the wolves all around him shifted.

Two came at him at once, jaws open, snarls building in their throats.

King twisted, dodging to the left as he sliced down, then up with his blade, efficiently lopping off two heads, one after the other.

Then the numbers built to three, and four. Five, six.

He was faster than most wolves, faster than most vampires. A terrifying tornado, he'd been called more than once.

In and out, he dodged a blow. Dodged teeth. Dodged claws. Dodged it all.

As he dipped down and to the right to fend off another attacker, claws scraped against his jacket.

He inwardly cursed at the destruction of his new threads. But all his focus was on taking down these fools. The wannabe Alpha had managed to get back to his feet after King had carved him up multiple times. Before he faced him again, King slammed his sword into the chest of the final attacking wolf.

The animal fell to the concrete with a dying whine. Quickly, he withdrew the sword and cut off its head in seconds.

The leader snarled as King turned toward him. The male had already shifted to wolf.

King sidestepped the uneven attack, and the wolf went flying through the air, landing on the concrete. His claws scrabbled against the pavement as he turned to face King once again.

He sheathed his sword, his wolf riding him hard, wanting to come out to play just a little.

The male rushed at him again, baring his canines. King feinted right and when the wolf twisted that way, he shifted to the left and released his own claws.

He swiped over the wolf's throat then underbelly, all before it hit the pavement. Then he pulled out a small blade and shoved it right into the male's stomach, pinning him into place.

The pure silver poisoned the beast, making it thrash in agony.

Delphine strode out of the shadows. "Impressive, though I wish you'd let me take some of them out. Ugh, and this is going to suck to clean up."

"The rest of the crew can handle it. Let's go."

She nodded as he lifted the wounded wolf off the concrete, carrying the whining animal out of the building.

He didn't have to tell her where they were going—to the Cheval vampire coven. The one this wolf had planned to target and blame his crimes on. He was going to leave this wolf with them to deal with. He was showing as much goodwill as possible right now, wanted them to know that he was trying to unify the city. Because he would do any damn thing except take a mate of convenience simply for a unification of the species. He had no problem mating with a vampire, but only if she was his true mate.

And after the stunning female he'd met recently, he didn't think his mate would be a vampire. Or a wolf, for that matter. Something that surprised him bone-deep.

He would sacrifice a lot, but he would not sacrifice the chance at a true mating because it would destroy his wolf. He loved both parts of himself—he couldn't betray his animal.

His wolf was annoyed as hell with him right now because he was certain they'd already met their future mate. Even if he wasn't sure what kind of shifter she was. His wolf sure didn't care. And neither did he.

But that was a thought for another day—when he didn't have the weight of the city, of the entire territory, on his shoulders.

CHAPTER 15

Star hurried around the side of the house, not even bothering to go inside first. Not when she heard voices coming from the back of her crew's mansion. She'd already checked in with Athena and Marley, who were patrolling the wall, and knew that Taya and Kartini were in their shifted eagle-owl forms, watching everything from nearby trees. Star knew that her sister was fine, but she still needed to see Aurora with her own eyes. That protective instinct had kicked into high gear and there was no stopping it.

Her heart rate started dropping back to normal the second she saw her sister stretched out on one of the lounges, an old, earmarked paperback in her hand. Brielle and Harlow were sitting at the wrought iron table playing a game of cards, though both were strapped down with weapons.

The tigers stood when they saw her, clearly sensing her distress.

"What is it?" Brielle asked.

"Maybe nothing." She quickly relayed what had happened in the cemetery as the three of them listened. She'd already told Athena and Marley everything, and as she spoke, Taya and Kartini flew down and landed on the pergola above the lanai, clearly listening. The Edison-style string lights waved slightly under the impact of their flapping before settling back down.

"At this point we don't know if it was one of Oscar's people," Axel said just as Lachlan—in dragon form—landed in the yard.

"He's fine," Star muttered as the twins tensed. She'd seen him following her—he certainly hadn't tried to hide.

"Is everything okay here?" he asked, striding toward them, all naked and glorious.

Star shoved back the strange urge to demand everyone turn away. She didn't want anyone looking at him, not even her friends and family. *Ugh.* Since when had she started caring about this male?

"We really need to see about keeping some clothes on hand for him," Aurora murmured, averting her gaze.

"It's not like this is going to become a habit," she said pointedly to her sister before turning to Lachlan. "Everything's fine here."

"Good. I found my phone in the cemetery and I've already contacted Reaper. He's on his way and will be keeping an eye on things here. I'm going to scour the rest of the city with my clanmates and see if we spot Oscar or his people. There's a good chance I'll pick up his scent as its familiar to me. If I do, I'll hunt him down and end this problem tonight." He might be in human form, but his dragon was in his eyes as he spoke.

"Thank you," Star said, meaning it. He didn't have to take part in this fight, but he'd chosen to side with them. "But we don't need Reaper here. We don't need babysitters." She liked the other dragon well enough, but he was still a dragon and a stranger, and it was hard for her to let people into her inner sanctum.

"I'm well aware of that. But extra protection never hurt anybody. Especially since you already know what Oscar wants." His gaze flicked to Aurora briefly.

Damn it. It was kind of hard to argue with him there. And she did like Reaper—mainly because she'd just plain liked his mate, Greer. It was hard to imagine that a female healer would mate with someone capable of kidnapping and torturing others. "Okay, fine."

The tension in Lachlan's shoulders eased, then he looked to Axel and the twins. "You want to come hunting with us?"

Annoyance burst inside her that he'd just asked her people without getting her permission first, but thankfully they looked to Star for guidance.

"Axel, Harlow, you guys go." She looked up at the eagle-owls and then at Brielle. "Return to your posts." Her shift was at midnight, something she didn't mind.

They all nodded, and as Lachlan headed off she forced herself not to stare at his retreating naked backside. His perfect, bitable butt.

"So how was your date?" Aurora asked after the three of them had gone, her tone teasing.

Surprised, Star stared at her sister. "That's what you want to talk about?"

"Uh, yeah. I so don't want to think about that bastard Oscar. And your man is seriously packing down there."

Lola, who had stepped outside, laptop in hand, started snickering. "So Star's male looks good?"

She stared at her sister in horror. "Oh my God, you looked?"

"I tried not to! It was just right out there. And for the record I didn't look the first time he dropped by and got naked. Come on, he's clearly into you. So...how was the date?"

"I can't believe you want to talk about that right now after what happened."

Aurora swung her legs off the side of the chair and stood. "We don't know if that was one of Oscar's people. It's not like he works with vampires, so it was probably just some weirdo stalking you. And besides, I'm not living in fear anymore. If he decides to come after me, or even you, if he's figured out what you are," she said as she shrugged, "I'm not going down without a fight. In fact, I'm not going down at all." Fire sparked in her sister's eyes as pale blue flames licked along her fingertips and up her arms for a brief moment. "I'm ready to start patrolling again. I'm ready to take my life back. I might be young, but I'm a warrior."

This was the Aurora that Star knew and loved. This was the sister who wouldn't put up with shit from anyone.

She lunged for her sister, pulling her into a hug.

Aurora returned the embrace tightly.

"I've missed you so much," Star murmured into her hair.

"It feels so good to be home. To be with my family."

"I'm getting in on this too." Lola jumped on them, wrapping her arms around them. And then Bella, who'd come out of nowhere, joined in too.

Star closed her eyes for a long moment, savoring it, because she knew death and destruction were on the horizon.

It was inevitable. Because Oscar would come for them or they would go after him. Star had tried to deny it, even to herself. She'd tried to push it off into this far-flung future event where she and her crew hunted him down. But it was happening and probably sooner than later.

She wasn't sure what tonight had been about and if that had been just a random vampire, but that little tingling in the back of her neck told her more was to come.

Soon.

CHAPTER 16

"Hey, guys." Kartini strode into the living room and eyed Star, Aurora and Lola. "What are you up to?" She'd just gotten off her patrol shift and looked incredible as always. The female simply didn't have bad hair days. With an Egyptian father and German mother—both musicians—she looked like both her parents, who Star adored. Her dark brown hair had natural caramel highlights, and her amber eyes were striking against her pale brown skin.

"Trying to convince Star to tell us what happened on her date." Aurora's grin was infectious as she glanced back at Star. "But she's being a little tease."

"You guys are ridiculous. And also kind of sad, if my nonexistent love life is all you want to talk about." It had only been a couple hours ago since she'd seen Lachlan, but it felt as if an eternity had passed.

"Well, considering I was locked up for a year, I need all the excitement I can get." Aurora lifted an eyebrow in challenge.

Star's mouth dropped open at her sister's words.

"Wow, Aurora. Pulling out the big guns, huh?" Kartini dropped onto the couch next to Aurora, then motioned for her to sit in front of her. "Come on, let me braid your hair. Otherwise it'll get all tangled when you go to bed."

"I'm not twelve," she grumbled even as she sat on the floor in front of Kartini.

"We kissed," Star blurted because yeah, Aurora had been locked up for a year. Even if her sister was using dark humor right now, damn. It hit Star right in the heart. And she could tell her sister this little bit about Lachlan and her.

Three pairs of eyes pinned her in place—even Kartini, who was working her magic on Aurora's hair with efficiency.

"And? Was it hot?" Lola asked from where she had her legs thrown over the side of an overstuffed chair.

"That's one way of putting it."

"What's that mean?" Lola asked.

"It was...weird."

Aurora winced. "Uh oh."

"Was he all slobbery?" Kartini asked. "Ugh, that's the worst."

"No! I mean, weird but good. Really good. But weird because I sort of lit on fire. And my skin started glowing purple." Again with the staring, which was why she hadn't wanted to tell them.

"Sounds like your other half likes him," Lola murmured, a grin on her face.

"I guess." But there was no guessing. Her beast was so intrigued by the dragon and it was frustrating.

Lola lifted an eyebrow.

"Fine. I know. I've never dealt with this kind of lack of control before. You guys know that." Even when she performed in front of thousands, she was able to control her fire. It was hard, but she did it. "My other half wants to come out and strut around in front of him."

"So?" Aurora asked, grinning.

Star stared at her. "Seriously?"

"I'm just saying, maybe telling him what you are isn't the worst thing in the world."

Now they all looked at Aurora.

Her sister shrugged as Kartini looped Aurora's braids around her head and pinned them into a crown. "I'm tired of hiding what I am. And maybe I'm not going to do it anymore. And maybe you shouldn't either. Maybe...screw it. Maybe we can come out too."

Low-grade panic hummed through Star at her sister's words. She'd practically raised Aurora after their parents had been killed. Her sister was a grown woman, had been through hell, and could make her own decisions. Still...the thought of Aurora revealing what she was, making herself a target to even more people, brought on a wave of fear. It wasn't common knowledge that they were sisters, but enough people knew at this point so if Aurora came out, Star was out too. "Maybe," she managed to rasp out, hoping her sister would reconsider.

"Or maybe you can quit stalling and tell us about the rest of that kiss," Lola added.

Star said a silent thank-you for the break because she didn't want to think about Aurora making herself even more of a target. And she really didn't want to talk about coming out. "It was…nice. More than nice. Hot and intense, and I was pretty damn close to letting him rip my clothes off in an alleyway." Which was not her style. Not even close. She hadn't slept with a male in…ahem, ever. Oh, she'd tried to more than once, though not in the last few years. But all males she'd tried with left her feeling cold. For a while she'd wondered if she'd preferred the opposite sex, but nope. She still found males attractive, she just couldn't find one she wanted to take that next step with. Until Lachlan.

"Oh, outdoor sex, my fave!" Kartini patted Aurora's head, indicating she was done, then motioned for Lola to come over.

"Sex anywhere is your fave." Lola sat in front of her. "Oh, make it double braids please. And do that fishtail thing."

"So why didn't you get busy with him, then?" Aurora asked.

"Well, I started glowing and we were interrupted by a human. Not to mention we were outside!"

"Shoulda let the human watch." Kartini made a tsking sound.

"You're such a perv!" She decided not to tell them she'd run away from Lachlan. What kind of Alpha ran away from a kiss? *Ugh.* She was so lame.

"Very, very true. So what are you gonna do about the dragon?" Kartini continued as she worked her magic on Lola's hair.

"I don't know." And that was the truth. She had no idea what to do about the big male. Her two sides were at odds about him. Well…that wasn't exactly true. All of her wanted him. But Star had to factor in far too many other things, which were holding her back. Because it didn't seem as if Lachlan wanted casual from her.

Axel strode into the room at that moment, a bottle of wine in hand as well as a glass. Star started to stand, figuring it was time for her to start her security shift, but he waved her back down. "Sit. I can't sleep. I'm still revved up from earlier. I'm gonna take your shift. You need some downtime anyway."

"You sure?" She felt bad and wondered if skipping her shift made her a bad leader.

He kissed the top of her head. "For the love of all that's holy, yes. You need a break. Especially since I'm sure you're gonna go to bed sexually frustrated after that smoking-hot kiss and no follow-through."

"Oh my God, you saw that?"

"Hey! You ordered me to tail you guys."

Shaking her head, she poured herself a glass. "You didn't have to watch."

"And you didn't have to run away from him." Axel tossed that bomb into the room before practically racing out.

Star threw a small throw pillow at him but he'd already escaped.

"You ran away from him?" Aurora demanded, reaching for the bottle and pouring some into her now empty glass.

"Axel was hit on the head on the way home. That silly lion doesn't know what he's saying. I think he might even be drunk." She snagged the bottle back from her sister and stood. "And I'm going to go get some sleep."

"No! Let me do your hair first."

But Star was done. "Sorry, ladies. I'm out. Maybe you can convince Axel to do his hair later," she said, laughing lightly, knowing the lion would never let Kartini touch his precious mane.

But Axel wasn't wrong about the sexual frustration. Unfortunately, the bad thing about shifters was that they could sense when you had a shift in pheromones. So if she kept talking about Lachlan—obsess was more like it—she was going to get even more worked up. Translation, turned on.

And she so did not need that right now.

* * *

Star opened her eyes and knew immediately where she was. Not in the literal sense, but she was in a weird dream state again. She sure as hell wasn't awake but this didn't feel like a random dream.

It felt like a memory locked inside her. They always did. Something she was starting to understand each time she ended up in one of them.

"You're awake?" The male voice spoke to her quietly, though she felt the voice more in her head than heard it aloud. The language wasn't one she should know either, but she did. Hell, Star couldn't pinpoint the language, but she understood everything.

"Hmm." She shifted and realized she was lying on his warm, bare chest. In the distance she saw sunlight peeking in from the opening of the cave. Instead of looking up at him—because it was impossible to think when she did—she made a noncommittal sound, though clearly she was up now since she was responding.

He pinched her backside. "Teasing female."

"Frustrating male." And he was. Always pushing her for more, wanting everything. Demanding it right before giving her all sorts of wicked pleasure. They'd done things she hadn't realized people even did—he put his mouth on her sex until she was writhing with the pleasure of it, until she scarcely knew her name. He also put his mouth...in another place. One she never would have imagined people did. But it seemed that there were no limits with him.

"Mate with me." A soft, familiar demand.

She stiffened slightly in his arms, the thoughts of this dream woman mixing with her own so that her mind felt even more fuzzy. "We've had this conversation." It wasn't her voice, but it felt like she was the one speaking.

"Aye, we have. And we're having it again. You need to make a decision."

"I'll never fit into your world." She was a human and he was other. So much more. Her villagers looked at his kind with awe and terror, and for some reason he'd chosen her. But he would grow tired of her, that much she knew. How could he not? Star felt the raw pain of the woman's thoughts echoing through her and tried to order her eyes to open. She didn't want to be here, didn't want to be seeing this. Didn't want to be with him.

Liar, her mind whispered.

"You will if you'll just give me a chance. Give us a chance. You must trust me."

She swallowed hard, wanting to say yes so badly that she trembled with it. She'd already given him her body, and if her family found out, they'd toss her out on her backside. Label her a whore.

"I never took you for a coward," he murmured.

She still wouldn't look at him. If she did, she'd cave.

He pinched her again, this time lighter. "All right, then." Now his voice was cajoling. "I still love you even if you're a coward."

"I'm not a coward! I see the world differently. Clearer than you, you

stubborn beast." Why couldn't he see that if he mated to her, it would ruin him? She was just a human and he would take over for his people soon enough. She was physically weak compared to him and his kind. But especially him. She didn't think he would ever hurt her, but she'd seen females in her village make the mistake of thinking that. Then after marriage their husbands showed their true selves. Though with him...he didn't need to hide anything. He was the strongest male she knew. When it came down to it, there was simply no way his own people would accept her, especially when he became their leader.

"If you trust me, mate me. You'll learn all my secrets. You'll understand why we'll work. Because there will never be another for me." The next words he said she couldn't understand, but she understood the soft tone and meaning nonetheless.

"There will never be another for me either," she whispered into the dark, cool cavern. This was a truth she couldn't hide from him. How could there be anyone after him?

"Then we're agreed on that. And that's all that matters." His big body shifted suddenly, his hand sliding up her body to cup her bare breast.

She shivered at the feel of his rough palm sliding over her smooth skin and— woke up.

Breathing hard, Star stared up at the ceiling of her room, trying to remember all the details of the dream even as they fragmented apart, little splinters dissolving into the ether. It was so real. So familiar. And the dreams were getting more intense each time. What the hell did it mean?

A deep-seated sense of loss for that woman settled in her bones. Frustrated, she sat up and punched her pillow. Then punched it again before flopping back down. It was going to be a long night.

CHAPTER 17

Star stumbled downstairs, grumpier than ever. She hadn't slept well and she'd had another stupid dream so now she was all sexually frustrated and out of sorts. When she found the dragon Reaper in the kitchen with Aurora and Lola, she frowned. She hadn't expected him to still be here. "Any news from Lachlan?" Ugh, she couldn't even manage a polite greeting this morning.

The big male shook his head. "No good news. He scoured the city with his clanmates but they haven't found anyone from Oscar's clan. He couldn't pick up any scent trails, and his brother is a skilled tracker."

Her frustration mounting, she headed for the coffee pot. "We appreciate you staying here, but why don't you go home? I'm sure your mate misses you."

He lifted a shoulder. "I know she does. I miss her too. But I promised I would stay put until Lachlan arrived here. I will not break my word."

Her frown deepened as she added sugar to the magic elixir that made her day better. Maybe she would write a song about her one true love, coffee. She inwardly snorted at the ridiculous sleep-deprived thought as she took her first sip.

"You know he's only a couple blocks over from here," Reaper murmured mildly when she didn't respond. "If you let him know you want me out of here and he agrees, I'll leave."

She paused, her mug halfway to her mouth. "Lachlan's only a couple blocks away?"

"Yep. He texted me all of five minutes ago saying they'd just returned, and gave me the non-news."

"What's the address?" And how did she not know he was staying so close?

He quickly rattled it off.

She looked at Aurora and Lola, who were silently eating pancakes that either Aurora or Reaper had definitely made—because Lola couldn't cook for shit. "I'll be back."

Aurora simply picked up her coffee and took a sip but Lola grinned. Today her rainbow-colored hair was still in the two long braids from last night and she had on a faded green T-shirt with the text, *I wear this periodically* over a picture of the periodic table. "Should we prepare for more fireworks?"

Regretting what she'd told them last night about the glowing and flames, she simply glared at Lola before striding from the room. The others were either out on their patrol shift or still sleeping upstairs but she was an early bird.

The sun was breaking over everything, birds singing, squirrels chirping as she strode down the long walkway toward the gate. She waved once at Harlow, who was sitting on the wall, eating an orange. "You good?"

"Yeah. We've got this." Harlow pointed to a nearby tree where Kartini, in eagle-owl form, was blending in well.

Lachlan's place turned out to be a three-story mansion similar to the one her people were staying in. Built in a different era and with a different paint color on the outside, it was still huge and big enough to fit a bunch of dragons.

She found the gate locked so she simply climbed over it. As she reached the front porch, she started to pull back the brass knocker on the dark blue door, but it swung open and she found a shirtless Lachlan staring at her.

Her gaze fell to his chest and she stared for a long moment. She'd seen him naked before but not quite so close and... *Damn it.* She snapped her gaze to his face.

His dark hair was damp and slicked back as if he'd just had a shower, and his expression was definitely one of surprise. And hunger. "Star." The way he rolled the R in her name sent a shiver of delight through her, but she fought it off.

What the hell? Her body just flared to life around him and it was maddening. She was here for a reason. "Don't you 'Star' me. Why haven't you contacted me?"

"Reaper said he wasn't leaving your house." He frowned at her. "Did he leave?" He came to attention then, all sexy and angry. Okay, he just seemed angry—she'd added the sexy part because, come on.

"He didn't leave. But I'm not dealing with some middleman. And you don't give me orders. You are not my Alpha."

"I could be your Alpha in the bedroom."

She blinked, staring at him for a long moment while her body heated and went haywire with a barrage of sexual images flooding her brain until someone cleared their throat.

"I dinnae want to get in the middle of whatever *this* is, but I think this is the last of the bags." The shifter she knew as Cody, Lachlan's younger brother, according to Lola's research, stopped at the end of the stairs. He dropped a green duffel bag on top of the stack of other similarly colored duffel bags in the foyer.

"You're going home?" Why did that thought fill her with disappointment? She should want the big dragon gone. But...after that kiss, she found she was more than ready for another taste. A slow one.

Jump him now before he leaves, her beast whispered. *Grrr.* She ordered herself to shut up, then felt a little crazy.

"Nay, lass. We were headed over to your place."

Her eyes widened. "Wait...my place? With bags? Why?" The answer seemed clear but apparently she was going to ask questions with obvious answers now. "And why didn't you ask me first?"

"We couldnae find any trace of Oscar last night but I didnae like what happened in the cemetery. And according to the sentries I have scouting his territory back home, they haven't seen him in twenty-four hours. So my clanmates and I will be guarding you."

"We don't need guarding." The words were automatic. She was so used to her crew being a unit and working together without any outsiders, and she bristled at his heavy-handedness.

"Fine, then you will humor me and we will be your bodyguards."

Her eyes narrowed. "Because we're mostly females? Because we're all pretty damn capable of defending ourselves."

"Oh, I ken you are capable, and your gender has nothing to do with it. Nonetheless, I will keep you safe."

She took a deep breath, centering herself and forcing herself to remain calm. The thought of him being under the same roof as her was too much. Especially since her strange dreams were getting her all amped up lately. "We don't have the room." That was a lie, one he probably scented. *Damn it.*

"Then I'll sleep outside in my animal form."

She let out a growl of frustration. Instead of responding, she simply turned and yanked the front door open.

She'd barely taken a step when she heard Cody say, "I call dibs on Bella."

She stopped in her tracks and turned to glare at him. She was ready to rip him a new asshole for talking about her friend as if she was a piece of property when she saw the mischievous look in his eyes. He was simply messing with her.

Sighing, she strode outside, not bothering to shut the door behind her.

"I'll see you soon, lass," Lachlan called out, more than a hint of wicked promise in his voice.

Gah. She really wanted to argue with Lachlan about staying at her house. The frustrating male hadn't even asked her. He'd simply packed a bunch of bags and informed her they were coming over. And he wouldn't have even given her a heads-up; he'd been planning to simply show up.

Who does that?

Ancient, stubborn, sexy dragons apparently, that was who.

She let out another growl of frustration as she started striding down the sidewalk, earning her a wary glance from two jogging females.

She grabbed her hoodie and tugged it over her head. Then she shoved her hands in her pockets and picked up her pace. Now she had to tell her crew that a bunch of dragons were on their way over.

A secret part of her was glad for the extra protection, especially if Oscar was on his way here. Or even here already. And at that thought, she started jogging faster. She needed to warn the others immediately.

* * *

As dusk fell, Star stood on the top step of the front porch as the four dragons headed up the walkway to the door. She'd expected Lachlan this morning but he'd been called in to see King, at least according to the text he'd sent her. So she and her bandmates had actually gotten some practice in. Singing and working on a new song had been a good way to mentally distract herself. Though nothing could fully distract her from thoughts of Lachlan. Especially considering the fact that she'd seen him naked. More than once.

Lachlan's mouth curved up into a sexy grin as he and his three dragons approached, his gaze sweeping her from head to foot.

She had to pretend she wasn't affected, but damn, it was hard. She cleared her throat. "The fact that you guys are here is ridiculous but I'm going to let it happen. You'll also be bunking with each other. I don't care how you figure out your sleeping situation, but there are only two extra rooms. One has twin beds." And she had no clue how they were going to even fit in them. "And the other is an office with a pullout couch."

"I could just bunk with you," Lachlan said mildly, even as heat flared in his eyes.

She rolled her eyes. "Second, if any of you make my girls, or Axel, feel uncomfortable, not only will they let you know in the form of a punch to the dick, but you will be out of here immediately, if not dead. I appreciate you helping us out, but you respect my rules."

"I like this one," the one named Teague murmured, a small grin on his face. "Already talking about dick punches and we haven't even crossed the threshold."

The one named Cian simply grinned in response.

"Damn, you really are Alpha," Cody added, his grin firmly in place. He looked similar to Lachlan, but there was a boyishness to him, even though she knew he had to be nearly as ancient as Lachlan. Unlike Lachlan, he seemed more playful, but maybe that was a symptom of being a younger sibling. His hair was also cut shorter, and his eyes, while indigo, weren't the same deep shade as Lachlan's, but a bit lighter. Still, he was huge in the way dragons were, built as if he'd been cut straight from a mountainside.

She gave him a hard look, and to her surprise he averted his gaze after a brief staring contest. *Ugh.* She hated it when people tried to stare her down. They always lost.

Lachlan raised an eyebrow at her.

"What?"

He lifted a shoulder. "We will respect all of your rules, though the second one is unnecessary. We respect all beings, lass."

She nodded then, ignoring the way her insides melted when he used the word lass. "Good."

He motioned to the other males. "Star, this is Teague and Cian, though I have a feeling you know that already." There was a slight question in his voice.

And yes, she knew their names because of Lola's research, but Lachlan and his clan were very good at keeping a low profile so it had been hard to mine much information. Instead of answering that question, she simply smiled at the males. "It's nice to meet you." She really hoped she wasn't letting the enemy into her house right now. Her other half scoffed at her, which actually made Star feel better. Her instincts had never steered her wrong. "Lachlan, you and I are on patrol now." If he'd decided to come to her place, then she was putting him to work with her.

"Not a problem." He handed his bag to his brother, and Cody and the other two filed inside.

"It's been pretty quiet around here so I'll take the east side, you take the west." It would give her a little space from him at least, but not nearly enough. When she'd thought he was returning to Scotland earlier some deep part of her had panicked, felt out of control. She didn't like or understand the feeling. But she couldn't deny the attraction between them. Or those damn dreams that kept haunting her. And she wasn't sure why she was thinking of those dreams and Lachlan in the same breath anyway.

His dragon peered back at her for a long moment. "What's it going to take for you to trust me?"

"I don't *not* trust you."

He scoffed slightly. "I helped get your sister and your crew out of Wales. I dinnae have any ulterior motives."

"You want to get me naked." And why did she have to go and say the word naked? Now she was thinking about getting him naked too. Something she'd been fantasizing about far too often lately.

"True, but I'm not hiding that. And I want more than just a quick roll in the hay."

Despite the tension coiled inside her, a smile tugged at her lips. "Look, you're a dragon, so the fact that I'm letting you and your clanmates in my house at all is a big deal."

He went still. "You have a problem with dragons?"

She was silent, watching him carefully. Her instinct told her she could trust him but she couldn't afford to put anyone in danger. "I don't know you enough to trust you. Not with everything."

"Fair enough."

She stepped off the porch and headed in the opposite direction of him. She took her patrols seriously even if they had set up a few traps. She needed to tell Lachlan about a couple of them and turned to do just that when she realized he was standing right next to her.

"You're quiet," she muttered, her heart fluttering with him so near. He smelled incredible, and all she could think about with him this close was that scorching kiss, and the damn dreams that left her aching for release.

"Aye." He lifted a broad shoulder. "When did you get chickens?" he asked, eyeing the new coop.

"Today. Bella has been a busy bee. She said she wants fresh eggs every morning so she made it happen. I honestly don't even know where she got them or who she got to build the coop." Star had come out from her practice earlier in the afternoon to find Bella ordering some guys around as they built the coop. And she had an instruction manual on how to care for chickens too.

"Impressive."

Feeling her cheeks heat up at his nearness, she cleared her throat. "Oh, we also set up a few traps around the property. Specifically for dragons. Nothing that will kill anyone, but they'll get tangled in the wires should they try an aerial attack or landing."

He nodded in approval. "Just tell me where they are."

She motioned toward the locations as they reached the eight-foot-high outer wall. Without waiting for him, she jumped up and pulled herself over the ledge so that her legs were dangling off the side. The street was quiet tonight and since Taya was also on patrol—something she wasn't telling Lachlan about—they had extra eyes in the sky.

She wasn't surprised when moments later, Lachlan crouched down next to her on top of the wall, then stretched his long legs out, letting them hang over the side too.

"We're supposed to be separated." But there was no heat in her words. She liked sitting next to him, breathing in his scent.

"I saw one of the tigers headed toward the west wall and Axel is in the backyard. And...I suspect you have another lookout somewhere." He simply pointed at the trees but in no particular direction.

"How do you know that?"

He gave her a sideways glance. "I can smell them."

Right. His olfactory senses were much stronger than hers. Since she was supposed to be a snow leopard, most shifters assumed her sense of smell was on par with theirs. But at this point, Lachlan knew she was something else.

"So did you always know you wanted to be a singer?" he asked as they watched a couple of wolves and a bear strolling down the street. The bear actually lifted a big paw and waved at them.

Star waved back, smiling at the brown bear. They were pretty rare as far as she knew. "I always liked to sing, but I only started performing on a bigger scale because I needed to save my sister. Between Lola and Bella, geniuses that they are, they understand branding and stuff like that. They helped get my name and voice out there and things took off."

His eyes widened in surprise.

"What? I never wanted to be famous. Not like I am now. I love performing on a local scale—I'm from Saint Augustine originally, which I think you know—but I never had aspirations of worldwide fame. Especially since I'm...supernatural. We'd already talked about how I would fade from fame and then start over somewhere eventually. Now I won't have to." Which was a relief at least.

"Your talent never would have remained a local thing." There was conviction in his voice.

She snorted softly. "I put on a good show."

"That you do. But you've still got incredible talent, lass. Someone would have discovered you no matter what your intentions."

She lifted a shoulder, feeling out of sorts with the praise, mainly because he was so blunt and matter-of-fact about it. And sexy. Far too sexy for her liking.

"Are you going to tell me what you really are?" he asked softly.

She froze. "What do you mean?"

"You know exactly what I mean. Because you're certainly not a snow leopard. Or not fully, anyway."

"It's rude to ask someone what they are."

"Yes, and I'm so worried about civility." Now he snorted.

She simply cleared her throat and glanced down the sidewalk as two female vampires strode by, their fangs on full display. One of them glanced up and gave her a half-wave. The other winked at Star and licked her lips.

All right, then. She waved back, laughing lightly.

"So how old are you exactly?" Star asked, deciding to ignore his question. Besides, if he wanted her to trust him, then she wanted more details on him. Because Lola had only been able to find surface information.

"I dinnae even know anymore. I went into Hibernation thousands of years ago. And I was thousands of years old then. Time is different for me."

She knew dragons often went into long sleeps and it made sense. The mind wasn't made to exist for thousands of years. That was far too many memories, too much pain, too much everything to store up for one individual. Jeez, talk about getting PTSD.

"Since you willnae tell me what you are, how about we talk about that fire show you put on in that alley?" Okay, so he wasn't giving up.

Too bad for him; she wasn't having this conversation. Jumping to her feet, she easily balanced along the top of the wall. "Not gonna happen, dragon." She headed east, keeping her strides steady though she was trembling inside. She didn't like all this pushing. "Stay on your side of the wall and I'll stay on mine."

To her surprise, and maybe disappointment, he didn't follow her. It was just as well. She needed to focus on her patrol, and if she was too near Lachlan—well, her focus was on him instead.

CHAPTER 18

S tar hurried down the stairs at the scent of bacon. After the night patrol shift, she'd showered and now she was starving. For more than food, but that was pretty much beside the point because that wasn't happening.

"How was patrol?" Aurora asked from where she stood at the stove, making scrambled eggs. A plate of bacon was sitting off to the side.

Star eyed the food, inhaling deeply. "Nothing exciting, which is the kind of patrol I like."

"I heard a party going on nearby last night."

"Oh yeah. A bunch of shifters were throwing down about two blocks over and the noise carried." The noise was better than silence in her opinion. It meant people were living their lives and trying to get back some semblance of normalcy. But after two in the morning, they needed to shut the hell up and go to sleep. Gah, she felt like a cranky old lady some days.

"Have you seen your boyfriend this morning?"

Star jerked slightly as she added sugar to her coffee. "Don't you start. That dragon is not my boyfriend. And he's a freaking dragon. Don't forget it."

Aurora shrugged, her oversized sweater falling down one shoulder as she added more cheese to the scrambled eggs. "Pretty sure I'm a good judge of people at this point, and this is a good group of guys. They're not like Oscar's clan. Not like the dragons who killed Mom and Dad."

She bit down hard before pushing out a breath. It was hard to think about what had happened to their parents. Aurora had been so young when they'd been murdered, but Star remembered everything in clear detail. "Maybe, maybe not." Okay, there was no maybe. They were good guys. She was just letting the past color her thinking.

"Star, it's not like dragons are the only ones responsible for killing our kind."

"I know." And this was a conversation they'd had many times.

"Anyway, since you haven't seen your not-boyfriend, look," Aurora said, holding a spatula up and pointing out the oversized window over the sink.

Warm mug in hand, she peeked outside and couldn't stop the startled burst of laughter that escaped.

Brielle and Harlow each had a volleyball and were tossing them at Lachlan, who was on his back in dragon form. He gently swatted the balls, as if he was a soccer goalie or something. But when he swatted them, the twins raced for them, trying to knock them back at him. It was like a bizarre game of ping-pong. "What the hell is wrong with them? Has the world gone completely mad?" she said more to herself than her sister.

"Pretty sure you know the answer to that."

She snorted because okay, it was true. "Still, this is…"

"This is your crew burning off some steam."

"True enough." Even Taya and Kartini were out there getting in on the action, throwing more balls at the giant dragon. "Where's Lola?"

"Sleeping. So is Bella. They're exhausted."

"They should be. I heard them playing poker until well after one in the morning."

"Pretty sure they cleaned those dragons out for everything they were worth."

Now that made Star smile. "Good."

"Have you heard any news on Aunt Cliona?"

Before she could answer, her phone buzzed in her pocket. "Maybe," she said when she saw the name on the caller ID. The back door opened then and Cody strode in, smiling at both of them as he rubbed his stomach. "Something smells good."

Star gave him a brief smile and answered her phone, then nodded once at Aurora who knew exactly why she was leaving. She didn't want anyone to overhear this conversation.

* * *

Lachlan stood as Star hurried outside. He'd been playing a ridiculous game with various sports balls that the females had been throwing at him. He wasn't sure why they'd been doing it but it had seemed to amuse them. Finally, he'd shifted back to human form and now all amusement fled as he saw the worry etched onto Star's face.

She flicked a glance at him, barely acknowledging his presence, and his dragon roared to the surface. But he kept him at bay even though his beast lingered, annoyed at being dismissed. *Silly female*, his beast thought. Then, *You need to court her better*, his dragon reprimanded. *Bring her food. Meat. Females like that. Mmm, so do I.*

He closed his eyes for a moment and ordered his dragon to simmer down even as he agreed with the beast. Maybe he should bring gifts like food. It was a primitive way of courting, but he was a primitive male at his core. He needed to do more than simply protect her.

"I have some errands to run," she said vaguely, even as she gave her sister a meaningful look.

And he didn't miss the subtle glances between the twins and the others. His own males were currently on patrol as he had ordered them to give Star's people a break. They deserved one after all they'd been through.

"I will go with you."

Now she looked at him, one eyebrow raised. Her dark hair was pulled up into a loose ponytail today and she wore jeans and a formfitting sweater that molded to all her curves. "I didn't invite you."

"Yet I am going."

She gritted her teeth, staring at him hard. "I'm not going into town. I have to make a trip out to the bayou."

"For what?"

"None of your business, nosy dragon."

"I can fly you. You'll get there much faster." He had a vague knowledge of where there were swamp and marsh areas surrounding the city as he had studied the geography before coming to New Orleans.

Her expression didn't change.

"I think it's a great idea," Aurora said, a smile playing across her lips.

Lachlan had come to realize they had a different relationship than

Star did with the others, and not just because they were sisters. Star wasn't Aurora's Alpha. Aurora was young, likely in her early twenties, but he could sense the Alpha simmering inside her. She just hadn't fully emerged yet, but it was there, ready and waiting.

Star shot Aurora an annoyed glance before she finally nodded once. Then she turned her back on him, giving him a shot of the most beautiful ass in the world. Unfortunately she had on pants. "I'll meet you out front in a minute," she tossed over her shoulder as she hurried back inside.

He frowned at her retreating back, a growl building in his throat. He had the urge to hunt her down, to take her to the ground and pleasure her until she was crying out his name. Bury his face and then his cock between her legs.

"You need to step up your game, dragon," the one named Brielle said. She shook her head slightly and then pulled out a switchblade and started peeling an apple.

He didn't respond, simply stalked after Star. Moments later he found her in the front yard, shoving something into a backpack.

"Had you planned to drive there?" It was his understanding that while people were driving right now, it was not as common. He'd only seen a handful of vehicles on the road, but he hadn't realized that Star's crew even had one.

She stood and slid the backpack onto her shoulders. "So how does this work?" she asked, ignoring his question. "Do I just climb on your back and hold on to your scales or..."

"I can carry you in my claws or you can ride on my back. Either way is acceptable."

"Your back it is."

"For the record, I would like you to ride me in other ways while we are both naked and—"

"Lachlan, you've got to stop saying that stuff!" Her cheeks flushed pink and she wouldn't look him in the eyes.

But he'd gotten her to say his name again. He lifted a shoulder as he started stripping off his clothes. Slowly.

She turned away then, making him smile. She lived with shifters—and was a type of shifter herself if he wasn't mistaken. She should not be shy about nudity.

"You can watch." He dropped his voice an octave. "I know you want to."

"You sure are arrogant."

Of course he was. "I'm a dragon."

She snorted and shoved her hands into her jeans pockets but he didn't miss the way she shot him a quick glance over her shoulder.

His gaze connected with hers and she jerked away, completely giving him her back now. He wanted to tease her some more but instead let the change come over him completely. Magic and pain exploded together into a kaleidoscope of bright colors and then he was himself again.

He stretched his wings out, happy to be in this form. *Kidnap mate, take her somewhere safe*, his dragon commanded him.

Unfortunately he liked this idea far too much, so he ignored it.

Star turned to him then, and reached back to quickly braid her long ponytail as she walked toward him.

He was glad she hadn't known how to ride him. It meant that she had not flown with a dragon before. He would be her first. He also wanted to be her last.

She stood staring at him with what he liked to think of as awe for a long moment, before she bundled up his clothes and tucked them into her backpack. When she approached him, she climbed up him in quick, agile movements, as if she'd done it before.

It surprised him and something about it bothered him, something in the back of his mind, but he couldn't grasp on to what it was. He still remembered her brilliant show of fire at the airport. It had been unlike anything he had ever seen. He didn't know of any shifters that could control fire—witches, yes. And some rare vampires. But she didn't smell like either species. She was unique.

That fire show she'd displayed was a very dragon type of thing—she had to be a hybrid of some kind. Maybe...half-demon? Not that he cared. The only thing he cared about was getting more of her kisses. Then all of them. Forever. That one glorious kiss kept replaying in his mind over and over. It was on repeat and making him mad with desire. He put those thoughts on lockdown, however.

As he launched into the air, he was careful to avoid the traps they had set in place. Now that he knew about them, he could easily see the wires, but they'd been skillfully woven into the vegetation and trees. Very smart, much like this whole crew of Star's.

He took to the air and she didn't make a peep. Lachlan had expected some kind of yelp of surprise or something, but she simply held on tight as he soared higher into the air. Wind rolled over his scales as he arced upward, far above the trees so that everything below them grew smaller and smaller.

"Head west," he heard her shout above the wind.

So he did just that, enjoying being in his dragon form even as much as he enjoyed her joining him.

If she wasn't a dragon hybrid, she might not have any idea how vulnerable he was letting himself be with her right now, letting her ride on his back. He'd never let anyone, save one human female, ride him before. And now Star. Pure instinct was the only reason he was letting her—his dragon recognized her for what she was. His mate.

It didn't take long for them to reach the destination. From the sky, he spotted the house she indicated clearly. A stilt house, he believed it was called—built up off the ground in case of flooding.

There was a huge grassy area perfect for landing behind it, so he suddenly shot downward, inwardly smiling at her inhalation of breath as he swooped in for a perfect landing.

The grass shimmered out in waves around them, making a faint swishing sound. She dropped from his body moments later and knelt in front of her backpack.

"I hope the ride wasn't too rough for you?" he asked once he'd shifted to human. He'd been careful, keeping his body angled so that the wind flowed around her instead of pummeling her.

Avoiding his gaze, she handed his bundled clothes to him. A few tendrils of her hair had escaped her braid and were wild around her face. The sight brought back a sudden memory of a different female, after he'd taken her on her first flight with him. She'd thought like Star and had braided her hair to keep it from tangling as well. He resisted the urge to brush the strands back from Star's face.

"No, it was exhilarating. I—" She abruptly cleared her throat and put distance between them.

He didn't smell a threat and he didn't think she did either—especially since her sense of smell seemed to be muted compared to his. No, she clearly hadn't wanted to tell him something. Sighing to himself, he dressed quickly, surveying the land and house. High off the ground on concrete pillars, the house was painted teal and yellow and had a coastal look to it. There was enough room to park two vehicles underneath the structure, but there weren't any vehicles in sight.

"Whose place is this?"

She paused, then said, "My aunt's."

Surprise filtered through him. As they strode across the grassy patch, he said, "I dinnae scent anyone here. And I didnae see any neighbors for at least a mile or two."

"Yeah, I saw that too." She glanced around at the swampy area to the left and then over to a greenhouse to the right of the home.

"Is she expecting you?"

"No. But that's okay. I guess she's out of town because I can't get a hold of her. And she moved recently," she grumbled. "Luckily I was able to find out her new address from an old friend." Star went straight for the stairs and he followed suit as she jogged up them. Immediately he spotted the security camera above the door. Star waved at it once before knocking on the door. There was no answer, though considering the faint scents surrounding the place, he hadn't expected any.

Star waited for a moment, then went to a potted plant and dug her fingers around in it until she found the key.

He simply raised an eyebrow as she unlocked the door.

"What? It's not breaking and entering if I have the key. And she won't care."

He simply shrugged and followed her inside as she quickly disarmed the security system. He didn't care what she did—if she wanted to break the law, he would help her.

The scent inside had a familiarity to it that he recognized as belonging to Star and Aurora as well. It was so subtle, the faintest hint of an underlying thread that said they were the same type of being.

He added all the puzzle pieces he had together, creating a picture of Star. It was an interesting one.

"Stay here and don't touch anything," she ordered as she hurried deeper into the house.

He glanced around curiously. There were a lot of brightly colored things everywhere. The furniture was mostly white and sturdy. A patchwork quilt with a starburst of rainbow colors emerging from the middle had been tossed haphazardly onto the back of the couch. The media cabinet underneath an oversized television that had a light layer of dust on it showcased different knickknacks. A bowl of sea glass, a dried starfish, a small vase with dried lavender. There were other little things dotting the room on shelves—some new and others quite old, creating an eclectic image of the owner. Likely someone much older than Star, considering the age of some of the things.

He went to the mantel and looked at an array of pictures, unabashed in his curiosity. He was a dragon after all, and cats had nothing on dragons when it came to being curious.

There were pictures of people he didn't know, clearly none related to the female, given the different shades of their skin tones. But on one shelf, the woman he assumed was Star's aunt, because of her frequency in all the pictures with other people, posed with a couple who he guessed were Star's parents. Because next to them was a Star who was maybe twenty years old, holding a little girl who was definitely Aurora. She couldn't be more than five in this picture.

"What are you doing?" Star asked from behind him.

"How old were you in that picture?" he asked, not bothering to answer because it was clear what he was doing.

"Nineteen." There was a wistful note in her voice.

"Aurora was adorable."

Star grinned at him then. "She really was. And she looks so damn happy here." Star touched the picture, a riot of emotions playing across her expression.

As he looked at the picture, he frowned as he focused on her aunt. For some reason the dark-haired female looked familiar, as if he should recognize her from somewhere. But he couldn't place her. "What happened to your parents?" he asked before he could stop himself from asking the question. In all his research, he hadn't been able to find out much about her—hadn't even known Aurora was her sister originally. But there was nothing on her parents, much less an aunt. No names, nothing. It was as if they didn't exist.

Just like that, the half-smile faded and she cleared her throat as she turned away. "They were killed two months after this picture was taken. By dragons."

CHAPTER 19

"What happened to the dragons who killed them?" Lachlan asked as Star locked up her aunt's place. His tone was even, but she could see the simmering anger in his indigo eyes.

She paused, surprised by the question.

"Dead." Star had hunted them down herself—weeks after she'd gotten Aurora to safety. "There were four of them. All males. I...had to run when they attacked, to get Aurora to safety. But once I regrouped, I found them and killed them one by one." Her crew had helped her in the actual hunt, but she'd been the one to pick them off. Each one of them had felt her wrath and died screaming in agony. Her parents had still been dead though. And she felt that loss every day.

"Good," he snarled.

She looked up at him as they reached the bottom of the stairs. "You don't even know why they came after my family."

"Dinnae need to ken." His jaw was set tight as he scanned the horizon, his indigo eyes searching for any sign of danger. "Multiple dragons attacking a family that includes a five-year-old? Besides, everything I ken about you... They deserved what they got. I'm sorry about your parents though. Sorry you were left to deal with everything alone. And...raise your sister, I'm assuming?"

"Yeah," she said. The sincerity in his voice punched up against that wall she had, creating little cracks. "And thank you. I wasn't alone at least. My crew—God, we were so young then—they helped me hunt them down while Kartini's parents took care of Aurora. It was the first time we'd ever acted as a unit. The first time I ever killed anyone." After that, they'd broken away from the co-op and had naturally formed their own crew.

"You all certainly make up an interesting group."

She shrugged as they reached the grassy patch he'd landed on before. "We work."

"Ready?" he asked, and she nodded.

He stripped and shifted—and she had to force herself not to stare at him, to pretend she wasn't interested in seeing his naked ass again. And...more. She stared a little bit, unable to tear her gaze away from all that bare skin. Heat blossomed inside her as she devoured him with her gaze like a giant perv. *Gah.* She turned away, giving him a bit of privacy even though she didn't think he cared if she watched him. But this was for her own sanity.

Once he was in his magnificent dragon form, Star climbed up Lachlan as if she'd done it hundreds of times. It was only the second time she'd ridden a dragon but it felt natural, normal. Which made no sense. But he was so powerful and protective so maybe it was why she wasn't experiencing any weirdness.

She was disappointed that she hadn't been able to find what she'd been looking for at her aunt's house. Not that she'd expected it to be out in the open, but she hadn't been able to find a safe or anything. If she could just talk to her aunt, get her to call her back. Star had thought about asking around New Orleans after her, but couldn't get past that intrinsic part that warned her to keep her secrets, to protect her family and herself.

Lachlan stretched out, flapping his wings once as if to ask if she was ready to fly.

She patted him twice and he made a sort of snorting sound which should not have been so adorable on such a fierce-looking animal. But he kind of was. She wasn't sure how it was possible, but fierce and adorable worked well on this huge male with the indigo-colored scales that glittered prettily in the sunlight.

He took to the skies, his takeoff graceful and smooth. She savored the feel of the wind rushing over her, wishing she was free to reveal exactly what she was. Her other half was getting antsy, wanted to come out and play with him—and show off for Lachlan, to show him exactly how beautiful she was. Yep, her beast was not happy.

Suddenly Lachlan's big body jerked. And then Star saw them.

Three shimmery blurs on the horizon. It had to be camouflaged dragons. Her stomach dropped at the sight of three blurs flying toward them from different directions. She glanced behind them. No one there. Suddenly, they dropped their camouflage, not bothering with it anymore. *Dragons.*

Her heart lurched in her chest as Lachlan angled upward, flying far and fast, bursting through a cluster of clouds. Realizing that he was hiding them, she held on tight to his heavy, thick scales and buried her face against them.

For a moment, she saw nothing at all except a thick white haze as he glided soundlessly back in the direction of her home through the clouds.

Heart racing, she glanced around them even though the clouds were pea soup thick. It was impossible to see anything, which was good and bad.

He banked left, dipping into another cluster of thick clouds. As the clouds started to thin, giving up all semblance of cover, Lachlan dipped downward, arrowing toward a huge forest and swampy area.

Fire blasted at them from above. The heat licked around her but her natural defenses kept it at bay. For now. Or...maybe Lachlan was somehow protecting her because her clothes didn't burn. She'd worry about that later.

He twisted midair and blasted a bright burst of raging hot blue fire at the nearest dragon.

She stared in awe and horror as the attacking dragon burst into flames, its screeches wild and terrifying as it began falling toward the earth in a billowing lump of scales. She'd never seen fire like that, never seen a dragon kill another dragon so quickly and efficiently. Normally dragon fire had to break down the other dragon's natural shields—and that took time. Immediately, the other two dragons split up, flying in opposite directions.

She wasn't stupid enough to think they were leaving. And neither was Lachlan. He raced after the closest one. His wings flapped with efficiency as he arrowed toward the giant gold dragon.

Hunkering down, she held on tight and trusted him to take out this threat. As they gained on the other dragon faster, faster, Lachlan let out another burst of bright blue flames, lighting up the entire sky in a brilliant show of color.

The other dragon's left wing burst into flames under the impact. As the beast started a downward spiral toward the treetops, she turned and realized the other dragon was gaining on them. And it had a rider!

Screw this.

Calling on her own fire, she sent out a burst of her own bright fiery magic, throwing a ball of purple fire straight at the dragon's chest. The rider held something in his hand. A gun, maybe. Some kind of weapon. Whatever it was, he aimed and fired at them as she released her own fire.

"Lachlan! Behind us!" She shouted on instinct even though he would have heard the dragon.

Her fire missed the beast as it barrel-rolled. The rider held on as she fired at it again. As Lachlan turned, something slammed into his wing. He let out a screech, his head whipping back as he started to fall. Lachlan shot flames upward at them, but the other dragon dodged the attack and started to fly away now. Trying to escape.

"No!" she screamed. Rage filled her as she hauled her hands back and threw another burst of fire at the fleeing dragon.

This time she didn't miss. Before the beast could fully turn, her fire slammed the dragon right in the face. It screamed, its head flying backward in pain before it whipped around midair and started flying in the other direction. Off-balance, she threw herself forward, clutching at Lachlan's scales as he flapped furiously, trying to steady them.

He let out a low keening sound, clearly in pain. She wasn't sure what the hell had hit him but it wasn't good and it ripped at her heart to know he was hurting.

He somehow managed to right them into a soft glide over the treetops as they descended a little too fast. Full trees ripped from their roots under the impact of his wings. Somehow he kept his body angled as they crashed through the trees, all the while trying to protect her from the flying debris.

Branches hit her in the face as they crashed to the hard earth below so she ducked her head against him. Her entire body shook under the impact, all her muscles tensing as he skidded to a halt, one of his wings knocking another tree out by the roots. Lachlan shifted to human form as Star jumped off him moments after they'd hit the soft earth.

"Lachlan!" She knelt next to him, scanning his body for wounds.

He reached for her, his eyes dilated and unfocused. "Poison... Get out of here... Save yourself." His back arched in pain as he tried to shove her away from him. "Go," he tried to order, though it came out as a thready whisper. "Might not...make it."

"I'm not leaving you!" And it pissed her off that he thought she would.

She shelved that thought for later and looked upward, scanning through the broken tree branches for any sign of danger. All around them was a muted hush of animals scurrying away. Their crash landing had clearly scared the local wildlife and sent everything into hiding. She just hoped that her blast of fire had stopped or at least slowed down their last attacker. She'd seen that dragon start to fly away, but what if it came back?

Or had backup nearby? Oh God, she really hoped there weren't more dragons coming after them. Not with Lachlan so vulnerable right now. She couldn't carry him and fight them off.

"Get out of here," he muttered, his body starting to tremble under the impact of the poison.

Completely ignoring him, she turned him over and started running her fingers over his body, looking for any type of wound. That was when she saw the slice against his right upper arm. It was where that rider had shot his wing. She couldn't see an arrow or bullet, but something had clearly been injected. He'd said poison and she wished she knew what kind. Not that it really mattered at this point.

"Lachlan," she said quietly, not wanting her voice to travel.

He didn't respond, his breathing deep and heavy. Hell, he was passed out.

Working quickly, she dug into her backpack and pulled out a knife. She sliced her palm open, ignoring the sharp sting. Then she placed her bloody hand over his wound. As an Alpha dragon, his wound should have already started healing, but it wasn't closing—until her blood made contact.

She breathed a small sigh of relief as she watched his skin start knitting itself back together. *It's working.* Wincing, she sliced her already healing palm again and placed it on him again. She wanted as much of her blood mixing with his so it would combat the internal poison. That was the key: her blood needed to destroy whatever was inside him. And fast.

In minutes, the wound closed, leaving an ugly red scar behind. That too would eventually fade, but her magical blood had worked its way into his system, healing him from the inside, fighting the poison. Depending upon what kind of poison it was, it could take up to an hour to destroy it. And she didn't think they had that kind of time to just wait out in the open.

She needed to get him to safety and that meant hiding. She could try to fly out of here but she couldn't fight off dragons while carrying an unconscious Lachlan. No, they would go into hiding for now.

Thankfully she had supernatural strength, so she hefted him up and fireman-carried him through the woods. Before they'd crash-landed, she'd seen a few random structures out here. She wasn't sure where they were going to hunker down, but even if she had to bury them in the swamp until she was sure the threat was gone, they were going to hide.

Anger roared through her as she stalked through the woods. She'd recognized the coloring of those dragons—gold and violet. Oscar had to have been the one behind this attack. She was going to kill him. Much sooner than later. Even if she had to go all the way back to Wales to put him down, it was happening. She wasn't going to sit around like a target and wait to be attacked like this again. No way in hell.

And now Oscar's people had poisoned Lachlan, a man she was starting to care waaaaay too much about. She would do everything she could to protect this wonderful male who'd protected her, who'd tried to get her to leave him to die. No matter what.

CHAPTER 20

L achlan moved slightly, his body stiff and pressed up against someone... *Star.* He scented her immediately, inhaled even deeper. That crisp, wild scent was in his bones. And he was naked. This could be interesting, his dragon purred. *Wait...* Fuzzy images racked his brain as he struggled to open his eyes.

"Keep quiet," Star whispered. "You're alive and okay."

The dragon attack. He remembered everything. He managed to open his eyes and looked straight into her pale violet ones. "Are *you* okay?" Images from their attack came rushing back: the dragons, that burning hot blue fire, poison flooding his veins...them falling. Crashing.

"I'm good," she said so quietly only he would be able to hear her.

Unlike him, she was dressed in the clothes she had on before. And...it wasn't daytime anymore. They were under some kind of boat or other structure, but the temperature had dropped and there wasn't any ambient light flowing in from...outside wherever they were hunkering down. Thanks to his dragon vision, he could see her clearly. He smelled wet marsh nearby as well as various animals—squirrels, a couple gators. Birds. Raccoons.

"Where are we?" he murmured subvocally.

"In the middle of nowhere, hiding in an old shack under a kayak." Her words were just as quiet as his.

"How long?"

"Hours. My sense of smell isn't like yours. I was worried I'd walk us into a trap, and this place would be impossible to see from the sky."

He nodded and shifted slightly, reaching out to pull her even closer to him. He felt oddly rejuvenated, and he sensed that the poison in his blood was gone. He knew what he'd been hit with too. He should still be paralyzed, maybe even dead, given the amount that had been shot into him. But something had happened. He wondered if it had to do with that weird blue fire he'd been breathing out...

No. This was something else and it must have to do with Star. He tried to focus but his mind was too fuzzy so he pulled her close, savoring the feel of her tucked up against him. She was safe and he hated that he'd been unconscious, unable to protect her.

To his surprise, she burrowed into him and laid her head against his chest. He turned slightly so that she was off the ground and halfway on top of him. He didn't like that she was here in this shite place when she should be treated like a queen.

"Have you heard any movement?" he asked.

"Not for an hour at least."

"We'll wait another hour, then leave." Though he was fairly certain they were alone, given that he couldn't scent any enemies, but he wanted to be careful.

She simply nodded, her hair swishing against his chest. "I...heard someone close by a couple hours ago. They opened the door and I expected them to see us or scent us but...they left. It was weird. I couldn't see who it was though, so maybe it was humans."

"My dragon half camouflaged us."

"What?"

He closed his eyes and kept his arm around her. "I'm ancient and it's one of my gifts. I can camouflage myself in dragon form obviously, but my body must have done it without thought, a survival instinct, and included you."

"Wait...I'm camouflaged too?"

"Yep." He rested his chin on her head, inhaled. She smelled like home.

"But I can see myself."

"No one else can see you though, except me."

"That's...pretty handy."

"It is indeed. How did you get us here?"

"I carried you."

"With magic?" he murmured.

She didn't respond, simply burrowed closer to him.

He decided not to push. It didn't matter anyway. "Thank you for saving me." His words came out rough. They hadn't known each other long—even if it felt as if he'd known her for a lifetime—and she'd risked her safety to protect him when he'd been vulnerable. It was a debt he wouldn't soon forget.

"You would have done the same for me." There was a note of conviction in her voice.

"Aye, true. I vaguely remember telling you to run, to leave me." He didn't think he'd imagined that.

"Then it's a good thing I don't take orders from you."

He chuckled softly. "No, you dinnae. And I have a feeling you never will, lass."

"Do you really want a female who you can order about?"

The fact that she was even asking meant she was considering something between them. Or at least it sounded like it. "I don't. Except maybe in the bedroom."

She snorted and mumbled something about him being a typical male.

Since he didn't scent anyone else nearby and he had her all to himself, he decided to ask more questions.

"What was up with that blue fire?" she asked before he could say anything else.

"I have no idea," he said with complete honesty. The intensity of his fire had taken him off guard. He'd never experienced anything like it and had never heard of it happening before either. He'd destroyed that dragon as if it was made of dried leaves. And the blue color? Definitely new. Powerful.

"Hmm."

He wasn't sure what to make of that so he said, "Will your family worry about you?"

"Very likely. I tried calling them but couldn't get a signal."

"You have a phone?"

"In my backpack." She patted the pillow beneath him to reiterate.

"Are my clothes in there?"

"Yeah. Sorry about not dressing you. I was in such a rush to get us hidden and then I was afraid to move again."

"It's fine. I dinnae mind nudity. And it gave you something to look at."

She giggled against him. "You're ridiculous."

The sound of her laugh made him smile, made the tight band around his chest ease. "So how did you end up as Alpha of your misfit crew?"

"Misfit?"

"I think that is the correct phrase."

She laughed again, quietly, her body shaking with it. "We've all been tight since we were kids. Our parents were all friends—or friendly. We grew up together in an artists' compound and I just sort of fell into the role of Alpha."

"I think you more than fell into it. I think you're born for it." He'd seen it for himself when his own brother hadn't been able to hold her gaze. He wondered if Star was even aware of her true nature, of how powerful she would grow to be.

"Maybe. But if I didn't have them...I don't know."

"If you didnae have them, others would still follow you. You have a...gravitational pull."

She snorted against him and he found he liked that sound too. He liked everything about her, it seemed. "I think you must have hit your head."

"I ken what I ken."

"Do you always think you're right?"

"Well, I usually am, lass."

She lightly pinched his side. "You're maddening."

"I get that a lot from my youngest brother." Cody made him crazy more often than not, but he loved him.

"You said youngest. Do you have more than one sibling?"

"Aye, I...do."

"Ah. And you don't want to talk about it," she said, clearly reading his tone. "It's okay."

For some reason he found he wanted to talk to her about his past. If he was ever to truly convince her to mate with him, they couldn't have a surface relationship. He would have to earn her trust, to put himself out there. That meant being vulnerable, something he was unaccustomed to. "I have another brother and I had a sister."

"Had?"

"Aye. She died. Was murdered."

Star shifted slightly against him. "Lachlan, I'm sorry. I...I'm just sorry."

He squeezed her once. "It's been thousands of years and I still think of her. Still miss her. She was a bright light in our family. So innocent and kind. She didnae deserve what happened to her."

"What..." She cleared her throat. "Never mind."

"It's okay."

Star shifted her head to look at him, pinning him with those pale violet eyes. Even in the darkness, he could see the soft glow of them. "You don't have to tell me. I didn't mean to pry."

"She was murdered by a witch who befriended her. A witch who wanted immortality and power and thought to use her dragon blood and bones for it."

Star blinked, horror bleeding into her expression. "I'm sorry."

"It was a long time ago."

"Did you kill the witch?"

He tightened his jaw. "Naw. We never found her, though we tried."

"Your clan?"

"Aye. My family. Me, Cody, my other brother Rhys and my parents. My mother started going mad in the way the truly ancient can and went into Hibernation before she burned half the world. My father joined her and...after decades of searching, I had to stop the madness. We'd lost a part of our clan in our hunt for her. And we almost lost Rhys to his need for revenge."

"How?"

"He...was going mad too. Letting hate consume him. I finally forced him into Hibernation and then not long after I went into it as well." But not before he'd met the female who would be his mate. Once he'd lost her, he'd nearly devolved into madness himself. He'd lost two females he loved—in very different ways—and had thrown himself into fighting and war after that. It had been a dark time in his life. One he didn't wish to relive. "The world wasn't connected like it is now with the internet and phones, and that witch well and truly disappeared. She's likely dead now, but…" He still had feelers out for her, had his people looking, because if he ever found her she would regret every crime she'd ever committed. She would regret the day she'd ever befriended his sister. Her death would not be easy. It would be long, painful and he'd make sure she ended up in Hell.

"You must hate all witches," Star murmured, laying her head on his chest once again.

"No. I would not paint an entire group of people based on the actions of one."

"Truly?"

"Truly."

"That's generous."

"Naw." And if Star was a witch, as he suspected, he didn't want her to think he hated her kind. "My brother Rhys, however…" Lachlan sighed, shoving thoughts of his other brother away. He was still in Hibernation and hopefully remained that way until his mind healed. "I think we're good to travel on foot now if you're ready."

"Can you shift? I wasn't sure if that poison affected you long-term."

"I think I can shift but I want to get my bearings first. Did you do something to me?" he asked as he quietly pushed the old thing she'd called a kayak off them.

She frowned, standing with him. "What could I have done to you?"

"I feel…different. Energized. Normally that poison has longer-lasting effects."

"You know what that poison was?"

He nodded and took the clothing she pulled out of the backpack. He also noticed that she didn't answer his question. "It's a toxin from a specific sect of dragon and hard to come by. And that was Oscar's clanmates. I recognized their coloring."

"They had a rider—he shot you with something."

"A bullet laced with the poison, likely. Something spelled so it was strong enough to puncture my hide. The bastards came prepared."

"Jeez," she muttered, a shiver rolling through her.

He thought about pushing her more about whether she'd done something to him, but the fact was she'd saved him and gotten him to safety when she could have easily abandoned him.

ANCIENT PROTECTOR | 161

And now, he would get them the hell out of there.

* * *

Star fought her exhaustion as they trekked along the dirt path. They'd managed to find their way out of the woods, both in human form. He'd shifted to his dragon form once, but hadn't been able to hold his camouflage long in that form, so he'd shifted back to human. Since Star had given up a good bit of her blood, she was a lot more tired than she normally would have been.

"How are you doing?" Lachlan kept his hand in hers—he'd told her he needed to touch her to keep the camouflage in place and she mostly believed him.

She was just glad he could maintain it in human form, in case there were any aerial spies trying to hunt them. "I'm good," she said quietly.

"Well I'm tired, so let's take a rest."

She shot him a sideways glance. "You're a terrible liar."

He shrugged and pulled her into a cluster of trees on the side of the clearly unused, dusty road. She wasn't sure where they were exactly, but they were headed in the general direction of the main highway. From there Lachlan said he would shift and head home, camouflage or not.

"What do you have left in your backpack?"

"A couple energy bars and one water bottle." They'd both already eaten two each. Today was supposed to have been a quick trip.

"I'm more than fine on energy." He seemed surprised by that and she knew it was because of her blood. "Go ahead and eat everything and take all the water."

"Then there won't be anything left for you."

"I'm good with that. Get your strength up." He frowned at her, his gaze roving over her in a purely clinical fashion. "Are you sure you weren't injured? Or you were inadvertently struck by the poison? It's dragon specific, but it might have an effect on you."

"I'm okay, I promise." She just needed sleep. And food. The energy bars would have to do for now.

"Do you hear that?" he asked, going preternaturally still.

She paused in opening up her bar and listened. "No." She could hear water running nearby and what sounded like maybe a helicopter far in the distance. "Wait, the helicopter?"

"The howling wolves."

"I don't hear them."

He gave her a curious look then motioned to the north. "They're in that direction."

"Hopefully it's King's pack." Otherwise they might have another threat to deal with.

Lachlan nodded and waited as she quickly ate the energy bars. Once she was done, she polished off the water even though she felt bad taking all the supplies. But she needed them if she was going to keep up with him.

After she put the trash in her bag, he took her hand again and they headed out. And that was when she heard the howls. The sound of the wolves grew louder the longer they walked. As they reached a fork in the dirt road, Lachlan stilled in that pure animal way of his.

She started to ask him what was wrong, but he held a finger to his lips.

"We know you're out there," a familiar voice called out. "Show yourselves."

King. Star glanced at Lachlan.

He released her hand and he must have dropped his camouflage as well, because she saw a sort of shimmer in the air but nothing really changed for her. It must have dropped their cover, however, because moments later King strode out from behind a cluster of trees, two wolves in animal form flanking him.

"What are you doing out here?" He eyed them, subtly scenting the air.

"I was visiting a friend," Star said vaguely. It wasn't a lie so he wouldn't scent one rolling off her.

"Who?" he demanded.

Dang it. She couldn't lie to a direct question. "A female named Cliona." Though she hated to reveal her aunt's name, she had no choice. There were certain rules when living in an Alpha's territory and right now she hated them.

He paused, true surprise in his expression. "You know her?"

Star simply nodded.

"She just moved... The place you were at is a new residence for her. Not many people have that address."

"I know. I used the key she keeps hidden and I took a guess on her security system code." And she'd gotten it on the first try.

He gave Star a thoughtful look. "She's out of town. She's working with a couple dragons on something—for me."

"She's working with dragons?" Star couldn't keep the surprise out of her voice. Damn it, if King knew where her aunt was, Star could have saved herself a whole lot of trouble.

"Yep. I sent them off on a mission, and no I will not share the details. We had a report of a dragon battle hours ago near here. I found the charred remains of two dragons a ways back."

Lachlan nodded, stepping forward slightly and angling his body so that he was half in front of Star.

Surprised by the move, she felt her heart warm at the gesture. He was so protective and she wondered if it was just part of his nature or if he was this way specifically with her.

"Three dragons attacked us. I killed two. They're from the Rabec clan. As you ken, Oscar is the one who held Aurora captive. I have no idea if he's here as well, but his people are. And they're clearly out for blood. To be fair, I killed three of his people six weeks ago, so he wants me dead for that alone, but he very likely wants to take Aurora back."

A low growl rumbled in King's throat as his gaze flicked to Star, perhaps for confirmation.

She nodded. "It's true. And they're fighting dirty, which is no surprise. They poisoned Lachlan but we managed to hide until it worked its way out of his system." Also not a lie. She just left out the part where she'd used her blood to help him and speed up the healing process.

"Come on, then. We've got vehicles a couple miles from here. You can ride back with us, or fly if you want."

"We'll ride with you," Lachlan said before Star could answer.

She was grateful for his response because she didn't feel like flying on his back. That was how exhausted she was. On instinct she reached out and squeezed his hand in silent thanks.

He squeezed back and didn't let go. For the first time that she could remember, she felt as if she had a true partner at her side, even if it was temporary. She loved her crew, loved taking care of them—and they took care of her in turn. But at the end of the day, the decisions made for her crew fell to her. So did all the worry.

Right now she didn't feel the weight of everything so heavily because of the incredible dragon at her side.

CHAPTER 21

King strode into Star's mansion after her, Lachlan and his wolves. They had a lot to discuss, including potentially moving Star's people somewhere else, since it seemed a new threat had descended into his city.

Which he was going to take care of personally. He was already dealing with enough shit—worrying about food supplies, manufacturing necessities, keeping the goddamn peace between the supernatural species. But this he would definitely help take care of.

"I want to talk to your sister," he said to Star as someone shut the door behind all of them.

"She's upstairs drawing," one of the tiger twins said as Star stepped into the foyer. "Thanks for the call letting us know you guys were okay," the tiger said to her. "We were starting to get really worried."

"Of course. Let's head to the kitchen and discuss everything there." Star motioned for Lachlan to follow and for the others spilling out of the kitchen to head back the way they'd come.

King pulled his cell phone out of his pocket and feigned answering a call. He motioned for his wolves to go ahead with the others. "I'll meet you there in a minute," he said as he held his phone up to his ear and said hello to no one.

One of his warriors gave him an odd look, but simply nodded and headed in with the others. As soon as he was alone, he tucked his phone away and hurried up the stairs, moving with the predatory silence of a wolf. It didn't matter that he was in human form, he was good at being quiet, good at blending into the shadows. He remembered what Star had said about Aurora being on the third floor so he simply followed her scent as he made his way. At the end of the hallway, the door was open and her scent was strongest.

He knocked lightly. "It's me, King," he said.

"It's open," Aurora's voice called out.

When he stepped in to the room, he found Aurora, the woman of his fantasies, standing in front of a canvas, a paintbrush in hand. He knew that wasn't her favorite medium, but she was good at this too. And...she looked as stunning as he remembered. Her dark hair was in two loose braids down her back, with strands coming out everywhere. Wearing baggy jeans and a breast-hugging T-shirt that must have once been a royal blue but was now beyond faded and covered in paint splatters, she was the sexiest woman he'd ever met. Yep, his wolf agreed. In that moment, King knew he was screwed where she was concerned.

"I looked you up online," he said as he stepped inside, taking in the room. "You're incredibly talented." She was painting now, but her sculptures were so detailed and realistic and he could only imagine how much time and effort went into creating them.

Her cheeks tinged pink as she met his gaze. "Thank you." She glanced past him as if looking for someone else.

"Your sister is home safe."

She met his gaze again, her violet eyes captivating. "I know. She texted me as soon as she had service and I heard you all arrive. She said there was a whole crowd so I decided to hang back until the place cleared out. Is there something I can help you with?"

He stood awkwardly in the middle of the feminine room and resisted the urge to fidget. He was an Alpha; he did not fucking fidget. "Did she tell you what happened in the bayou?"

Aurora's gaze shuttered as she set her paintbrush down and turned fully to face him. "Yes."

"Why did the dragon take you? Why does he still want you? Because his clan members are now in my city, attacking people—your sister. I need to know everything about this enemy if I want to destroy him." King could understand why any male would want Aurora, but there was an element here he was missing. A dark one, he feared.

She watched him for a long moment, clearly assessing him. "If I tell you, do I have your word that you will tell no one?"

"I will tell no one. Not even my second-in-command. You have my word as an Alpha."

Standing, she moved past him and he inhaled her sweet scent as she shut the door. Then she laughed to herself as she half turned. "If anyone wants to eavesdrop, they easily could, I guess." She went to the corner of the room where he noticed a bunch of stacked canvases leaning against the wall, all turned backward. She rummaged through them, pulled one out and turned it toward him. "This is what I am."

He stared in shock for a long moment. *Oh...hell.* "Cliona isn't your friend, she's a relative."

Aurora nodded. "My aunt. Did Star tell you she was a friend?"

"Yes." He hadn't scented a lie, so obviously she must consider the woman a friend as well. "That's why he took you?"

She nodded, still watching him carefully. "What do you know of my kind?"

"Well...that you possess the ability to control fire." He spoke quiet enough for her ears only. He didn't want to say more in case someone actually was listening.

"There's more to it than that, and that's why Oscar took me."

"What aren't you telling me?" He didn't know much about her kind, but not for lack of trying. He knew Cliona was powerful and a bit older than him, maybe by a hundred years or so. Even though he trusted her after her allyship during The Fall, she was still secretive by nature. Hell, he only knew her real name was Cliona because someone else had told him. He'd met her under a different name.

Aurora half-smiled and went to sit by the window. She seemed to have an internal sort of glow, giving her skin a soft hue. "I don't trust many people, but from everything I've heard you're a good Alpha. And you gave us shelter even knowing we might bring trouble to your doorstep. And," she added, placing her fist in the middle of her chest, "I can tell you're honorable here."

He sat on the edge of her bed, relaxing slightly. Though he was glad she was opening up to him, he hated that she'd come to his city needing shelter—that someone wanted to hurt her. "I'll give you shelter as long as you want." *How about forever?*

"Our blood is powerful. It heals," she said quietly. "Among other things," she added.

Healing blood? Oh damn. He could see the value in that, but there was no excuse to take another being, to keep them captive for your own greedy needs and desires.

"I will kill him for you," he said quietly, a soft vow, his words not conveying the rage his wolf felt, the rage he was keeping at bay.

Her eyes widened slightly in surprise. "I don't need anybody to fight my battles. I know I've been cooped up here—hiding—because I'm still processing everything. My power level is back to normal. The only reason he managed to take me is because they ambushed me."

"How many were there?"

"A dozen."

It had taken a dozen dragons to bring her down? She was strong, something he sensed regardless, but twelve was overkill.

"Does Lachlan know what Star is?" he asked, curious at this point.

To his surprise Aurora snorted. "No. She isn't sure she can trust him yet. But I think she'll get there."

"You sound very sure of that."

"I know my sister. Dragons killed our parents, and over the years, dragons have killed many of our kind. She's...very careful. And I understand why. Obviously." She gave a bitter-sounding laugh. "But it doesn't matter how careful I was, someone found out what I was. I've been thinking that maybe hiding what I am isn't necessarily the best thing."

"I'm sorry for all you've been through." He couldn't change her past, but he could sure as hell protect her from any future threat.

She gave a dismissive shrug. "It's not your fault, but thank you. So tell me why you're really here."

"I wanted to talk to you about Oscar, get any insight from you that I can." That was a lie. He had his people on research duty, as well as his sentries scouring the city looking for the male.

"He's a greedy bastard. And he's powerful. He never goes on the front line unless he has to because he views everyone as expendable—not because he can't handle himself. And he used my blood to increase his power. That much I know. I was literally in an underground prison for a year. It was a nice enough space and he did give me certain entertainments like television and books, but it was a cage nonetheless.

And..." She paused, her jaw tightening, but when she went to say more, she stopped herself.

"What?" he asked, his gut clenching.

"Nothing. I don't know anything that can help you. But if he's here, he won't stop until he gets me back. His pet," she spat.

King only realized he was growling when she blinked at him.

"Sorry. That's what he used to call me. His pet."

He stood then, forcing his wolf back because he didn't want to scare her, even as he wanted to tear Oscar apart with his canines and claws. "I'll make sure no one ever takes you again. This is your sanctuary city as long as you want. And hopefully it becomes your home." *With me.*

She gave him a truly surprised look. "Don't make promises you can't keep."

"I never do." He intended to keep her safe—no matter what it took.

* * *

"I'm not sitting by idly and letting him get away with this," Star said to Lachlan.

Brielle, Harlow, Taya and Athena strode up to them after breaking away from King's wolves and Lachlan's dragons, who were currently talking.

They'd all gathered outside and Star wanted to know what was taking King so damn long. She understood that he was Alpha and had to take emergency phone calls but she wanted to talk about hunting Oscar down—wanted to go after him right now.

"We go where you go," Athena said, crossing her arms over her chest. "I can't believe that bastard is here and his dragons attacked you guys." The snow leopard's eyes flickered to her cat then back to human.

Before Star could respond, King strode out the French doors and immediately zeroed in on her. Next to her, Lachlan stiffened slightly but King approached, nodding at all of them. "I'd like to talk to you alone," he said to her.

Star simply nodded and strode off with King, ignoring Lachlan's growl of annoyance, or maybe it was anger. She wasn't sure and hadn't known him long enough to read all his growls.

"I talked to your sister," King said as they reached the other side of the expansive yard.

She blinked in surprise. That was the last thing she'd expected him to say. "Wait, what?"

"I went upstairs and talked to Aurora."

Star felt her fingers start to tingle with fire as her instinctive need to protect Aurora rose up.

"She told me what you are."

Her fire died just like that. "*What?*" she demanded, feeling like a parrot as she repeated herself.

"So you were going to see your aunt out in the bayou, not a friend."

No point in denying it now. *Damn.* Why had Aurora told him? "Yep."

"I've sent a message to her. She's gone dark, but once she gets it she will contact you or Aurora."

"Thank you," she said carefully.

"Why did you go to see her?"

"She has a weapon that can bring down our enemy." Only in the technical sense. The "weapon" would give Star or anyone touching it the ability to see dragons even if the dragons were camouflaged. So in her opinion, it was a weapon. It evened the playing field a bit. Of course her fire could kill dragons as well but battling a dragon was still difficult as hell and she would have to expend a whole lot of firepower.

He gave her an arrogant sort of look that was pure Alpha. "I can bring one down too. And I will help you destroy his clanmates. Anyone who is in my city helping him—they'll all die." Raw, savage words that revealed the wolf beneath the surface.

"What are you doing to find him?" she asked.

"I've got sentries and warriors out hunting for any and all of his clanmates."

"What about pockets of the city where people don't...necessarily respect your authority?" she asked carefully. It was no secret that certain vampires and other groups hadn't fully recognized him as the Alpha. The majority of the people in the city did, especially after his show of power during The Fall, but she wondered if the place was a powder keg waiting to explode at this point. She'd been so focused on getting Aurora to safety and settling in that she didn't have as good of a pulse on the city as she should. But after meeting Reaper and Greer, she got the feeling there was a lot going on behind the scenes.

He was silent for a long moment. "There are some vampires who would like to see me removed from power. They want to keep humans under their thumbs, as no better than slaves." His jaw ticked, his wolf peering back at her.

"I want to know who they are."

He frowned. "Why?"

"They're certainly not going to talk to you. But maybe if my crew and I approach some of them separately about Oscar's presence in the city, they'll talk to us. It's worth a try at least. Because I'm finding it hard to believe he's in hiding with absolutely no help. This city isn't that big and he's a dragon Alpha."

Lachlan approached, his long strides eating up the distance of the yard. Yeah, he was clearly done with giving her any sort of space. She inwardly sighed, kind of surprised he'd waited this long to head over here.

King gave him a neutral look.

"You feel like going hunting tonight?" Star asked Lachlan, knowing that even after all they'd been through in the last few hours, Lachlan would want to go hunting if there was a chance they might find Oscar tonight.

"I'll go wherever you go."

King rubbed a hand over his face. "All right, I'm going to go over all this once because I know the rest of your crew is going to go too." He simply turned and walked away then, assuming they would follow him.

He didn't stop at the lanai, but kept going inside. So they all followed him into one of the living rooms with floor-to-ceiling real silk drapes, a glittering chandelier, heavy, antique pieces of furniture and funky tufted couches.

King pulled out a detailed paper map of the city and surrounding areas and set it on the oversized trunk that doubled as a coffee table. Then he looked up at all of them. "Anyone got a pencil?"

Harlow, always ready for anything, held one out.

"Thanks," he said and turned back to the map. "This area is run by the Gray coven. Caesar is the leader. He chafes at my rule but he has done nothing outwardly to defy me." *Yet* seemed to be the unspoken caveat, as if King was waiting for it to happen. Then he went on to circle three other areas. One was a witch coven in the Garden District, and the other two were in the suburbs, on the other side of the bridge. Another vampire coven and witch coven.

She didn't know why she was surprised they lived in the suburbs, but some small part of her kind of was. It made sense though, since supernatural beings assimilated everywhere.

"I know Caesar—not his real name, by the way," Cody said, nodding to the first circle that King had drawn. "I did some business with him about eight years ago. He's a real prick."

"What kind of terms are you guys on?" Lachlan asked.

"As good as any. The deal went fine and we both walked away happy. I just don't like him on a personal level."

Lachlan nodded. "We'll talk to him first, then."

"We can split up with the others," Athena said, stepping forward. "I don't mind talking to one of the witch covens. Witches always like me." She shrugged.

It was true, witches had always had an affinity toward Athena. Star nodded and then broke up the rest of her crew, giving them their assignments. She thought about telling Aurora what they were doing, but didn't want to take the chance her sister would insist on coming. Once she was done, Lachlan ordered his own warriors to accompany them, splitting them up as he saw fit.

"Caesar's place isn't too far. We can just walk," Lachlan said as he eyed the map.

"There's something else," King said as they were all getting ready to leave. "You guys should move. Temporarily at least, until this is all over. I've got a place set up for you, big enough to accommodate your whole group."

Next to her Lachlan growled low in his throat and on instinct Star gently touched his forearm. To her surprise, he calmed, so she left her hand there as she said, "Thank you, but that isn't necessary. I texted Cynara on the way back from the bayou and she has a place for us." She looked at Lachlan. "All of us. You and your dragons can come as well if you want." She'd specifically asked because she had a feeling this big dragon wasn't letting her out of his sight.

He simply nodded, not questioning her, which she appreciated. Though it did surprise her that Lachlan didn't try to steamroll her with everything and take charge. He seemed to take charge when necessary but it was clear he didn't get caught up in his ego. It was a good trait in an Alpha. And it made her want him even more. Things had shifted for her in the bayou, and now...she found herself more and more curious about Lachlan. Okay, more than just curious.

"That's not necessary," King started.

"Look, I really appreciate the offer. But I've known Cynara longer and I'll feel safer staying with her."

The Alpha wolf finally nodded and she had a feeling he wanted to keep Aurora under his own roof. Well, too bad.

"Okay," King said. "Everyone keep communication open. Meanwhile, I'll escort Aurora to Cynara's and my wolves will trail after you."

"All right, but I'll tell Aurora we're moving." And Star had a feeling Aurora was going to be annoyed she wasn't letting her come tonight. But Star trusted King to get Aurora to safety and luckily he was the Alpha of the region so Aurora wouldn't argue with him.

Lachlan cleared his throat. "If the vampire coven gets the sense that we have backup in the form of your wolves, do you think they'll talk to us?" His tone was mild enough, even though it sounded more like a statement than a question.

"I'm not sending you guys in anywhere without backup," King said.

"I would be a pretty mince Alpha if I couldnae handle going to talk to a bunch of vampires alone," Lachlan snapped out.

It took her a moment to realize that mince meant rubbish. Star inwardly winced as the two Alphas started digging their heels in. Now wasn't the time for a pissing contest.

Thankfully, King didn't push back. "Fair point." Then he looked back at Star. "Keep communication open. That is one thing I will not bend on."

She nodded, excused herself and hurried up the stairs. She knew Aurora would be annoyed at being left behind, but it had to be this way.

If Oscar was at any of these places and he got Aurora's scent, he would full-on attack them. And Star wasn't going to risk her baby sister getting taken ever again.

Because something told Star that if Oscar got Aurora again, he'd hide her somewhere no one would ever find her—and eventually kill her.

CHAPTER 22

A head of Star and Lachlan, Cody, Teague, Brielle, and Axel strode in pairs on the sidewalk with Cody trying to flirt with Brielle—while she ignored him. Star had noticed that Cody seemed to flirt with everyone but didn't really seem to show an interest in anyone in particular. He was an equal opportunity flirter. It seemed like more of a habit for him than something serious.

Star knew that Harlow was nearby as well, but she'd gone full tiger and was likely lurking in the shadows.

"Have you ever been to Scotland?" Lachlan asked her suddenly.

She was surprised by the question and almost said yes. Some deep part of her was compelled to answer in the affirmative but she shook her head because that made no sense. "No, but it's on my list of places to go."

"I'm surprised you didnae go after your London concert."

"Why are you surprised?"

"Scotland is far superior to any place on earth. Why would ye nae go?" His question was dead serious too.

Despite the intensity of the situation and the fact that they were headed to question vampires who might know where Oscar was, she laughed. "You're quite certain that Scotland is the best place."

"I'm ancient. I've been everywhere. For *me* it is the best." There was a deep longing in his voice as he spoke of his homeland. "Of course it wasn't always called Scotland. It has been known by many names."

The ache in his voice was subtle and suddenly she felt guilty for keeping him away from his homeland. Even though she wasn't actually doing anything to hold him here. He was in New Orleans of his own free will. Still, she hated that he was missing his people and land.

"Maybe I'll visit someday."

"Aye, maybe you will. And then you will love it so much you willnae leave."

She smiled at his teasing words, even though she didn't think he was teasing. "We'll see."

"There are fields of green there so lush and beautiful, they make a dragon want to nap all day."

"Maybe a dragon like Cody, but not you. You don't have a lazy bone in your big body." She wasn't sure why she was so positive of those things, but she was.

Lachlan gave her a strange look, his eyebrows drawing together.

"What? Why are you looking at me like that?"

He shook his head. "Just had a bit of déjà vu."

She'd been having weird flashes of déjà vu as well but she didn't tell him that as they turned the corner onto the next street.

"Pretty sure this is our destination." Her tone was dry as they glanced across the street at a huge mansion. Multicolored lights were strung up throughout all the Spanish moss-covered oak trees, and there was a sort of strobe light show flashing off the house, creating creepy shadows. As they approached the wrought iron gates, she could hear the definite sounds of people having sex in the front yard.

"Vampires," Brielle muttered up ahead of them.

Teague snorted in agreement.

Harlow jumped down from the trees onto the sidewalk in tiger form, her black and orange tail swishing. She made a snuffling sound as if to agree with her twin.

"Did Caesar respond to you?" Lachlan asked Cody as they approached the open gates.

"Yep. He knows we're coming. Well, he knows you and I are coming," Cody said, glancing over his shoulder. "Not the rest of us."

"He chose the name Caesar for himself?" Star muttered more to herself than anyone, but Lachlan made a sound of agreement next to her.

Star rolled her shoulders once as they headed through the gates with Lachlan, the two of them automatically taking the lead. It was clear from his stiff shoulders that he didn't like being here.

She wondered if it was a vampire thing. Or if it was just, this was an uncomfortable place type of thing. In her experience, pure-blood vamps and the really old ones were the only vampires who had their shit together and didn't act like complete morons. The newly turned ones tended to live completely hedonistic lifestyles—much like the fools here tonight. It was like an orgy 24/7, hence the very public sex currently going on in the front yard. Who had time for all that? She didn't understand how they didn't get bored. Not to mention, it just felt lazy to her. Lying around all night screwing. *Bah.* There went the cranky old lady inside her again. Maybe if she'd actually had sex, she would want to do it all day long. But this right here? No thanks.

"You and I stick together," Lachlan said quietly.

On instinct she moved a bit closer to him as they headed up the long walkway—through the thick of all the sex. It felt strange to be leading the rest of the group with him, as if she was the Alpha of these dragons as well, but she couldn't deny that the role came naturally. And the others didn't seem to mind. Which was kind of strange as well.

She wasn't going to think about what that meant for her and Lachlan. Just like she wasn't going to think about the strange feelings he evoked inside her. There were far too many reasons they would never work. They were from different worlds. That was enough. Add in all the other stuff, like the fact that they lived on different continents, and it was a whole lot of hell no. Still...if she let herself dwell on the fact that he would be leaving soon, it sent a spiral of panic through her. She didn't want him to leave.

A few of the vampires glanced up from the lounges in the yard to look at their group, but most of them kept on doing what they were doing.

"Well that's new," Brielle murmured behind her.

Star wasn't sure which act she was referring to—there were so many things happening at once.

Lachlan leaned his head down close to her ear. "If you would like to try out anything you see here tonight, I'm available for your—"

"Don't finish that thought." Star elbowed him in the side and to her surprise he simply chuckled, the deep sound wrapping around her like a comfortable embrace.

In that moment he looked like such a typical male as he shrugged. "I'm just saying."

"Oh I know what you're just saying." There was a weird familiarity as they joked with each other, as if they'd done it before. The thought made no sense but she'd discovered that around him some things made no sense at all.

She straightened, prepping herself for battle as they strode up the stairs to the main doors. Two huge ornate wood doors were thrown open, beckoning them inside.

Acting like the superstar she was, she strode inside like she owned the place, with Lachlan at her side. He walked into any room as if he owned it and now was no different. She might be young, but she could sense the power level of the people in this place—and she controlled fire. She wasn't afraid of these vampires.

Luckily, they didn't have to go far to look for Caesar. The male was in a formal sitting room, lying on a red tufted chaise lounge with a male's head between his legs, getting his dick sucked.

"You're Caesar?" Lachlan asked, though clearly he was.

Why was it clear? Because the male was wearing an actual Roman emperor-style headdress. Like...what, he was a former Roman emperor? Star knew from Cody that the vampire wasn't even close to old enough to have been an emperor and that his real name was Leonard, so apparently this was just something he'd decided to dress up as. It took every ounce of willpower she had not to roll her eyes. Or maybe laugh aloud at the moron. She didn't want to offend this male even though everything about him was offensive in that moment.

The male nodded and shoved the guy off his lap. "I am." Frowning, he zipped up his pants and stood. "I thought it was just you," he said to Cody over Lachlan's shoulder.

"You thought wrong," Lachlan said mildly. "I'm Lachlan, Alpha Laird of the Donnachaidh clan."

"I know who you are." As he dismissed Lachlan, his gaze strayed to Star with interest, his dark eyes sweeping her from head to foot in a very sexual manner.

Oh, this guy was a peach—and was very close to getting his ass kicked. Probably by Lachlan—because she couldn't tell if he would be able to control himself. Next to her, the growl that rumbled out of him was a deep, harsh sound she felt ripple through her.

The vampire straightened, his gaze snapping back to Lachlan. "No disrespect intended. I was just admiring a beautiful work of art."

"She is a person, not a work of art or a piece of meat. Apologize to her, not me, ye daft bawbag." Lachlan's words were a savage growl, his beast right underneath the surface.

On instinct, Star reached out and placed her hand on his forearm. Lachlan immediately stilled, but his dragon remained in his gaze. While she really, really wanted to throat-punch this vampire, she called on her diplomatic nature. "We need to talk to you in private."

"Anything you say to me, you can say in front of my people," Caesar answered.

Okay, screw diplomacy. "I wasn't asking you," she snapped, even as fire tingled right under the surface.

The male gave her an insolent look, then snapped his fingers and all but two of his people left. Both remaining vamps were well armed and dressed in tactical gear.

Lachlan nodded his acceptance and she let a ghost of a smile pull at her mouth. The truth was, he could simply set this whole house on fire and kill everyone in here, but she kept the thought to herself. This vampire was clearly too stupid to realize that—or else he wouldn't have been so disrespectful to an ancient dragon with waves of power rolling off him. If Star had been a betting female, she'd wager that Caesar wasn't long for this world.

"I'm going to ask you some questions and if you lie to me, I'll burn your house down. Then I will start slicing off your body parts, one by one." Lachlan spoke so matter-of-fact, his body language deceptively casual. "I'll take your favorite one first."

The vampire stepped forward, his fangs descending as he tossed off his headpiece. In that moment she saw the predator in his gaze, but she could sense that his power was no match for Lachlan's. Not even close. "I don't answer to you. You can get the fuck out of my house right now."

"Do you know where Oscar, Alpha of the Rabec clan is?" Lachlan asked, completely ignoring the threat and the command to leave.

Star was also aware of other vampires entering the room, of her own people and Lachlan's spreading out as they faced off with each other. This was going to get bloody fast if less than level heads prevailed.

"I've never heard of him," the male answered.

A lie, if Lachlan's response was any indication. He moved so fast, her eyes barely tracked him as he grabbed the vampire by the throat and held him up off the floor as if he weighed nothing more than a pillow.

The vampire released short claws and stabbed Lachlan through the ribs but Lachlan grabbed Caesar's wrist and broke it as he yanked the offending hand away from him.

Moving on an instinct she didn't bother to question, Star shifted position and put her back to Lachlan's. She didn't think he needed her protection, but he was getting it anyway. She released her own fire in a show of power, keeping it neatly contained in a ball of bright purple flames between her hands. The little ball hovered in midair in front of her. For theatrics only, she tossed it back and forth between her hands as she swept her gaze over the vampires.

The vampires in the room froze, staring at her instead of rushing forward as she figured they'd planned to do.

Lachlan's dragons and her own people stood at the ready, including Harlow who was growling low in her throat, the crouched tiger eyeing everyone like a tasty treat she might indulge in with a side of barbeque sauce.

"Unless you guys are fireproof, today is not the day to fuck with us," Star snarled. "We've got three dragons and me. You really want to tangle with us over some asshole?"

The vampires in the room shifted nervously on their feet, some of them taking subtle steps backward. Oh, there was no loyalty in this coven, that was for sure.

Star tossed a tiny fireball at the chaise lounge by the window where Caesar had been getting pleasured, watching it slowly start to burn.

Behind her, Lachlan said, "I'm going to try this again. Where is Oscar Rabec? And dinnae tell me again that you've never heard of him. He goes by Osgar as well if you're confused."

"He's got a place outside the city," Caesar rasped out, struggling to speak. "It's an old colonial mansion. Used to be a plantation. His people

ANCIENT PROTECTOR | 181

took it over. No one else knows he's staying there."

"Are you allies with him?" Lachlan asked, and shook the male when he hesitated.

"Yes."

"And you know why he's in town?"

"Of course. He hates King," the vampire rasped out. There was truth in his voice and in the subtle scent she could smell rolling off him. It was hard to tell over the scent of flames and his fear, however.

"He wants to kill King?" Lachlan asked.

"Yes. He's going to help my coven take charge of the city. Vampires should be in charge, not wolves. They're allied with humans. And witches!"

Oscar wasn't in New Orleans to kill King, but he'd very clearly found a foolish vampire he could manipulate into working with him. "Have you been feeding him information about King?" she demanded.

"Yes."

"What do you get in exchange?" Lachlan's tone was even, but she sensed the barely leashed dragon underneath the surface.

"His allyship," the male gasped out. "The world has changed and..." He coughed. "Need allies."

"Did you send one of your vampires after Star the other night?" Again, Lachlan's tone was deceptively mild, but Star swore she could actually feel his dragon pulsing in the room, his heat ready to blast this vampire away.

"He was...just supposed to tail her. Wanted to see where she went and who she met with." Another cough. "He never came back."

Yeah, because he was dead.

Star couldn't see, but she guessed Lachlan was still squeezing the male's throat tight. The sounds of struggling had since ceased, but Lachlan hadn't moved a fraction so she guessed he was still holding the male up in the air.

"You're a bloody fool." Disgust dripped from Lachlan's every word. "You will give me the exact address for Oscar."

After the male managed to rasp it out, there was a thud on the floor.

"If you warn him we're coming, I'll come back and raze this place to the ground with all of you in it. I'm older and more powerful than your tiny brain can comprehend. There will be no place you can run from me. No rock for you to hide under." A millennia of power reverberated in Lachlan's words, his rage rippling throughout the room, dripping off the walls with its raw truth.

Star was comforted by it instead of repulsed. She loved the feel of his power surrounding her, and for one insane moment, reveled in it.

"Understand?" A soft, deadly whisper.

"Yes," Caesar rasped out.

Star reached out a hand and ordered her fire to subside. Just like that, the flames that had already devoured the chaise disappeared, but the damage to the chair remained.

There was a gasp of surprise from one of the vampires, but she didn't bother glancing in their direction. She didn't care what they thought.

"If I were you, I'd get out of the city no matter what," Star added, facing Caesar. "There's no room for troublemakers like you. And if you go up against King, know this—every single one of us are his allies." She nodded at Brielle, Harlow and Axel to head out. They did, but not before snarling at the vampires in their way to move.

Once outside, Star pulled in a deep breath of fresh night air. The vamps who'd been in various stages of screwing on the lawn had all disappeared back inside—or somewhere—in the time they'd been talking with Caesar. So they weren't all complete fools.

"You were pretty savage in there." The way Lachlan said it kind of sounded like a compliment.

Her? *He'd* been the savage. "Thank you?"

He simply shrugged. "You're a true Alpha."

She decided not to respond to that. She was young and Alpha of her crew, but that was different. Waaaay different than him. He had the responsibility of a whole clan and territory. "You think he'll call Oscar?"

"I think it's a possibility," Lachlan said. "I embarrassed him. I also scared him. Who knows which emotion will win. So we go there now."

She nodded in agreement. There was no time to waste, not after their attack earlier. And if they did wait, it might give Caesar time to regain some bravery. Or stupidity.

"You can ride on my back. The others can ride on Teague or Cody's."

She was tempted to tell him she could fly—to show him what she was. But for her safety, her sister's safety, she held back. And because okay, she was protecting her heart. Giving him the most vulnerable part of herself was a risk she wasn't prepared to take.

Even so, she recognized that he was making himself vulnerable by letting her ride him in dragon form. He'd given her an honor.

"I like riding on your back," she murmured, the shadow of a memory bubbling up inside her. She knew she'd done so before on the way to her aunt's place, but... She brushed away the edges of whatever was lingering in her mind, trying to hold on like static cling. She glanced at Lachlan when she saw he had his cell phone out.

"I texted King," he said, though she hadn't asked him who he was contacting. "I let him know about this coven so he can do what he needs to."

"Good." Star didn't think this coven would last the night, though something told her King would give them the option to leave of their own accord.

Because that was the kind of Alpha he was.

CHAPTER 23

The flight to the outskirts of the city was fast and hard, the clear sky and near full moon lighting their way. There were other random dragons in the sky simply out for an evening flight, but they kept a healthy distance as Lachlan and his two warriors flew Star and the others.

Barely fifteen minutes into their flight, Star smelled the acrid scent of smoke on the wind. Faint, but growing stronger, and the heavy ball coiled inside her told her where it was coming from.

She didn't want it to be true, but in the distance, bright orange flames danced into the sky, smoke curling up against the backdrop of the moon. Lachlan picked up speed and that was when she saw it.

A huge house and outbuildings in the middle of fields were burning.

Her heart rate kicked up as they reached their destination, landing a hundred yards from the burning house. Sharp disappointment surged through her. She'd been ready to find Oscar, to burn him to ashes, to get vengeance for her baby sister. But he wasn't here.

"Can you scent him?" she asked Lachlan after he changed to human form.

"No. But the fire is thick. It's covering it up." He motioned for Cody to circle around the house and to sweep the property.

"You can go too, if you want." She tried to push back the rage building inside her, the fire that wanted out, that wanted to burn everything in sight.

He shook his head. "Cody's fast and he's a good tracker. And I'm not leaving yer side, lass."

She shot him a look of surprise even as Harlow stripped down and shifted to her tiger form and raced off into the darkness.

"We need to get someone out here to put out the fire," Teague said. "Or else it's going to spread, and innocent people will lose their homes."

"I can take care of it." Star stalked forward and let her power flow through her. She didn't just create fire, she controlled it.

The rage built, a suffocating pressure in her chest. When she was barely twenty-five yards away, the heat from the house potent, she held out her hands and let out a scream. She screamed for the year her sister had lost, for the death of her parents, for the memories that scraped at her mind, making her feel crazy, and for a hundred other things as she unleashed the power of her own fire.

The purple fire burst from her fingertips, swooping upward and obeying her command. Another burst of flames exploded in an outward arc, circling the crumbling home as yet another jet of flames headed directly at the house.

Her fire created a giant circle around the house, pushing back against the dragon-made fire. Pushing, pushing, pushing.

She strained against the dragon fire, sweat beading against her upper lip, dripping down her spine, until nothing remained but crumbling concrete blocks and ash.

She might have extinguished it, but her fire didn't destroy the scent, and the stink of charred wood and furniture and whatever else had been in there filled the air, making her nauseous.

Breathing hard, she bent forward and put her hands on her knees. Expelling that much fire at once took a large amount of energy and focus. Next to her, Lachlan rubbed a comforting hand up and down her back, and damn, did she savor it. He didn't question how she'd done what she had with her fire, didn't ask for details she didn't want to give. No, instead he simply provided comfort.

This man was determined to break down all of her walls. Just kick them all down with his kindness and protectiveness. And when she thought of walking away from this growing thing between them, of not exploring it...pain lanced through her chest.

She sucked in another deep breath, feeling more steady. As Star straightened, feeling nominally better after that release of energy in spite of the fatigue, both Cody and Harlow returned. Cody didn't shift forms, and he looked so similar to Lachlan—with both his huge size and the

ANCIENT PROTECTOR | 187

indigo coloring it was clear they were related. He just shook his head.

Harlow changed back to human and gave the same news as she started tugging her clothing on. "Nothing. They were definitely here but I scented different trails spreading out in four directions. I guarantee they flew off in random patterns to intentionally throw anyone off their scent trail."

More disappointment surged through Star even though it was what she'd expected.

"Go on ahead of us," Lachlan said to the others, his order soft.

Star simply nodded at her own people. She needed a few minutes to clear her head anyway. Once the others were in the air, she said to Lachlan, "Do you want to attempt to hunt them down tonight?" Because she was game. The energy inside her couldn't be contained. She could feel her fire pulsing under her skin, wanting out. It didn't matter that she wasn't at full capacity, she was still on edge. And if she had the chance, she would go after Oscar.

Lachlan shook his head. "No, it would be a fool's errand. We need to bring them out into the open, get them to come to us. We need to set a trap for them and kill him on our turf."

He was right, she knew that, but she still had too much pent-up energy. "So why are we hanging back?"

Reaching out, he cupped her face with his big, rough palm.

Surprise and something else slid through her, soothing her nerves. Against her better judgment, she leaned into his hold, enjoying the feel of his callused palm against her cheek. Damn, she liked it way too much. "I don't want to talk about what I just did," she whispered. She didn't have the emotional capacity to hold anything back at the moment and if he pushed, she would tell him what she was.

"Good, because I wasn't asking. I simply want to know why you're fighting the heat between us, lass."

Um, how about for her sanity? "You want to ask that now?" When they were standing near a burned house in the middle of nowhere. And...all alone, she thought. Just the two of them.

"It seems as good a time as any. And we *are* alone. No one's coming back here. No one is here to see your fire if you lose control." His eyes went pure dragon then, as if he liked the thought of her losing control.

"I don't know if it will come back." Though her gut said it would. She'd been nineteen when her parents had died and they'd never had a sex talk. Not one about fire showing up anyway. And she'd never talked with Cliona about mating. The fire had never appeared in the past with the few males she'd made out with so she wondered if maybe...this was something to do with a potential mate. Or maybe it was because they were better suited for each other. Or...who the hell knew. For some reason, the thought that this might be a mating thing didn't appall her. Not when it was Lachlan. Though it did scare her.

He stroked a thumb over her cheek, gently and sensually, sending curls of heat spiraling through her.

Her fire was already simmering under the surface now, her fingertips tingling with it. Still, she cleared her throat. Even though they didn't need to worry about STDs or anything—not with them both being supernaturals—or pregnancy right now, since she wasn't in heat, they still needed to talk. "I'm not cut out to be the Alpha mate to a dragon. And I know you're not asking to mate me but...I'm just putting it out there so you know where my head is at."

He gave her a wicked, sexy smile as he shook his head slightly. "You were pretty damn Alpha in the vampire coven, and just now with your fire. Your people listen to you without question. And my own brother couldn't hold your gaze. He's a powerful dragon even if he is young and reckless. He's also thousands of years older than you."

She lifted a shoulder. Okay, so if that didn't scare him off, then... "There's something else you need to know. I've never done this."

He frowned, his thumb still gently stroking her cheek. "This?"

She wanted to lean into his soft strokes even more, but forced herself to get the words out. "Ah, I mean, I've fooled around with males of course."

He started growling, making her blink in surprise.

She didn't want him to think she was completely inexperienced. "I just meant, I've made out with them and you know, done other stuff."

His growls deepened.

Despite the situation, her mouth curved up. "Oh my God, I just meant—"

"I dinnae want to hear about you and other males." A soft, deadly growl. "Or I may feel the need to hunt them down and relieve them of their heads. And other body parts."

"I'm clearly doing this all wrong. I'm trying to say that I'm a virgin." When he stared blankly at her, she continued. "You know, I've never done the whole 'penis in vagina' thing."

To her surprise, he snorted out a laugh. "I dinnae think I'll ever tire of that mouth, lass," he murmured, his gaze then dropping to said mouth.

"So...we're good?" *Oh, please be good.*

"Oh, we're very, very good." Again with the deep, intoxicating voice.

Relief slid through her that he wasn't making a big deal about this or treating her like a freak. Or even worse, putting the brakes on.

Because she could see the hunger in his gaze grow even brighter as he bent his head and crushed his mouth against hers. Yep, apparently they were done with the talking portion of the evening.

Oh, thank the goddess. She didn't want to talk either. The only thing she wanted to do with her mouth was put it on him, all over. In that moment she let go of all her worries because they didn't matter.

They were alone, and for this one moment she could be herself. Mostly.

She didn't have to consciously think about it—her flames burst free, not burning him, as if they knew not to hurt him. *Never* him. The flames danced along her arms, legs, and even her skin glowed violet as their mouths melded and their bodies came together.

In seconds he'd picked her up, carrying her farther away from the house until he stretched her out on a soft patch of grass. She didn't care about the lingering scent of fire, about the fact that they were outdoors. In fact, she liked being under the night sky this way with him. She didn't want a nice, soft bed, she wanted something raw and earthy with this huge male who'd already burrowed his way under her skin. He was ripping down all of her defenses one by one just by being himself. It was a miracle she'd lasted as long as she had against him.

"I'm tasting between your legs," he growled against her mouth.

And he wasn't asking. Her flames licked higher at that and he let out a low, wicked laugh.

"You like the thought of that, lass."

"I'd like it if you'd *do* it and stop talking about it," she rasped out.

He threw his head back and laughed, the rich sound rolling over her and making her nipples tighten against her bra cups. Holy hell, she loved his laugh. There was a freedom to it she felt to her bones.

"You're a feisty lass."

For some reason those words struck home right to the heart of her, as if he'd said the words to her before, which she knew was ridiculous.

He made quick work of her clothes, and she did the same to him, frantic and manic as she stripped him fully naked, desperate to run her hands over every inch of the powerful body she'd only been able to admire visually until now.

As his shirt went flying behind her, her eyes widened as she realized he was emanating a soft glow himself. The indigo seemed to light him up from within, and when he realized that he was glowing he didn't seem at all surprised. No, he had an intense, pleased look on his face as he covered her body with his again.

She liked the feel of his chest covering hers, of the whole weight of him pressed against her.

"Mine," he murmured as he slanted his mouth over hers and pressed her into the grass. Without pause, he reached between their bodies and cupped her mound, testing her slickness as she rode his hand. She loved the friction of his palm against her clit, grinding into him harder and harder as they tasted each other. She was already soaked for him, desperate for everything he could give her.

As she clutched onto his back, digging her fingers into the hard planes of his muscles, she flashed back to one of her dreams, reminded of...something. But the thought at the edge of her mind quickly dissipated as she lost herself in the sensation of him stroking her.

Moaning, she slid her hands lower, raking her fingernails lightly over his back until she reached his ass. Then she dug into his muscles hard, groaning into his mouth. The man was all power and she loved the feel of him against her, his hand between her legs.

It was a heady feeling to have that kind of power at her fingertips. To know this male was hers to command—and she wasn't sure how she knew that with absolute certainty, but it was true.

He started kissing a path down her neck, to her breasts, and when he slowly started teasing her nipple with his tongue she made an impatient sound. She wanted his head between her legs, wanted that wicked tongue bringing her pleasure.

"Impatient lass," he murmured. "You were always so impatient."

She frowned at the wording but when he slid a second finger inside her, all thoughts fled. The sensation of him stretching her like this felt amazing.

"Right there," she said, not even sure what she was referring to. She just knew she wanted more of this. His talented mouth, his thrusting fingers, or maybe the way his thumb was now teasing her clit in a rhythmic little pattern. She wanted everything he was doing and more. So much more.

Everything was perfect yet not enough. Goddess, she was so greedy for him. Greedy in a way she was having a hard time wrapping her head around.

He chuckled low again and then took pity on her because he continued southward. By the time his face was between her legs, her entire body was trembling with want and need. Her flames had now burst out at least twenty feet in every direction. She was so confused by how massive they were, how they weren't burning anything—how he was the one who seemed to bring them to life.

When he sucked on her clit, her entire body jerked and she let out a groan of pleasure, the erotic sensation spiraling through her in soft waves. Hot damn, her toys had *nothing* on his talented mouth.

Just as quickly, he gentled his tongue, barely teasing her and definitely not taking the edge off. Tension buzzed through her as a climax drifted on the edge of her consciousness. If he just picked up the pace, she would come. But he knew what he was doing, knew he was making her crazy as he started thrusting his fingers inside her faster now. He was getting her worked up and then slowing down.

She speared her fingers through his hair, clutched onto his head. "I need to come," she somehow managed to get out. She didn't care how desperate she sounded, how hungry. Her body was on the precipice, and damn him, she needed a release. Needed him.

Without a word, he slid another finger inside her and found the perfect rhythm with his mouth and tongue.

She arched against the grass, falling into a sharp orgasm, her flames wrapping around both of them now, embracing him as he ramped up her orgasm higher and higher.

She'd barely come down from her high when he crawled up her body, his expression wild and a little feral.

"Yes?" he asked.

She knew what the question meant. "Yes." She wanted him, all of him. At least right now, in this moment. There would be no more barriers between them.

Keeping his gaze pinned to hers, he positioned his cock right at her entrance and soooo damn slowly, he pushed forward.

Her inner walls clenched around him as he took his time, easing her into this. Suddenly she rolled her hips upward, taking all of him. *Oh, yeah.* Too much and not enough.

Her head fell back even as she arched up and held on to him tight. She shoved at his chest once, the urge to roll over and take control, to ride him hard, punching through her. But he grabbed her wrists and held them above her head in a show of pure power.

She'd never been dominated before, and was surprised how much she liked the feel of him pinning her to the grass, thrusting into her hard, over and over. She loved the sensation of completely letting go as he took over everything.

He kept his eyes pinned to hers, the moment impossibly intimate, until she felt another orgasm building. It should be impossible, but it was happening.

"I need more hands," he growled out in pure frustration as he dropped one hand to cup her breast. "Because these are perfection and should be worshipped." Another animalistic growl.

Pleasure rolled through her at his words, at the truth of them. Then his mouth was on hers again, devouring and taking as she wrapped her arms around him, needing to hold on to him. As if he could somehow ground her, anchor her.

She felt as if she was caught in a storm, an out-of-control tornado that wouldn't stop, and Lachlan was her anchor.

She started orgasming again and as she let go, he did too, emptying himself inside her as he groaned out her name. "Star!" He raked his teeth against her neck but didn't break the skin as he came deep and hard inside her.

For some reason it disappointed her that he didn't mark her, but the notion was swept away with the wind as they both found release, cresting together until they collapsed against the grass, sated and satisfied. For now.

Because she wanted more from this male. So much more, and she wasn't sure if she should tell him the truth of what she was. She wondered if postcoital bliss was muddling her brain, making her even consider telling him.

Sighing at herself, she curled up against his chest, enjoying these few quiet moments under a blanket of stars. Because she knew this peace wouldn't last.

CHAPTER 24

As Star rode on Lachlan back toward the city, she wasn't sure where her head was. Her body? Oh, she was feeling incredible—and ready for round two. Then three and four and oh holy hell, she had to stop this madness train she'd jumped on. She'd never imagined sex would be like this. Yeah, she might have fooled around a little, but she'd never been able to let go of her control.

For so long she felt like she'd been playing a role, especially after becoming famous. She'd constantly had to be aware of what she said, where she went, who she associated with.

But tonight with Lachlan? Having sex with him—no, making love? That sounded weird, but even though it had been raw, it had felt somehow familiar and incredible aaannnnd she needed to get out of her own head or she would start spiraling. Lachlan had clearly done something to her because he was making her think things she shouldn't be. Considering things she might want for just herself... *Nooooo.*

Star shut all those thoughts off and buried her face against his scales, simply inhaling the wild scent of him. Enjoying the pureness of this quiet moment.

Thankfully the flight back to the city was uneventful and short, not giving her much time to get lost in her thoughts.

Lachlan flew in a loop around the city before camouflaging himself and landing in an empty park about a mile from Cynara's club. After he shifted back to human, he immediately took her hand in his once he'd dressed, making it clear he wasn't going to break the connection between them. She loved the small, possessive way he held on to her, as if he couldn't bear to not be touching her. Because she felt the same way.

The walk through the Quarter was mostly silent as they strode along the uneven sidewalks. Once they made it back to the heart of the Quarter, nearing Cynara's club, tension curled in her belly as she glanced at the people on the sidewalk. There seemed to be more people out tonight, the city coming alive this late. There was a nip to the air so everyone had on light scarves or sweaters and boots.

"Come on." Lachlan dropped her hand and hooked his arm around her shoulders before guiding them into the street. There weren't any cars since driving had slowed exponentially after The Fall. In the street there was more room for the two of them and Lachlan definitely needed it, given his size.

She also liked the feel of his arm around her, wanted to wrap her body around his again once they had some privacy. Still, that tension settled low in her belly and she scanned the people they passed, humans and supernaturals alike. All her muscles were bowstring tight and she had no doubt that Lachlan could sense her worry. Worry that Oscar or his people were lurking nearby, watching and waiting to strike right here on the street.

"We're almost there," he murmured quietly, tightening his grip on her.

She laid her head on his shoulder. "I know. I just hate knowing that he's here. Or nearby. Just stalking my sister, thinking he's going to take her. I want to rip his head off and throw it into a volcano."

"We'll find him." A soft, deadly promise. Then he kissed the top of her head as they turned into a quiet alleyway.

For some reason, him kissing her head felt ridiculously intimate. Like something a couple did. But they weren't a couple, were they? She wasn't sure what they were, she just knew that she was confused—and that she wanted to get him naked again as soon as possible. It was like a switch had flipped inside her and now she kind of understood that whole hedonistic vampire lifestyle. It wasn't laziness! It was raw, burning hunger pulsing through her.

"I want to get you naked again soon," Lachlan murmured as they rounded the club building toward the back—as if he'd read her mind.

"Are you a mind reader now?" she asked as they approached the back door. The place took up nearly a city block, so it explained how they had extra space here for bedrooms and living spaces.

"No, I'm just reading *you*." His rich, dark scent intensified, wrapping around her and giving her comfort.

At the back door, the same security guy who'd been there before nodded when he saw them and opened the door without question. "Head the same way you did before and bypass Cynara's office door. The bedrooms are farther down the hallway and loop around the rest of the club. It's all insulated and you'll see clearly marked doors. Your people have already settled in."

"Thanks," she said, stepping inside with Lachlan.

They hurried up the stairs, and as she reached the top she spotted Marley stepping out of one of the doors in the long hallway. Of Barbadian and Irish heritage, she had amber eyes, sharp cheekbones, pale brown skin, and often wore her long braids pulled up into a ponytail so they stayed out of her way. Tonight she actually had on regular, whole jeans instead of the ripped-to-shreds ones she normally sported, sparkly black heels and a skimpy, black bandeau top that just covered her breasts.

"Hey! Was wondering when you guys would get back. I heard about what happened. I hate that he got away—" Her eyes widened slightly as she reached them. Then she inhaled not so subtly.

Star cursed, because of course Marley would scent the sex lingering on them. Damn snow leopard senses!

Her friend looked between the two of them, a smile tugging at her lips, but she contained herself from saying anything. "Everyone has assigned rooms. Aurora is downstairs with Cynara right now in the VIP section. I'm headed to see Kartini, but I'll be downstairs in a little bit. Your room is around the corner. The blue door. Number twenty-seven."

"Which room is mine?" Lachlan said.

"Pretty sure it's number twenty-seven too." Marley snickered as she headed back down the hallway, her braids swaying against her back.

"Go find your sister," Lachlan said to Star, surprising her.

"What?"

"I can read your expression. You're worried about her."

"Come with me," she said, slipping her hand into his and squeezing his fingers.

He blinked once, but squeezed back. She knew that them holding hands—not to mention that she smelled like sex—would signal to her crew that she and Lachlan were a thing. And screw it, she needed his touch. Needed him, something that was hard to wrap her mind around. For so long it had been her and her crew, literally since birth. Now? She couldn't imagine Lachlan leaving, not being part of her life. And that terrified the hell out of her.

It didn't take long to make it back downstairs—using an elevator and navigating a bunch of complicated hallways until they stepped out into the VIP room. At least they didn't have to walk through the main floor of the club, which was nice. Though she could easily see over the railing below. There were tons of people dancing, a huge dance floor, multiple bars, high-top tables, flashing strobe lights, males and females walking around with shot trays—pretty typical club stuff. Well, if you discounted the random shifted animals partying it up on top of the platforms. Seriously...was that... She blinked. Yep, that was a brown bear wearing a fluffy pink skirt.

"I...have never seen that," Lachlan murmured.

She looked up at him, glad he appeared as bemused as she felt. As they strode across the VIP section, she immediately spotted her sister sitting with Cynara and a female who was likely a dragon, given her height. Man, it was like dragons were everywhere.

"Go sit with your sister," Lachlan murmured. "I see some people I know."

She looked up to find him nodding at two males sitting at a table near her sister's table. One of the males—with red hair, a red beard and broad shoulders—smiled in surprise when he saw Lachlan and shouted something she couldn't understand. Maybe ancient Gaelic? She wasn't sure what the words meant but it was clear that Lachlan liked the guy if that genuine smile of his was anything to go on.

Star also acknowledged to herself that she was glad the people he was going to talk to were males. She shouldn't care at all—had never thought of herself as the jealous type—but now that she'd gotten a taste of him, she'd decided he didn't need to be talking to any females. Which yeah, was beyond banana crackers crazy but whatever.

Winding her way through high-top tables and bypassing a small dance floor, she nearly stumbled when a familiar song came on the speakers. It was weird to hear herself singing in a setting like this, but she recovered and kept walking.

"You're here!" Cynara slid off her chair when she saw her and gave her a brief hug. "Good timing too." She looked at the tall female with slightly tangled jet-black hair sitting at the table next to Aurora. Ooooh, Kartini would love to do this female's hair. Even with her sitting down, it was clear the female was tall, and she had the kind of cheekbones Star could envy. "Prima, this is Star, Aurora's sister. And she is who you hear singing over the speakers right now."

"Oh, I like this song very much." The female leaned forward slightly and inhaled in a way that was very much not human. Like, she wasn't even trying to hide what she was doing. Not to mention her gray eyes flashed to her dragon and stayed there, the dragon peering out at Star with pure curiosity. "And I like your scent."

Okay, so Star was going to just push past that. "Are you guys having a good time?" she asked as she sat down.

Aurora looked relaxed for the first time in ages, so she wasn't going to bitch at her for being out in public. Because this really wasn't public anyway. Star was just being an overprotective big sister and she knew she needed to pull back on that. It was just so damn hard not to worry about her. Until Oscar was dead, Star wouldn't be able to completely rest. Especially after the long-ass day she'd had—being attacked by Oscar's dragons, trekking through the bayou, giving Lachlan her blood to heal him, threatening a jackass vampire coven, then hunting down Oscar and finding him gone. Seriously, how had this only been one day? It felt like four years had passed.

"You and your sister really do have very unique scents," the female named Prima said suddenly as she watched her.

Cynara simply face-palmed herself. "Prima!" she groaned.

"Thanks, I think," Star said as Aurora just laughed and took a sip of her martini.

"There's a uniqueness to the two of you, but yours is different. It's almost like one scent overlaying the other, a dual thing. As if you have…" Her eyes narrowed ever slightly as she looked at Star, but then she shrugged. "So, your sister tells me that you and your band will be performing here in the coming weeks."

"That's right."

"I have never been to a concert before. I'm quite looking forward to seeing you perform."

Star found herself smiling at the almost formal way the woman spoke. "Thank you."

They talked for a few more minutes, though Aurora was mostly quiet, sipping on her drink and looking out at the crowd, taking everything in.

When Cynara and Prima started talking, Star scooted closer to her sister. "Did you get settled in okay?"

Aurora reached under the table and squeezed Star's hand once. "I'm fine. And I know I can't tell you to stop worrying about me, but I can feel your tension. And I really am fine. It's okay for you to not worry about my needs 24/7."

She frowned at her sister. "What are you talking about?"

Aurora had started to respond when the bearded male that Lachlan had been talking to came up behind Prima and wrapped his huge arm around her front, sort of caging her against him. He murmured something to Prima in a low Scottish brogue, then bit her earlobe.

Prima nipped at his shoulder, then slid off the stool. Without a word to any of them, she dragged the male away.

As soon as she vacated the seat, Lachlan slid into her empty seat and gave Star a heated look she felt all the way to her core.

"I'm probably going to get out of here," Aurora said, slipping off her chair. "I'm pretty beat."

Star started to do the same, but her sister shook her head.

"Stay," Aurora said.

"I'll walk you to your room." She'd barely gotten a chance to talk to her.

Her sister sighed, clearly annoyed with her or maybe just frustrated. "Okay."

"I've got my phone on me," she said to Lachlan, loud enough for him to hear over the thump of music and people.

He gave her a heated look, his eyes practically glowing. "Dinnae worry about me, lass. I'll meet you soon."

Oh, God, she hoped so. As she stepped away with Aurora, Teague and Cian appeared out of nowhere and joined Lachlan and Cynara at the table.

"What were you doing downstairs?" she asked as soon as they got to Aurora's room, which ended up being pretty incredible. The bed was round and huge enough for five people. A purple tufted headboard made up most of the wall. In one corner of the room a softly humming hot tub was running, with flower petals already in the water. There was a soft purple glow to the room, giving it a soothing, spa feel. "I didn't think you were going to be out in public while we were gone," she added.

"I'm thinking I don't have to answer the question because the answer is obvious. I was perfectly safe and enjoying the company of other people." Aurora's tone was dry as she looked at Star.

Star winced because she knew she was being way too over protective. "I know. I'm sorry. I'm trying not to be such a psycho. Even if it doesn't seem like it. I swear I'm trying."

Aurora grabbed her hands and tugged Star toward the oversize bed. At the edge of it, she pulled Star so that they were both sitting. "Look, I love you. Soooooo much. You raised me and I have more memories of you than I do of our parents. You've always been more like a mom to me than a sister and I know those lines get blurred for you as well. I just..."

"You need me to unclench a little bit?" Star asked, already knowing the answer.

"Yes. I know why you're stressed. You always take care of everybody, and I'm releasing you from that duty."

Now Star snorted. "First of all, it's not a duty. And I will always worry about you, that's just the way it is. But...I do know that I need to relax a little bit. I know you were perfectly safe tonight. It's just...Oscar wasn't there when we got to that house but his scent was left behind." And that meant he was nearby, lurking somewhere. Just waiting to make his move. "I'm sure you've already been filled in on all the details."

Aurora nodded. "He clearly got wind that you guys were headed that way."

Star rubbed a hand over her face. "I hate him so much. You're my baby sister, I should have protected you." The guilt that her sister had been taken at all still weighed heavily on her. They'd always been so damn careful about hiding what they were.

"You didn't do anything wrong. This is all on him. And if he's here... Maybe I should just make myself bait and bring him out into the open."

Star's eyes widened even as her heart jumped into her throat. "No!"

Aurora lifted an eyebrow, her expression challenging. "You can't really stop me."

"I bet I can."

They stared at each other for a long moment before Aurora dropped her head back and let out a long-suffering sigh. "Can we not talk about him just for a minute? Tell me about you and the dragon. I know something happened between you guys."

She felt her cheeks heat up and knew she must be flushed pink. "We had sex in the middle of a field not far from the burned-down house. It was insanely hot and I'm falling for him." Okay, there was no falling. She'd flat-out fallen for the male. Headfirst. And saying it out loud was freeing and terrifying at the same time.

Her sister stared at her, eyes wide. "Oh...my God. That's awesome!"

"Is it? He lives in Scotland and he's made it pretty clear that he doesn't want anything casual. He hasn't said the words, but he wants a mate. He wants me to be his mate," she added. Or she was pretty sure he did.

"You don't want casual either. I know you, and no matter what you say, you could never do casual. Not with a male like that—not one who looks at you like you hung the damn moon."

Star rubbed the back of her neck, trying to erase some of the tension. "But our home is here."

"Is it really? We came here for safe harbor. But you don't have roots here. And even if you did... You get one life, Star. Nothing is tying you here—"

"Uh, my whole crew, my family, is here."

"True. And not gonna lie, if you move, the whole crew might not go with you. But at the end of the day, you have to make the right choice for you. Nobody will hold it against you if it turns out he's your mate, if you decide to start a new adventure with him. So is he?"

The word yes was on the tip of her tongue but she held it back and cleared her throat. "I've been having these really weird dreams. For close to a year." And she'd never told anyone.

Aurora frowned at the change in topic. "Ah, okay, about what? And what does that have to do with Lachlan?"

"I don't know. The dreams are always about this woman, and this dragon whose face I never actually see. He's trying to convince her to mate with him. But I get the feeling they're not actually dreams but memories, which as I say it out loud sounds nuts. But some part of me feels like..." *Oh, God, just say it.* "They're my memories," she whispered.

Aurora's eyes widened. "Well that's interesting."

"You don't think I'm crazy?"

"You're the most sane, wonderful person I know. If they feel like memories, maybe they are. I wouldn't discount anything as a possibility. And whatever you decide with your big dragon, go with your instinct. You *always* tell me to listen to my gut."

"Okay, I will. And when did you get to be so wise?"

"I've had a good teacher." Aurora's mouth curved up ever so slightly. Then her smile fell as she spoke again. "Oscar won't stop until he has me again. It's not just the blood thing. He really is obsessed with me. He thinks...I'm his mate." She whispered the last part.

Star sucked in a breath. "His mate?" The idea filled her with revulsion.

Aurora nodded, her expression getting more grim. "I know I told you it wasn't a sexual thing in captivity, but..."

Star's gut tightened. *Oh God, no. No, no, no.* She bit her tongue and kept quiet, letting Aurora talk.

"Near the end of my captivity, I was getting desperate. I didn't know if you would ever find me. He was draining my blood constantly and I was so damn delirious. But I'd seen the way he looked at me sometimes, so..." She closed her eyes and looked away as if ashamed.

Star reached out and grabbed her hands. "Whatever happened is not your fault. You didn't do anything wrong. You survived."

Aurora opened her eyes and swallowed hard as she squeezed back. "I put the moves on him basically. I mean, I get that it was rape. Intellectually, I know that's what it was. I didn't want it and I was in captivity. There was a huge power imbalance—because I was in a prison. But I thought if I could use sex to get out, then at least I would be free. Then I could come back once I'd regained strength, and kill him."

Her eyes sparked a bright purple then as she continued.

"I was able to have sex with him twice—barely. After the second time, he had a weird kind of energy rolling off him. But he was so relaxed and almost lethargic, so I attacked him. I was so damn weak from the blood loss, but I had to try. I managed to escape and make it to the elevators. But he was fast, too fast. He was enraged and dragged me back to my room. After that he was angry all the time. He drained me near to death almost every single time after that but he wouldn't touch me. He was enraged that I'd faked wanting to be with him." She snorted in disgust. "As if that was a big shock. He said he would never let me go. He said I belonged to him, that I was his pet and that I'd better remember my place." She closed her eyes for a long moment.

Horrified, her rage against Oscar building even higher, Star leaned forward and pulled her into a tight hug. "I'm so sorry."

Aurora hugged her in return, letting out a shuddering breath. "I'm just glad to be free," she said as she pulled back, wiping away a few stray tears. "And I set up an appointment to talk to your friend Greer. I just need to talk some things through, but thank you for listening. Once he's dead I know I'll be able to move on. I just...I don't know how to move on with him still out there looking for me."

"We will kill him." Star would do whatever it took to make that happen.

"I know you want to keep me safe, but...I'll never be safe as long as he's out there. I need to be part of the team to bring him down. I just do." There was a desperation in her sister's eyes and in her voice.

After this, Star could deny her nothing. "I'm not your boss. I'm just your sister, and even though I hate the thought of you putting yourself in danger... Whatever it takes to bring him down, whatever it takes for you to move on with your life. Even if..." She couldn't say the words. She absolutely hated the thought of Aurora being in any more danger. Because Aurora was right, the line between mom and sister had always been blurred with Star because she truly had raised Aurora.

"I love you," Aurora said finally. "I really am exhausted though. Why don't you go find your dragon?"

"I'm staying with you tonight." No way was she leaving her side.

Her sister shook her head and stood. "Honestly, I just want some hot tea, a soak in the tub and to go to bed."

"Are you sure?"

"I'm completely sure. Please go find him. Tomorrow is a new day and you've had a hell of a one today. Go indulge in some fun with him, and tomorrow...we'll tackle whatever we need to."

Star hugged her sister once more and left, even though she didn't want to. She was resolved more than ever to destroy Oscar—and anyone in his clan who had been part of her sister's kidnapping. Anyone who had even known about it.

And she knew Lachlan would be right by her side, helping her. That thought alone should be startling, but it wasn't. She knew without a doubt that Lachlan was in this thing until it was over. She was glad he was on her side.

CHAPTER 25

Star stepped into her room and froze when she found Lachlan already there, leaning against a column of the four-poster California king-sized bed. Waiting, as if he had every right to be there. "What are you doing here?"

He simply cocked an eyebrow. "That should be obvious, lass," he murmured.

She shut and bolted the door behind her. Not only were the living quarters secure here, the whole place had also been spelled by multiple witches with a specific spell to keep Oscar and his clanmates out, which made Star feel better. But after what Aurora had just told her, nothing could ease the pain inside her now.

As if sensing her distress, he shoved off the column and stalked toward her, concern in his expression. "What is it, love?" He cupped her cheek, and against her better judgment she leaned into it, closing her eyes at the feel of his hand on her skin.

And yeah, she liked the way he'd just called her love. Oh God, she liked it way too much. "It's just... I don't want to talk about it." Because talking about her sister's captivity wasn't something she'd been given permission to do. She would never betray Aurora's trust that way.

He didn't push, but pulled her into a tight embrace instead, rubbing his hand up and down her back. It felt so familiar that she leaned into it even as that sense of déjà vu threatened to overwhelm her again.

"You don't even have to be here. You can just go home and forget all of this ever happened," she said against his chest, her words muffled. "I'm not holding you here."

"But you are, because you're here. And if you think I would just leave you, you're a foolish female." There was a bite of censure in his words.

She groaned and pulled back to look up at him. "I don't think you would leave. I'm just trying to push you away." And not doing a good job of it—probably because she didn't want to push him away. Not anymore.

"You willnae have any luck with that." His gaze landed on her mouth, hungry and intense.

Just like that, a rush of heat burst through her and flames started dancing along her fingertips, up her arms, until all of her was engulfed. It was like he'd opened some kind of floodgate and nothing could stop her reaction to him now.

"I know you willnae tell me what you are, but when dragons find their mate, and become intimate, a mating manifestation appears."

She blinked at his sudden admission. "Is that why you were glowing before?"

"Aye. And I can't help but wonder why you light on fire when we become intimate," he murmured, watching her carefully.

"I don't know," she said honestly.

"Well whatever you are, you are mine." Then his mouth was on hers.

Deep inside, she felt like his. As if they'd been made for each other. As if she'd been searching for him without even realizing it. And she wanted to claim him right back. So she grabbed onto his shirt and wrapped her whole body around him as they started kissing. She couldn't get close enough, needed skin to skin like she needed her next breath.

He pinned her against a wall, his huge fingers spanning her throat as he looked down at her. His hold didn't feel aggressive, however, just...possessive as his indigo eyes lit up with pure hunger. "You're mine, love." His words were all gravel and heat, and she didn't know if he was repeating them for her benefit or his own.

She couldn't find her voice so she nodded. She was his. All his.

"Say it," he demanded, rolling his hips against hers, keeping her pinned in place.

Another rush of heat flooded between her thighs. "I'm yours." Saying the words out loud felt freeing.

Their mouths collided again and it took only moments to shed their clothing in a frantic rush. She didn't even remember ripping his shirt off or how she got naked.

As she rubbed her bare breasts against his chest she groaned at the friction, at the sensation of being skin to skin with him. This was what she'd needed. God, she'd missed him so much.

"I haven't gone anywhere," he murmured against her mouth as they landed on the bed together.

She hadn't realized she'd said the words out loud and she wasn't even sure what they meant. How could she have missed him? She'd only been away from him for maybe half an hour. Dismissing the thought, she rolled on top of him, rubbing her slick folds against his thick, erect cock. Thanks to her shifter genes, she wasn't sore from earlier. No, just fired up and ready for more.

He arched up into her, the head of his erection rubbing over her clit. She groaned at the sensation, her tongue teasing against his as they basically mimicked sex with their mouths.

He ran his big, callused hands down her back, before palming her ass and squeezing. "I love everything about you," he said against her mouth.

She jerked slightly at the use of the L word. She wanted him...was starting to feel more than obsessed with him. Maybe even... She kissed him harder, deepening their connection, wanting him inside her again with a wild desperation. That first time hadn't been nearly enough— would never be enough.

He growled against her mouth, and flipped them so that he was on top, guiding her wrists above her head. He held them in place as he plundered her mouth, taking everything she had to offer.

In that moment she wanted to give him everything, wanted to make up for past mistakes— Wait, what the hell did that even mean? *Past mistakes?*

Her thoughts were so jumbled as she arched into him, wanting him to completely fill her. Wanting to block out the whole damn world as they found pleasure with each other.

"You are the most fascinating female I've ever known," he murmured against her chest before sucking one nipple between his teeth.

Her wrists were free so she speared her fingers through his hair. She held on tight, not sure if she wanted him to go lower or higher. Her body was in flames, literally, and they were spreading across the room, not burning anything, just growing higher and higher, creating a haven around them. His own indigo glow was just as bright so that she saw everything between them clearly.

By the time he knelt between her legs, she was slick with need. When he finally teased his tongue against her folds and clit, he sent her over the edge.

Really all he had to do was blow on her at this point and she would have climaxed. So when he started teasing her with the perfect amount of pressure, something inside her broke free, her orgasm cresting in a sharp explosion.

Her orgasm seemed to go on forever, but before she'd even come down from her high, he let out a soft growl and flipped her onto her knees.

She lifted her ass, spreading her legs wider for him—and let out a yelp of surprise when his teeth raked against her butt. He didn't break the skin, but he did it again, his teeth pressing into her in a way that had shivers spiraling through her. Groaning, she pushed back against him, wanting to be filled by him again.

"Absolute perfection," he murmured before she felt him press his thick erection against her folds.

She sucked in a breath, her body still sensitive from her orgasm. As she pushed back against him, she dug her fingers into the covers. She needed more, so much more from him.

She wanted him to completely claim her, even though she knew that was insane. They didn't know enough about each other and yet she felt as if she'd known him for her entire life. Longer, even.

Some deep-seated part of her felt like he was the man from her dreams but that made no sense. Because that meant she was that female from a different time.

He thrust deep and she lost all ability to think as he pistoned inside her, over and over, his thickness filling her.

"Lachlan," she cried out as he found that perfect spot inside her, another orgasm building up with each stroke.

He placed one big hand on her back, pinning her down in place so that she could barely move. She struggled against him, but found the sensation wildly erotic as he pressed even harder. Her inner walls clenched around his cock and when he reached around with his other hand and began teasing her clit, she jerked against the sheets.

The friction should have been too much, she shouldn't have been ready for another orgasm, but one built inside her nonetheless. She let out another cry as pleasure rose up and knew the moment he let go of his control.

He grabbed onto her hips, no longer holding her down. "My morning star," he growled as he found his own release, coming hard inside her.

For some reason the nickname ricocheted through her as she fell over the edge again, her orgasm mixing with his until she collapsed against the sheets, him on top of her.

Breathing erratically, she lay there, enjoying the feel of his chest against her back. But as lethargic as she felt, she knew he was keeping most of his weight off her. She wasn't sure how long they lay there but she opened her eyes when he finally pulled out of her.

"I'm just going to sleep this way," she murmured against the sheets, not bothering to turn over. The material of the sheets felt cool against her cheeks and breasts and she really, really didn't feel like moving. No, she just wanted to savor the sensations still humming through her body, to hold on to this for as long as she could.

Behind her, she heard a dark chuckle and then the en suite door opened. A moment later he came back out and began wiping between her legs with a warm cloth.

For some reason the act sent her emotions into a free fall and she wasn't sure why. Okay that was a lie—she'd never had anyone take care of her before. Her crew didn't count because yeah, they took care of each other. But that was different; that was what family did.

With Lachlan there were no rules. He busted through every single wall she had, and not only was he taking care of her, he was fighting alongside her to find the monster who had hurt her sister. She couldn't put him in a little box, couldn't relegate him to one part of her life and forget about him. No, he'd insinuated himself into every facet of her life and she liked it. More than liked it.

To her horror, tears welled up inside her. She couldn't believe she was crying, couldn't even remember the last time she *had* cried. Even when Aurora had been taken, she'd gone into a sharp, determined rage and had kept all other emotions locked down tight. Now, however, it was as if all those emotions she'd been trying so damn hard to keep hidden just came pouring out.

"Hey now, lass." Lachlan pulled her into his arms and didn't stop moving until they were curled up against the pillows and headboard, with her in his lap, crying on his shoulder.

His powerful, capable shoulder. It was like he'd been made for her. He didn't ask why she was crying, simply wiped away her tears as she buried her face against his neck. She wasn't going to apologize for crying because screw it, she had emotions and they wouldn't remain inside her any longer.

He simply held her close, almost rocking her as he rubbed her back in a gentle soothing rhythm.

"You're killing me, Lachlan," she murmured.

"I dinnae think that word means what you think it does."

She laughed lightly even through her tears. "This was just supposed to be physical between us." And it was anything but that. She couldn't deny it even to herself. She didn't want to.

"You can lie to yourself and tell yourself that it's still just physical if it makes you stop crying." He kissed the top of her head and pulled her even tighter against him.

She wasn't sure how on earth this male had come to invade every facet of her life but she held on to him tight. Even with all the crap going on, she was so glad he was here. She clutched onto him just a little bit tighter as blessed sleep started to pull her under. It was as if all the events of the last twenty-four hours came crashing down on her at once and she couldn't keep her eyes open any longer.

And for the life of her, she couldn't remember the last time she'd felt so safe, as if she could put her burdens on someone else and let him take half the load. Hell, even a fraction would be wonderful, but Lachlan was strong, and though he was arrogant, his ego could handle a strong female.

That much she knew without a doubt. He was...he was *her* dragon. Always had been, always would be.

Some elusive thought played in her mind at that, but she was exhausted, and the darkness was beckoning. So she let it take her as her male held her tight in his arms.

CHAPTER 26

Star woke up, feeling completely wrung out, if completely physically satisfied. But emotionally, she felt raw and vulnerable.

When she realized that Lachlan wasn't next to her, her stomach tightened in disappointment as she got off the bed. That was when she saw the white piece of paper on the nightstand and a note in Lachlan's big, scrawling script. *You looked so peaceful sleeping I didn't want to wake you. I've just gone to talk to my brother but I've got my phone on me. —L*

The tension inside her immediately eased. Her head might be all over the place, but knowing that Lachlan hadn't just left without any thought of her shifted something inside her. He really was a male worth…everything.

After a quick shower, she changed into jeans, a plain black T-shirt and boots—and realized she was starving. When she stepped out into the hallway, she nearly ran into Cynara, who smiled at her.

The demon-vampire hybrid wore a black dress this morning along with hot pink lace-up boots that stopped right over her knees. She always looked so fierce and put together. "Hey, I hope you slept well?"

"I did, thank you." She couldn't actually remember the last time she'd slept so solidly. That had more to do with Lachlan than anything, however.

"Your whole crew is in our eating area and there's plenty of food—unless that lion ate it all."

Star snickered because Axel definitely packed it away. Lion metabolism and all. "Would you mind directing me to it? I know you told me last night but I can't remember how to get there."

"This place is huge, so I'll just walk you there."

"Thanks. So where's your mate, anyway? And why haven't I met him?" Star asked.

She laughed lightly. "Justus has been doing all sorts of night patrols on King's orders—which I think he loves. He does *not* like to sit idly by and do nothing. But we get to spend most of our days together."

"I can't believe you're mated. And not because you don't deserve it! It's just—you used to make barfing sounds anytime anyone ever brought up the word mating and you in the same sentence."

Cynara laughed as they reached the elevator doors. "I know. I was ridiculous."

"So...can I ask you something personal?" They stepped onto the elevator and as they descended Star realized it was heading to a sublevel underground. "Hey, how'd you even have a sublevel built in an area that's below ocean level?" she asked.

"Really good construction. It's waterproof too. And there's also a little bit of magic that went into building it," she said proudly. "But I don't think that's what you wanted to ask."

"It's not. I know Justus moved here and basically gave up his coven for you."

Cynara nodded. "He did. I offered to move there with him but..." She shrugged. "He said no. He wanted to be here with me, said it was time for a change and that he was tired of all the vampire politics. He'd already put someone else in charge, someone he trusted to run the coven the right way so the changeover in power was seamless."

"How has the adjustment been for him?"

"Really good as far as I can tell. And he wouldn't lie to me," she said as they stepped off the elevator into a quiet hallway. As the doors shut, Cynara stopped and leaned against the wall. "He likes King and admitted that he thought it would be hard to listen to another Alpha give orders."

"It's not?" Star shoved her hands in her pockets.

"Eh, I mean, they butt heads sometimes, but the whole structure in New Orleans is different than a lot of territories. King isn't a jackass overlord who gets off on telling people what to do. He's a true leader. Different rules for a new world, I think. This is King's city, no doubt about it. And while he's arrogant, he doesn't let his ego get in the way of making decisions. He's putting strong people in charge of different areas and trusting them to run them right without micromanaging. Justus used to be a Roman general and this kind of thing is right up his alley. I told him that if he ever wanted a change, that I'm willing to move for him. We're basically immortal and I don't have to live here. I'm open to change if it makes him happy. And he feels the same way. So for now we're living here and trying to get things back on track, back to a new normal. But if my mate needs a change, I'll make one with him. His happiness means everything to me."

"I'm happy for you," she said, pulling her friend into an impulsive hug. Cynara was one of the kindest females she'd ever known. As she stepped back, she said, "And thank you again for letting us stay here, for the protection of your club."

"You don't ever have to thank me. Besides, you're totally going to pay me back with some free shows." She winked at Star and pointed down the hallway as she pressed the elevator button again. "If you keep going, you'll run straight into the cafeteria."

"Thanks." Her rubber-soled boots were quiet against the tile as she hurried down the hallway. She could see two double swinging doors, and when she was about twenty feet away, she heard a multitude of voices, all her crew. When she stepped inside the room she found Aurora standing in front of everyone, hands on her hips, while the others lounged on various chairs, and some were sitting on tabletops.

They all turned to look at her.

"You guys are having a meeting without me?" she asked, frowning at everyone.

"You needed the sleep," Aurora said, completely unapologetic.

"Yeah, we know that dragon of yours tired you out last night," Marley said, smirking.

Kartini started making obscene thrusting motions and cackling. "It's about time you got some!"

Star rolled her eyes and stepped farther into the room. "I swear you guys turn into fifteen-year-olds at the mention of sex."

"Of course we do," Kartini said. "Talking about sex is fun. Thinking about sex is fun. Engaging in sex is—"

"Fun, we get it," Axel muttered, though he was smiling.

"So what's going on down here?" Star asked, her eyes widening when she saw a huge table display of muffins and different assorted pastries. Oh, and sweet, blessed coffee. She made a beeline for the food, her mouth already watering.

"We've come up with a plan to bring Oscar out into the open," Aurora said.

If she'd had anything in her stomach it would have curdled at her sister's tone. She had a feeling she wasn't going to like whatever this plan was. Star paused at the table, then turned away from it to face the others. She shoved her hands in her pockets. "Why do I think I'm not going to like any of this?"

"Because you're not," Aurora said, meeting her gaze dead-on. "Because it involves me—and you—acting as bait in an effort to bring Oscar out into the open. I'll do it without you, but the whole plan will work better if you're part of it. And I'll explain why if you don't start arguing with me right now."

Her instinct *was* to argue with Aurora, to tell her she wasn't doing anything to put herself in danger, but Star took a deep breath. She was not Aurora's mother. And even if she was, she didn't control her. That bastard had controlled everything about Aurora's life for an entire year. Star knew it would be selfish if she tried to do the same, no matter how noble the reasons. "Okay, let me hear your plan."

Aurora's purple eyes flashed in surprise but she quickly recovered. "The plan itself is simple enough. Cynara has completely spelled this place so it's impossible for Oscar to get past her defenses. Or at least really hard to, since technically nothing is really impossible. But if she agrees to release some of the spells, and if you put on a rooftop show here—with me in attendance—we'll spread the word around the city that you're doing a charity show and anyone is welcome. Bella and Lola have already come up with online images to post. All the surrounding streets will be cordoned off so that no vehicles are allowed—as long as King is okay with it. People will line the streets to see you and just listen to you and it will be VIP access only in the actual club. In reality, everyone on the roof and in VIP will be our people, including Lachlan and his dragons and any of King's people who agree to help us."

"Have you talked to Lachlan or King about this?" she asked.

"Of course not." Her sister seemed offended by the question.

"I was just asking," she murmured.

Aurora frowned at her. "I sort of expected you to interrupt me or argue with me by now."

Star gave her a ghost of a smile. "So far it's a pretty good plan, though I do see at least one hole in it."

Her sister narrowed her gaze but continued. "If we do this show, he'll come for me. Even if he thinks it's a trap, I don't think he'll be able to resist making a play for me if I'm up on stage with you or right near you, out in full public view. He's incredibly arrogant. When he makes his move, we work as a team to bring him down. He's already sent his people after you once. I don't think he'll risk someone else screwing up again. And if Lachlan's dragons are on board, I don't think we'll have a problem taking Oscar and his clanmates down. He didn't bring his whole clan with him anyway. The majority of them were left behind, according to Lola. And you guys already killed some of them so I think we have good odds."

Star took a second to digest everything, running it over in her mind. "What about all the supernaturals and humans on the street during the show? Do we really want to start a fight with dragons and potentially injure innocent bystanders?" She knew the answer but had to ask the question. It was one of the holes she could see—none of them would want to risk innocent people. Not even for revenge.

"No. Which is where another part of the plan comes into play. Cynara is friends with a couple witches. We can ask them to cast a protection spell over everyone on the street so they don't get hit by any of the fallout or dragon fire if there's a battle in the sky. And if it turns out that some of Oscar's people are in the crowd, they won't be able to get past the witches' barrier to the rooftop."

Okay, so that was a really good idea. "If he comes for you—and we'd basically be waving a giant red flag at a bull, so I think he will—the only way we can fight him back is by shifting to our true selves."

"I know. It's the only thing I was worried about telling you." Aurora's expression was grave. "I'm tired of hiding what I am. I've hid what I am forever. You and I hid our relationship in case anyone realized what one was, so the other wouldn't be targeted. And look what happened. I got taken anyway."

They'd hidden what they were for their whole lives. Look what keeping their secret safe had gotten them in the first place. Aurora was right. She'd been kidnapped anyway. "Okay."

Everyone shifted almost nervously in their seats and even Aurora dropped her arms from her hips. "Are you serious? You're going to come out to the world?"

"If I have to. And if I'm being completely honest, it's been wearing on me regardless, having to hide what I am. I don't think anything we do will keep us completely safe. And if we reveal what we are, especially to our allies, it will only strengthen those bonds. Look at Aunt Cliona—she's allied with King and working with dragons now."

Aurora gave her a brilliant smile, the sister from before her captivity shining through in that moment. "We're going to kill this bastard," she growled.

Even though fear lived inside Star at the thought of her sister having to face the man who'd hurt her, she nodded. "We're certainly stronger as a team. And we're going to have to plan this down to the last detail. There can be no room for error." She started to say more, but stopped when she heard footsteps out in the hallway. She turned to find Lachlan and his dragons striding into the cafeteria.

His gaze immediately landed on hers, pinning her with those intense eyes she could drown in. "Cynara told us you were down here. Is everything okay?"

"Sure is," Aurora said before Star could answer.

She shot her sister an annoyed glance over her shoulder and immediately recognized the mischievous glint in her sister's eyes. Before she could say anything, Aurora continued.

"We're going to bring Oscar and his clanmates to us. Star and I are going to be bait. And we really hope you guys will help us take them out."

Star winced and turned back to find Lachlan staring at her with a *Hell no* expression on his handsome face.

"You're not making yourself bait!" he snarled, his dragon in his gaze.

She winced again. Then she looked over her shoulder at Aurora. "Am I this annoying when I tell you what to do?"

Aurora simply snickered.

She turned back to Lachlan. He'd been so incredible last night, letting her cry all over him like some kind of maniac. And then of course all the sexy times. He'd taken care of her and let her be vulnerable in front of him without using it against her. She wanted to respect his feelings, because she did. But it didn't change what they had to do.

She stepped forward, gently placing her hands on his chest. "This is the only way. And with your help, we'll be able to take him down and gain our freedom. Unless you don't think you're strong enough to take on Oscar?"

"I know what you're doing," he snarled, covering her hands with his. "Do you?"

"Don't try to bait me."

"I'm not baiting you. I'm asking a serious question. Can you take him on with us? Can you kill him?"

"Of course I can." His Scottish brogue was thicker in that moment.

"Then our plan will work. Because all of us are strong as well. We just need to function as a team."

She could see that Lachlan wanted to argue. His jaw clenched tightly and he watched her for a long moment. "Once he's dead, you come back to Scotland with me."

She stared at him, aware of her entire crew and his own dragons watching them, listening intently.

"Lachlan," she rasped out. Now wasn't the time to have this conversation, not in front of everyone else. She needed to talk to her crew about her leaving; she owed them that. They'd all been together for decades—they'd put their lives on hold for an entire year as they worked as a team to save Aurora.

"It's not an ultimatum. I'm just saying that when this is done, I want you to come home with me. Where you belong."

She stared at him, trying to find her voice. She wanted to go with him. In that moment, she deeply, completely wanted to go. She would miss her sister, miss her crew, if they decided not to come, but she wanted to be with Lachlan. She could live with the sadness of missing her people as long as she had her dragon.

Not giving her a chance to answer, he crushed his mouth to hers in full view of everyone, plundering her mouth with wild abandon. Her flames burst to life, and without opening her eyes she knew he was glowing too by the gasps from all those around them. Then he pulled back suddenly, his dragon looking back at her. "Let me hear this asinine plan," he growled out.

In that moment she wanted nothing more than to return to Scotland with him. To start a life with him—to be his mate. But she was terrified to say the words out loud. Because what if she got ahead of herself and then jinxed everything before they could take Oscar down?

She was terrified at the thought of losing Lachlan just when she'd found him.

CHAPTER 27

*S*tar knew she was back in that dream world, where nothing made sense. All around her were green fields—a lush color so incredibly beautiful and bright it felt fake, but she knew it was real. A blue sky dotted with puffy white clouds—and impending storm clouds on the horizon—were high above her, but she felt as if she could reach out and touch them if she strained enough.

"I'm going to marry him," she said, standing up to her father for the first time in her life. Fear slid through her as she defied the man who'd raised her, but she was a woman now. She made her own choices about her future. A low rumble of thunder sounded in the distance, making her shiver.

His eyes blazed with fury as he stared at her. "You are a fool," he snapped. "He is just using you. He will not marry you. I just hope you haven't spread your legs for him yet!"

She gritted her teeth, even as her cheeks flushed.

"You're a stupid little girl," he snarled again. "What happens when he becomes displeased with you? Do you not think he won't take it out on your people? On our village? You have put us all in danger! You have shamed us all!"

"You don't know what you're talking about. You don't know anything about him!" she yelled back. She'd never raised her voice to her father before in her life and saw the surprise in his red, mottled face. She had always thought of him as the tallest, strongest man she knew. But as she looked at him now she saw fear in his weather-lined eyes, in eyes the same color as hers. "And I'm done with this conversation. My decision is made."

"Fine, just don't come crawling back to us once he's discarded you like the common whore that you are." Disgust dripped from his every word. "If your mother was still alive—"

"I wouldn't finish that thought if I were you," she said so quietly she wasn't sure he would even hear her. But whatever he saw on her face made him snap his mouth shut. Her mother had loved her, would have wanted the best for her. Would have wanted her to be happy.

Feeling her own disgust rise at her father, she turned away from him. There was no use having this conversation any longer. She wouldn't change his mind and she had made her choice. Her future was with her dragon. Even if she only lived a few decades compared to his many, at least she would have that time. At least they would have those years together. And maybe, once her father had time to cool down, he would see reason, see the truth of her relationship with her dragon.

As she stalked through the grass, pain exploded in her skull. Crying out, she fell onto her hands and knees, trying to push up, but another burst of pain fractured inside her and darkness completely engulfed her.

Star jerked awake at the feel of a gentle touch on her shoulder and looked up into Bella's concerned, dark eyes. Aannnnd that was when Star realized her entire body was engulfed in purple flames. Her heart rate was an erratic tattoo in her chest but when she looked at her friend, she felt more grounded in reality.

"Are you okay?" Bella frowned down at her, her expression pinched. "I think you were having a nightmare."

Taking a deep breath, Star mentally shook herself and shoved up from the lounge chair, the flames immediately dying. She must have dozed off. Inwardly she cursed herself—now was *not* the time to sleep. They had a show to put on in less than an hour. But her mind was all over the place, a hotbed of chaos she couldn't control. Hell, she was barely able to keep her fire in check at this point and it seemed in sleep she couldn't lock it down.

"I didn't sleep well last night." It didn't seem to matter that she'd slept in Lachlan's arms—after toe-curling orgasms. That's right, *orgasms*, as in multiple. She'd lost count after six. She should have been able to sleep like the dead. But she'd tossed and turned, her mind in overdrive about today.

It had been two days since they'd made the plan to bring Oscar out into the open, and today was the day. She glanced around the quiet room where the band was all getting ready. The show mattered more than anything for their plan to work and Cynara had allowed them to use what was basically a private bedroom with an en suite to get ready. It was the equivalent of some kind of penthouse room in a hotel, given how gorgeous it was. All whites, grays and sparkling, shiny surfaces.

"I just need some water and I'll be fine," she added.

Bella nodded and hurried away as Star stood and stretched. She couldn't believe she'd actually fallen asleep, much less had that nightmare. And she knew it hadn't been a simple nightmare, but a memory. Deep in her bones she knew what it meant even if she wasn't going to voice it aloud just yet. She would after the show, however. She needed to talk to Lachlan immediately about it. Far too many emotions punched through her as she realized what that memory meant—or what she thought it meant. It was...a whole lot to digest and she could admit she was rattled by it. Right now she didn't have time to focus on the past. Not when her future depended on today. Because killing Oscar was her first priority.

Marley strode up to her, dressed in jeans so shredded that Star could tell Marley wasn't wearing anything underneath them, a sparkly green top, matching stilettos—and her drumsticks were tucked into the back pockets of her jeans. "You ready to rock this thing?"

Star nodded and forced a big smile on her face. "We've got this." She set the tone for everything and that meant she had to be upbeat about not only the show, but about destroying Oscar. And they *would* do it. She refused to accept any other possibility. "We've got a bunch of dragons on our side and we're all badass bitches—except for Axel. What could go wrong?"

"Speaking of," Axel said, approaching dressed in full-on tactical gear—and his gorgeous hair pulled back in a man-bun. "Your big dragon is waiting outside for you. And you can call me a badass bitch too," he said, grinning.

Feeling a little lighter, she broke away from Marley and headed to the door. She could actually scent Lachlan on the other side before she pulled it open, as if she was more attuned to him now. She smiled the moment she saw his face, the tightness easing inside her now that she could lay eyes on him. It had only been like maybe an hour since she'd seen him and they'd spent the last two days making love over and over in their limited downtime. But she was pulled to him like a magnet. She wanted to tell him what she suspected about her dreams, but now definitely wasn't the time. After this show, however, she would.

He cupped both of her cheeks with his hands and brushed his mouth over hers once. "I have something for you.

"I don't think we have time," she murmured.

He blinked then laughed, full and throaty, as he shook his head. "Not that. Here." He gave her a rectangular box.

Surprised by the gift, she opened it—and then frowned some more. It was a thin bracelet made out of...huh. As she looked at it, she wasn't even sure what material it was. A strong type of metal with intricate carvings in it. Definitely not store bought. And the symbols reminded her of something—it was on the edges of her consciousness.

"It's made from my fire," he said, securing it around her wrist. "It took a while to create or I would have given it to you earlier. It will give you the ability to see any dragons that attempt to attack you even if they have on their natural camouflage—you can see dragons with this anytime, anywhere, regardless if they're attacking you or not. This is very valuable for anyone who wants to stand against dragons."

Her eyes widened as the gravity of his gift settled in. "Are you serious?"

He nodded. "This is yours forever. Not just until Oscar is dead. I want you to always wear this—whether we mate or not. I always want you safe."

Oh damn. Tears wanted to spring up but she blinked them back. The reality of what he'd just given her touched her deep inside. And he'd given it with no strings attached. They hadn't officially talked about mating and she knew why. They needed to get through today. She needed to make sure that her sister was safe and able to live her life before anything else. And Lachlan seemed to understand this. Hell, the man seemed to get everything about her. "When we went to my aunt's house, I was searching for something there. A knife made from dragon fire. It does the same thing. She took it from... Well, it doesn't matter. I cannot believe you made this for me." She understood the significance of it, understood that he'd made himself vulnerable in this as well. Because if she lost this, if this fell into the wrong hands, it could give an enemy an edge over him or any other dragon. "Thank you so much for this gift," she rasped out.

"I would do anything to keep you safe." Strong, quiet words.

That was something she was coming to understand. "I have a question you might not be able to answer. I know dragons have their secrets. If you made this for me, why not make something like this for yourself too?" Maybe he had and she just couldn't see it.

"Ah...it goes against dragon survival instinct to do that. If I'm attacked by dragon fire, I'll survive the blast. And once I blast back at an attacking dragon, their camouflage usually falls. We dinnae make things from dragon fire often in case they fall into the wrong hands. I willnae risk losing it when shifting. It's one of those ingrained things. But I want you to have this."

Because she was worth the risk were his unspoken words. She swallowed hard as she looked into his eyes. "When this is over...I want a life with you," she whispered. "I want a future—I want to mate with you." Because without him, her future would be stark and lonely. And they'd come too far to walk away from a future.

He stared at her in stunned silence for a moment before he kissed her swiftly and with a toe-curling possessiveness, stealing her breath away. "As soon as he's dead, we're returning home, love."

She nodded because she couldn't find her voice. Her home was wherever Lachlan was.

The door opened behind her and her bandmates spilled out even as Lachlan lifted her wrist and kissed it and the bracelet. "I'll be there the entire time. I'm ready for him. I willnae let anything happen to you or your sister. Or your crew."

"I know. We've got this. And look, I need to tell you something." She'd been holding off telling him what she was, but she was going to mate with this male. She loved him, even if she hadn't said the exact words. And she knew he loved her too, even if he hadn't said it either. They were meant to be together.

"Save it for after the show. I can see it's stressing you out, but I'm not pushing. We'll talk about what you are after."

"How'd you know that's what I wanted to talk about?"

"Because it's the only thing still between us." He kissed her again in that possessive way she felt to her core. "And I dinnae care what you are. You're mine, love. That's all that matters."

"Star!" Marley called from the end of the hallway, standing halfway in between the open doors that led outside.

Lachlan was right. They belonged to each other and that was all that mattered. She didn't want to just toss this information at him before the show. "We'll talk as soon as this is over. I've really got to go." She slid her robe off and handed it to him.

His eyes widened with a whole mess of emotions as he took in her costume, one of them raw heat. Though she hated to leave him even for a few minutes while they set up, she knew it was necessary as she hurried after her bandmates. They had a show to do. The most important show of their entire lives.

CHAPTER 28

As Star and her band stepped outside onto the roof, Star could hear what she hadn't been able to inside the upper floor of Cynara's building. There were thousands of people in the streets, their voices and laughter reaching up to her. Not to mention all the supernaturals spread out on the rooftop. Though they were all here as security and part of their backup, in case Oscar showed his face today.

Star prayed he did. She was amped up and ready for this fight. Ready to destroy him with her fire.

Considering the hard work Bella and Lola had put into spreading the word about the show—and considering how many people were in the streets for this afternoon concert—she figured he'd heard about the show by now. She didn't think he would be able to resist. Not after what she'd taken from him. Especially now, since Aurora was with her, right out in the open. Her sister was wearing a bright red dress with red feathers in her hair. She was a shining beacon, practically taunting him.

Star's costume wasn't any different really; she had on her signature purple, of course. A lycra bodysuit Bella had found God knew where, sparkly purple tights, and the ensemble was completed with kickass purple boots. The bodysuit had been chosen with her shifter form in mind—because when the time came, she might have to shift. That was the only part of the plan she was nervous about.

"I hope you guys are ready for the show of a lifetime!" Her sister's excited voice came over the microphone as she introduced the band on stage.

Okay, it was showtime. Star and the others raced up the set of stairs on the side of the stage to the sound of thousands of clapping and cheering fans down below. It was like the entire damn city had come. Someone had set up a huge screen across the street on a different building and tilted it downward so that everyone had a great view of the rooftop show.

Star waved with both hands, smiling broadly, and another cheer went up. She could see Lachlan out of the corner of her eye edging toward the stage. The sight of him eased some of her tension. She also saw King blending into the background on the other side of the rooftop, keeping an eye out on the streets below. He hadn't been thrilled about this plan but once the witches had agreed to spell the streets below from any fallout, he'd agreed. Plus, Star didn't think he'd been able to say no to Aurora, but that was a whole other thing she wasn't worrying about right now.

Her heart was in her throat as she strode up to her sister and took the outstretched microphone. A moment later Marley started tapping on the drums, jumping straight into their first song.

Star sang her heart out, dancing around on stage as if this was her last show—and it very well might be. The cheers from the crowd were constant, the energy feeding her, and she was tempted to release her fire now, to give them the best show ever. But she held back the flames, and tried to smother the tension inside her.

They'd already performed three songs and she'd expected Oscar's presence by now. As they started performing the fourth song, she glanced over at Aurora. Lachlan was right next to her, his big arms crossed over his chest, protecting her sister. Damn, she really loved that male.

As she belted out the chorus, she caught a glimpse of gold in the distance, a flash of something against the white-cloud backdrop. Star kept singing and looked to her right again. She saw the flash again, the brightness glinting under the sunlight. She looked over at Lachlan but he didn't appear to see anything as he scanned the skies.

When their eyes made contact, she jerked her head to the right, not caring what she looked like. She just wanted him to understand her meaning.

He straightened, and glared into the distance but it was clear he didn't see what she did.

So Oscar was camouflaged.

At that moment she spotted four, five, six more spots of gold and purple in the distance. They were only a few blocks away now and there could be more coming. Stepping back, she dropped the microphone and all pretense of singing.

"Get ready!" she shouted to her crew. Calling on all her inner fire, she created a giant flaming ball of purple and hurled it in the direction of Oscar—the huge obsidian patch across his left wing giving his identity away. Her fire arrowed straight for Oscar and his clanmates, but they dodged them, splitting up in all directions. One dragon dove low in between buildings and slammed into the invisible barrier below. She would have smiled at the sight but all her focus was on the incoming dragons. "To the west, right above the brewery building!" she shouted to Lachlan and his clanmates.

He raced for the edge of the building, shifting midair, his clothing shredding as he transformed into his gorgeous dragon form.

She was vaguely aware of screams and shouts below, but ignored it all as she hauled back and tossed another ball of flames at the incoming dragons.

She struck one dragon, her fire ricocheting off and hitting another. The firepower that fell beneath them dispersed against the invisible barrier, being absorbed and causing no threat to the humans directly below.

She realized the moment the dragons' camouflage dropped because they became clearer to her.

On a scream of rage at the clear sight of Oscar coming for her sister, Star let her fire take over, let her energy burst through her as her flaming wings emerged from her back.

She was aware of a whole lot of gasps going through the crowd but ignored them as she dove off the building, wings extended.

Aurora was right behind her, her dress in tatters as her own wings burst out behind her.

Two dragons dive-bombed straight for Star but she was ready. Flapping hard, she shot upward like a bullet, drawing the attacking dragons. As they raced after her, she twisted in midair and threw a ball of fire at one of them. Then the other.

Her aim was true, smashing both of them in the face.

One screeched in agony, spiraling downward under the onslaught, but the other shook it off and let out a roar.

She flew harder and faster, banking to the left as he shot fire at her. Out of the corner of her eye, she saw Lachlan battling with two dragons even as her sister threw wild fireballs at Oscar.

Below her, the humans stood stock-still, staring up at the battle, and she was pretty sure the witches had done something to everyone so they didn't stampede and get hurt. Because no one had moved.

She wanted to get to Aurora, to Lachlan, but had to take care of the dragon flying at her first.

Something pierced her shoulder—a dart. She pulled it out, but didn't feel any effects of what had to be poison. Lachlan had told her the poison was dragon specific and he hadn't been kidding. And that was when she saw the rider on the back of the dragon's back crouching low and nearly blending with the gold scales because of his clothing.

Another burst of rage shot through her, and she threw a ball of fire directly at the rider's midsection.

The male tumbled backward, falling off the dragon. She didn't bother to see where he fell as she flew straight at the dragon now. Fire shot out of her wings this time, in a huge swooping arc, arrowing straight at her enemy. He shot fire back at her, but she swooped under it and watched as her purple fire engulfed the dragon in a burst of flames.

Decades of untapped fire and power all came pouring out of her in a deluge as she fought to protect Lachlan, her sister, her friends and family and everyone below. The dragon's screams filled the air as it started falling toward the earth in a smoking, burning mass.

Lachlan felt the darts slamming into him even as he battled with the warrior dragon. The effects of the poison started pumping through his system but a shot of adrenaline pushed it back. He would not let his Star down. He wouldn't let Aurora down. They were going to destroy this cowardly dragon who used poison to fight his own kind.

His brother and clanmates were in battles of their own, their fire streaking across the sky in shocking, vivid waves of color. And King was somehow on the back of an attacking dragon, slicing through the beast's neck with a giant sword.

But there was another dragon flying straight at Star—who could apparently fly! She was so damn glorious, so stunning that he wanted nothing more than to just stare at her, to bathe in her beauty. But he had to protect her, had to protect his own people.

A rage like he'd only known once burst through him, and a brilliant blue fire emerged from his throat as he shot flames at the nearest dragon. The male incinerated, ash and dust flying down across the city and falling against the invisible barrier. He flew straight through the still tumbling ashes, fighting the pain of the poison pumping through his system.

Star had just killed one dragon and was arrowing straight for Oscar—who was in a battle of fire with Aurora. One that would end in the death of one of them.

Oscar was huge, as big as Lachlan, and breathing stream after stream of red-hot fire at Aurora. And she was fighting back with her own bright flames.

Aurora was strong but she was so young and Oscar's fire was pushing harder and harder against hers as he slowly won the battle.

No! Lachlan flew faster. If Star lost her sister, it would destroy her. That same rage built inside him as he flew like an arrow right at Oscar. He released another burst of blue-hot flames.

Oscar saw him and barrel-rolled, missing the brunt of his attack.

The blue fire hit the tip of one of his wings, burning it to nothing. The dragon screamed in agony, the screeches causing the humans below to scream in terror even though they didn't move.

Lachlan kept flying hard for Oscar, but Star was faster. She held a giant ball of fire in her hands and threw it directly at their enemy. Fire from her wings followed, arcing like bolts of lightning at the male. She was utterly magnificent, a fierce avenging warrior.

The bolts hit Oscar in the chest, sending him tumbling into a nearby building. Brick and stone flew in all directions as he slammed into the rooftop.

Aurora screamed something at him as she flew downward, raising another ball of fire in her hands.

Lachlan saw everything play out in slow motion as he flew at the male. His own fire built in his throat, but as he started to release another stream of flames, Aurora flew into his way.

Then he understood what she'd screamed at him.

My kill.

He banked to the right to go around her, wanting to help her bring this bastard down.

But Oscar turned to the right, focusing on Star, who'd landed on a building next to him, her own hands raised as if to call on more fire.

A burst of orange and red flames emerged from the bastard's throat, shooting directly at Star.

No! His dragon screamed even as Aurora released a ball of fire at Oscar.

Lachlan did the same, his blue fire slamming into Oscar's head as Aurora's fire incinerated his middle.

The dragon burst into flames, but Star flew backward under the impact of the red fire, her delicate form slamming into a neighboring building top.

Despite the poison pumping through his system, Lachlan arrowed toward her. The moment he crash-landed on the building, he shifted— and watched as Star's body burst into flames.

"Noooo!" he screamed, the echo of it ricocheting throughout the city. Agony engulfed him, a thousand times more painful than the poison searing his insides. "No!" He couldn't have lost her again. After thousands of years he'd finally found his mate again—knew it deep in his soul that Star had finally come back to him. He'd realized it days ago, had been too afraid to say anything to her in case she didn't feel it too.

But she was his morning star, come back to him. He fell to his knees, the raw agony of his loss ripping his chest apart. Star, his funny, fierce and protective Star. All she'd ever wanted to do was protect her family, to care for the people she loved.

And she was gone.

"Lachlan." He heard his brother's voice, then Aurora's gentle one behind him. He ignored them and stared at the ashes of Star.

"No!" he screamed again, unwilling to accept this fate. He screamed again and again, fire releasing from his throat in a wild wave of heat and anger at the unfairness of it all. What kind of fucked-up shite was this that he'd finally gotten his mate back only to have her torn from him again?

"Lachlan!" Star strode out of the ashes and rubble, naked, her brilliant purple wings ethereal but growing more solid by the second as she raced across the rooftop toward him.

He stared for a long moment, his fire gone even as his heart jumped into his throat. "Star?" he rasped out. She was alive. *Alive!*

He didn't even remember getting to his feet but suddenly she was in front of him, clutching onto his shoulders as he continued to stare in disbelief.

She sliced her palm and held out her bloody hand, rubbing it all over the wounds from the poison darts, but he batted her hand away and crushed her to him. "Star," he growled against her neck, overcome with too much emotion as he clutched her body against his. "My Star."

"Lachlan." Her own voice was thick.

"You're alive." Of course. She was a phoenix, rare and unique. Oh God, she was here and never leaving him again.

"I am, and I'm not going anywhere. Never, ever again, I swear it. I won't make the same mistake twice."

Her words registered in his brain. She knew the truth. "I've loved you for thousands and thousands of years. There was never anyone else for me after you. Never." He hadn't been able to touch another female. Not until he'd met Star. "I went into Hibernation because I couldnae stand the pain of losing you."

Nearby he was vaguely aware of Aurora and his brother on the ledge of the rooftop.

"I think he's delirious," Aurora murmured, watching them.

But Lachlan wasn't. He knew that his morning star had finally made her way back to him.

"I know," Star said to him. "I remember everything. I remember being a foolish human, but in the end I had planned to mate you. I was on my way to tell you but was killed. By my father, I think."

He closed his eyes, reliving the agony of finding her at the bottom of a cliff, her fragile body broken against jagged rocks. Everyone said she'd fallen and died far too young. He'd been so angry at the world, so angry at the unfairness of it all. He'd never suspected anyone of taking her life, much less her father. Her family had all mourned her deeply, their agony real. And she'd never had any enemies. She'd been a sweet, giving human he'd met by chance while in human form. She'd been fixing the broken leg of a goat, cooing at the little thing, and Lachlan had been completely enchanted by her. If he'd known that her father... Maybe it was better that he hadn't. It wouldn't have changed anything, and here she was, in his arms again.

"The fates gave us a second chance," she continued, tears in her eyes. "Gave me a second chance because I was such a fool to wait before. I am your morning star."

He felt her blood working through him, healing him as he pulled her even closer, his heart so full he feared it might burst. "I'm never letting you go again," he growled out. "I dinnae care where we live. I'll stay here. I'll give allegiance to another Alpha. Anything for you. Or we can find a new territory altogether. But I willnae live without you ever again."

"I'm ready to go home," she said, her throat thick with tears. "Scotland is calling me and I would never ask you to give allegiance to another. You're my mate, and if your clan accepts me, I want to be their Alpha as well."

"If they dinnae, we'll leave. You are all that matters. You're all that ever mattered." Lachlan turned to his brother. "Take care of this mess." Because he wasn't sticking around one second longer.

Cody simply nodded, his gaze on Star with a bit of awe. He'd known Danica, the human Lachlan had loved so long ago, and he'd liked the wisp of a female then too.

Star looked at her sister. "Aurora, are you okay—"

"He's dead and I'm fine. Go, be with your mate. You deserve this." Aurora's wings were still visible, pale blue flames against the sky.

Thank the gods, because Lachlan wasn't waiting to mate his Star. He'd do it right here in front of everyone, the need was so great.

"My place," Lachlan said as he stepped back and shifted to his dragon. It wasn't really his true home, but it was close and that was all that mattered.

Star jumped off the side of the building, her huge wings lifting her into the air. He followed after her, in complete and utter awe of the beauty of her phoenix.

His beautiful phoenix, risen from the ashes.

CHAPTER 29

Lachlan felt as if his heart would explode as they raced into the Garden District mansion. He had his mate back. He had his Star, something he'd never even imagined possible, not if he lived another thousand years. But she was here, the soul of the female he'd always loved returned once more.

Inside the house, they fell on each other, him wrapping his arms around her as she entwined her body around his. Her flames danced everywhere and his own indigo glow lit up the entire foyer. He couldn't hide his mating manifestation even if he wanted to. But he did not.

He was ready to claim his female. The female who had stolen his heart millennia ago.

"I was coming to tell you that day that I wanted to be your mate," she said as if she didn't quite believe the words coming out of her mouth. "And I've been having dreams for the last year. I thought at first that they were just strange dreams brought on by who knows what, but in the last week I've come to realize they're memories. And then today I knew the truth even if I didn't fully understand until I rose from the ashes. When I did, all my memories came flooding back, every single one of us together." Her voice cracked on the last word as she cupped his face, stroking her fingers over him as if she couldn't believe he was real.

"I woke up a year ago. Probably when your dreams started." No wonder he'd been so drawn to her, been so called by her music.

She leaned in at the same time he did, their mouths connecting as he pinned her to the nearest wall. A painting fell to the floor next to them, but he didn't care.

She moaned against his mouth as he cupped one of her breasts. He wanted to stroke every inch of her body, kiss every sensitive area until she was writhing underneath him.

But first, he had to claim her. There was no more waiting.

Somehow he drew his head back, needing to tell her what he'd never gotten to tell her when she'd been human. He'd been waiting to tell her until after she agreed to be his. "In dragon matings, if you die, I die. And vice versa." He had to tell her the truth, needed to make sure she understood what the risk would be if she mated with him.

She clutched onto his shoulders and kissed him hard in response.

That was all he needed. He reached between their bodies, found her slick and ready for him.

There would be thousands of years of foreplay after this. But heat was riding him hard, the need to take her a wild, living thing pushing against all of his senses.

"Now," she growled against his mouth, just as desperate as he was. "We've waited long enough."

She rolled her hips, pushing the lower half of her body up slightly so that she was centered on top of his cock.

Oh, fuck him. He thrust upward, grabbing her ass with one hand as he kept her pinned against the wall. They fucked in a raw, wild mating. He was vaguely aware of the plaster cracking beneath their bodies before they fell onto the ground.

She wrapped her legs tight around him as he pinned her to the floor, meeting him stroke for stroke as he thrust into her over and over. Purple fire covered every surface, the glow beautiful, just like his Star. He loved the sight of her flames covering him, as if she was claiming him in return.

His canines descended, the need to pierce her with his teeth, to mark her, to claim her now and forever overwhelming. Without thinking, he buried his mouth in her neck and let his instincts take over, marking her even as she dug her fingers into his back, hard.

The pleasure/pain of her nails spurred him on.

She cried out as he bit her.

"Lachlan." Hearing his name on her lips just about had him climaxing inside her but he held off. He wouldn't find release until she did.

Instead he reached between their bodies, all his muscles pulling taut as her inner walls tightened around his hard length. When he started teasing her clit, she called out his name again. Hold off, he ordered himself.

As soon as he found the right tempo, she started coming around him, all heat and fire.

He lost himself then, finding release at the same time as she did, his climax punching through him until they were a sweaty, unmoving pile on the foyer floor. Spent and sated.

He had no idea how much time had passed when she finally pushed gently at his shoulder.

Groaning, he rolled off her and fell onto his back, staring up at the huge chandelier above them.

"I love you," she said, tilting her head in his direction. "I can't remember if I said it."

He rolled over to look at her, drinking in every inch of her face, memorizing it. "I love you back, lass. I always have."

"And I always will," she finished, reaching for him.

It was true. He had waited a lifetime, thousands of lifetimes, for her and he would do it again. She was worth the wait, worth everything. He gathered her in his arms and raced up the stairs. They weren't even close to done.

CHAPTER 30

Lachlan strode out onto the back porch, his heart skipping a beat to see the sadness on Star's face. "What is it?" he demanded as he hurried across the patio of her crew's place toward her where she sat with all of her people. He would destroy anyone who'd put that look on her face.

"Nothing," she said, a smile tugging at her lips when she saw him.

He sat on one of the chairs and pulled her into his lap, wrapping his arms around her. He was constantly touching her now, unable to get enough of her. They'd mated a week ago and they'd only left the house twice—both times so Star could play a charity show with her band. After the insanity in the Quarter, and the fact that she would be leaving soon, they'd decided to put on the charity shows for the city.

Other than that, he and Star hadn't left her bedroom. And the only reason they'd come out today was because Star had been hungry and had wanted to personally check on her crew before they packed up and left. Otherwise he'd have stayed buried deep inside her for another week. Or five.

"We've just decided who's staying and who's going with you guys," Aurora said, looking between the two of them. "And Star is feeling a bit blue."

"Ah." He'd known this was coming. He and Star were leaving this evening with his clanmates and whoever wanted to come back to Scotland with them. His private jet was on standby whenever they finally figured things out. "So who is coming with us?"

"Marley, Athena, Taya and Kartini."

So the bandmates were all coming, but the others—Bella, Lola, Axel, Brielle and Harlow—were staying. And of course Aurora.

He knew this would be hard on Star but he liked to think that he would make the move worth it. He also knew that she wasn't surprised by this either—she'd already told him she knew who was staying and who was going. She'd told him this morning that her warriors had come to her, all separately, and had told her they would be staying to keep an eye on Aurora until the time she was ready to mate or to start her own little pack. They knew Star would never be truly at peace unless there were people watching after her baby sister. For that, he loved her people as much as she did.

"You guys are welcome to visit anytime you want," he told the ones who weren't coming with them. And he hoped that one day in the future, some would come live with them as well, so his Star would have even more of her people at her side.

"I'm definitely taking you up on that," Bella said, crossing the distance and pulling Star into a tight hug even though she was still sitting in Lachlan's lap.

"Why don't you guys leave in the morning and let's have a party tonight?" Lola asked, eyebrows raised.

"I think that can be arranged." Anything to make his female happy. And it wasn't as if she'd even packed, he thought in amusement.

Star leaned back and kissed him on the cheek. "Thank you," she whispered. Then she turned to look at her friends, her family. "I can fully say I want to get a buzz on, so let's get some good stuff for this party."

"I'm going to make a few phone calls," Bella said, clapping her hands together. "I'll make sure we have enough champagne—I think Cynara will hook us up with some stuff from her stash."

"Can I steal my sister for a minute?" Aurora asked as she approached them.

"Of course." Though Lachlan hated to do it, he released his hold on Star. Soon they would be headed home and right now she needed to spend as much time with her family as possible.

He leaned back as the sisters walked away, his heart aching for the pain he sensed coming from his mate. He wished he could take it all away. That was another revelation to him, the mating link he felt between them. It was strung so tight between them, as if it was a physical thing. Combined with the new scent on both of them—the one that proclaimed to the whole world that they were taken—he felt more at ease being around other people knowing she was fully claimed.

And in that moment he felt like the luckiest male in the world.

"I still can't believe she came back to you," Cody said as he sat next to him, squeezing Lachlan's shoulder once.

"Aye, me neither."

"It's a miracle." There was a bit of awe in his brother's voice. "You are a lucky dragon, brother."

"That I am." He didn't say anything more because he didn't trust his voice in that moment. His mate had come back to him. Something he still hadn't fully wrapped his mind around yet.

He wished his brother Rhys was here to meet her, to see that miracles did happen. But Lachlan wouldn't dwell on that. The only thing he was focused on was the future. With his mate by his side.

* * *

"I probably should have called first," Star said as she and Lachlan approached King's headquarters in the Quarter.

"I dinnae think he'll mind," Lachlan said. The Alpha seemed to have an affinity for Aurora and Star.

"He's probably just going to be glad to have us out of his territory."

"Me more than you," Lachlan said, laughing lightly. The other Alpha hadn't minded Star's presence at all.

"True. He will likely be sad to lose me, since I am made of pure awesomeness. It will be a true loss to the city," she said cheekily. "You, however?" She shrugged, giving him a mischievous smile.

He kissed the top of his mate's head as the heavy door swung open. The female wolf who had guided him to the inner sanctum to meet King before was the one who opened it. She lifted an eyebrow. "Can I help you?"

"I would like to talk to King if he's available," Star said, all sugar and sweetness.

Which earned a real smile from the wolf. "Of course. I've been given instructions that you or your sister are always welcome." Then she shot a level look at Lachlan. "I'm only allowing you in because you've mated with this badass."

Star bit back a laugh at that.

The female looked at Star again. "I'm a huge fan, by the way. I saw you perform in Austin last year and you were amazing. Seriously, one of the best performances I've ever seen."

Her cheeks flushed. "Thank you."

The wolf nodded then beckoned them to follow. They found King in the courtyard, with his shirt off, sparring with four wolves at once. They were attacking him with various weapons and he was dodging all of them, a practical whirlwind. His speed was impressive but when Lachlan saw the awe on Star's face, as if she was admiring the male, he frowned.

She looked up at him. "What?"

"Nothing," he muttered.

"Are you being weirdly jealous?" she asked, quiet enough for his ears only.

"His moves aren't that impressive."

She patted his chest once and looked back at the sparring session.

King called a halt to it, however, and dismissed his wolves, surprising him. Lachlan had expected him to make them wait, since they'd dropped by unexpectedly.

"You're here to tell me you're leaving?" King asked quietly, looking between them.

She nodded. "We're headed back to Scotland. We're headed home."

"Your sister—"

"Is staying," Star said before King could finish.

Lachlan liked that Aurora was the first thing the male thought of. It told him all he needed to know about this Alpha wolf and his intentions toward Aurora.

The relief rolling off King was a palpable thing.

"I've seen the way you watch her," Star continued. "And I'm not here to give you a big-sister speech, but I am here to tell you that she's an artist. And yes she is a fighter and more than capable, as you've seen, but she has a gentle soul. Whoever finally claims her heart had better be gentle with it."

His smile was genuine. "I know."

"Good. Now, if I *was* here to give you the big-sister talk, I would tell you to be good to her, and that if you're not, I'll rip your heart out and incinerate it with my fire. But I don't think I need to tell you that, because you're a good male."

"And I dinnae need to tell you that I would rain fire down on the city if you hurt my mate's sister," Lachlan added.

"I won't hurt her." There was a wealth of truth in King's voice. "I'd gut myself first."

It was clear that was what Star had needed to hear. Lachlan knew she hated leaving her sister, but Aurora needed to spread her wings. She needed to be allowed to come into her own. And King was a good male—so good that if Aurora rejected him, she would still be allowed to live and grow here, under his protection. Lachlan could clearly see that.

Star pulled the big Alpha into a hug, definitely taking him by surprise, but King patted her back gently, if awkwardly. Lachlan restrained his dragon from reacting like a total jackass at the sight of his female hugging another male. He could be understanding for two seconds. Probably.

"Thank you for the hospitality. Thank you for having my crew's back. We're not all leaving, however. A few of my people are staying behind with Aurora." Star stepped away and wrapped her arm tight around Lachlan, as if she knew he needed her touch.

"They have safe harbor here as long as they need. Oh, I spoke to Léonie. She'll be returning soon and is looking forward to seeing Aurora. She's still dark for the most part, but she promised to contact you as soon as possible."

Star smiled at the wolf. "I forget that she goes by Léonie now. To us, she'll always be Aunt Cliona."

"She saw some of the footage from the battle and was quite impressed with both of you."

Star leaned closer to Lachlan then, wrapping her arms tighter around him. "I'm glad she's allied with you."

"And you have an ally with my clan, for life," Lachlan said, holding a hand out to the wolf. That male had jumped into the battle with Oscar's clan and killed one himself. He'd given Star shelter in exchange for nothing. Lachlan would always have the male's back.

King nodded. "You do as well."

And that was that.

"Oh, we're having a little party at the house tonight. Mainly our crew, but a few others, so if you want to stop by before we head out, feel free," Star said before they left. "Aurora will definitely be in attendance."

King nodded once, a smile transforming his hard face. "I might. It's been a pleasure having you in the city. I'm sure it won't be the same without you."

Star grinned. "I certainly hope not."

Lachlan wrapped his arm tight around her shoulders as they headed out. New Orleans wouldn't be the same without her for certain, but now Scotland was calling her home. "Once we get back to Scotland, I plan to hole up with you for at least a week."

"At least... Hey, is it true that dragons have big hoards of gold and stuff?" she asked as they stepped out onto the sunlit sidewalk.

"Aye. I've got a whole pile of it. Why?"

"I kind of want to roll around in it. Like Scrooge McDuck. But naked."

He didn't know who Scrooge McDuck was, but the idea amused him. Lachlan threw back his head and laughed, ignoring the few looks from passersby on the sidewalk. "I can definitely arrange that. And you will most definitely be naked when you do."

"I'm totally on board with that."

CHAPTER 31

Sitting in Lachlan's lap, Star looked out at all her friends, her family having a good time at the party, and felt something shift inside her. It had been easy enough to set everything up in the backyard—and even the chickens were strolling around pretty as you please, not one bit concerned that they were surrounded by shifters.

Even King had shown up, and though he was currently talking to Cynara and Justus, his gaze kept straying to Aurora, who was nestled against Axel, her head on his shoulder. Star and her crew all knew the relationship with Axel and Aurora was platonic—they were like siblings—but it was clear King didn't know. Or maybe he didn't care, because he was not a fan of her lion right now. And Star knew Axel well—he was very aware of the Alpha's glares and it seemed to spur him on even more. Oh, she was going to miss her mischievous lion so much.

"I'm fairly certain that cat is going to use up one of his nine lives soon," Lachlan murmured into her ear, as if he'd read her mind.

She let out a startled laugh and turned to her mate before kissing him on the mouth. God, she loved this male.

"You guys are so cute." Greer's voice tore her back to the present as the female and her mate sat across from them, all smiles.

Reaper simply fist-bumped Lachlan once before settling back in his chair.

"I still can't believe you're a phoenix," Greer said quietly, staring at Star with a bit of awe. "That's so amazing. I always thought your kind were myths until Léonie... Oh, I guess Léonie is your aunt, right?"

"Yes." Star didn't bother telling Greer that she'd always thought of Léonie by her given name. It didn't really matter. "I was hoping to see her before we leave."

"I know," Greer said, sympathy in her gaze. "But you'll be back to visit, I hope?"

"We will," Lachlan answered before she could, making her snuggle up against him even more.

Star knew that she wasn't leaving for good. And she knew that someone who was as long-lived as her would have to be open to change. And she was, always had been. But that didn't make the leaving portion any easier.

"Good." She nodded, taking a sip of her wine.

"Do either of you know what that blue fire was?" Lachlan asked quietly, for their ears only. He didn't have to specify what he meant either; a good portion of the population had seen it.

Star knew he'd been wondering about it—she had been too. That fire of his had burned so hot, so bright, and with laser precision, destroying everything in its path.

"Ah, yes." Reaper nodded, exchanging a look with his mate.

"It only appears when your mate is in danger," Greer continued. "It's a defense mechanism for dragons. And it doesn't *always* appear even when your mate is in danger—just in dire situations, it seems. Or it could be based on the emotional state of the dragon emitting it. Basically, there's no science to it."

"Thank you," Lachlan said simply.

Star was glad he finally knew what that fire was. The knowledge seemed to settle him. She was coming to learn that her mate did not like surprises and he liked to be in control.

A blur of motion appeared behind them and suddenly Lola—wild, rainbow-colored hair and all—was in Star's lap. Clearly she didn't care that Star was still in Lachlan's lap. She wrapped her arms around them both and kissed Star loudly on the cheek. "I'm going to miss you, and I've decided that I forgive you for taking her from us," she said to Lachlan. Then she gave him a smacking kiss on his cheek too, making the male snort.

"I think you have imbibed too much alcohol, Lola."

This made Lola snicker as Bella tugged her out of their lap—and then Bella tackle-hugged Star and Lachlan too.

Star wrapped her arms around her best friend, unable to believe they wouldn't be living in the same house anymore, let alone the same continent. Change was good, she reminded herself. And she loved Lachlan more than life itself.

"I'm gonna take care of your baby sister, promise," Bella murmured. She'd known Star a long damn time and clearly knew where her head was at.

"I know. Thank you." Her throat tightened and she couldn't get any more out.

"All right, lasses," Lachlan said, standing so that they all had to move. "Star, I think it's time for you to make the rounds before your crew all jumps on us at once."

"They can all jump on me," Cody said as he approached, beer in hand, a wicked grin firmly in place.

Lachlan simply gave his brother a dry look even as Star laughed.

"I think you're right." She kissed her mate on his lips, a soft claiming before stepping away.

He sat back down with Greer and Reaper so she headed off across the yard, stopping where the twins were talking with Avery and Avery's dragons. The human female hadn't been kidding. She'd brought four of them plus her younger brothers to the party. Three of the dragons and her brothers were all mingling, if they were all a bit on the quiet side. But one of those dragons was ancient, brooding and most definitely into Avery, if the mere two feet he allowed between them was any indication. Unfortunately for him, it was clear that Avery had no clue.

As Star approached, Harlow wrapped an arm around her shoulders and pulled her close. "Gonna miss you, girl." Probably some of the only words she'd heard out of the quiet tiger all night.

"Gonna miss you too. Though I won't miss your chatterbox ways." Harlow rolled her eyes.

But Brielle laughed loudly. "God, right? I can never get her to shut up."

Avery giggled into her champagne glass as she looked between them. "Are you excited about going to Scotland?" she asked as the laughter died down.

"Very. And if you ever want to visit, you're more than welcome to." She was the Alpha's mate now; she figured she could invite anyone she wanted.

Avery's eyes widened. "Seriously?"

"Seriously."

"I've always wanted to go. And I thought...with everything that happened to the world, it would just never happen. Not anytime soon anyway."

"Well the invite is there." Star wasn't sure how air travel would work. There was still some commercial travel, though on a smaller scale. However, she'd be heading to Scotland on Lachlan's private jet.

Avery beamed at her as Axel and Aurora joined them. And oh no, Axel greeted Avery in a very friendly, teasing manner that got the hackles up of the big male next to her. When Axel wrapped his arms around her and pulled her into a hug, she worried the dragon would incinerate her lion right then and there.

As Aurora said something to Brielle, Star shot Axel a look that said *behave.*

He simply grinned and winked at her as he wrapped a casual arm around Avery's shoulders—and left it there.

Lachlan joined her at that moment, pulling Star close. "Now your cat has lost two lives. Poor, poor, lion. A dragon and wolf are now plotting his dismemberment and death."

Turning her face into Lachlan's chest, she barely smothered a giggle. In that moment, she knew her crew would be fine without her. Though Axel might get into a few tussles sooner than later. She was going to miss all of them desperately, but if they remained here for good, they would thrive.

She had no doubt. And she was going to live her life and be happy with her dragon. Her mate. It had taken millennia and they'd found each other again. Being with him was exactly where she was meant to be.

CHAPTER 32

Star couldn't fight the nerves buzzing through her as she flew next to Lachlan, her phoenix fire bright, a shining purple beacon against the gray morning sky as they headed deeper into his territory. They'd flown on a private jet into a small airport, then he'd told her they'd be flying in their shifted forms to his castle. His brother, clanmates and her own people had driven there ahead of them and were helping to prepare the way.

Lachlan wanted everyone to see what she was, and to know that they were a unit. It was hard not to be touched by the male's thoughtfulness. Because the truth was, she was worried that a dragon clan wouldn't accept her as the Alpha Laird's mate. Sure, they had the whole fire thing in common, but dragon clans had been very insular until recently. And phoenix fire could destroy a dragon if the phoenix was powerful enough.

His brother and Teague and Cian had accepted her, but a whole clan? That was a different story.

At least it was crystal clear that their animals fully accepted each other—Star's wings of fire were now shot through with flashes of indigo and Lachlan's scales now had jagged streaks of the deepest purple intertwining with his own indigo. They were true mates, now and forever.

As he flew lower she followed suit, her heart brimming to full with happiness at the sight of the beautiful green landscape and mountains below them. The landscape was as rugged and wild as the male flying next to her. This place called to her soul almost as much as Lachlan did. After she'd resurrected from the ashes, more and more memories had emerged every day and she very clearly remembered this place. Her home.

Their wings disturbed the long blades of grass they passed over, creating a ripple effect as they arced up another hill. As they crested over the top, her heart caught in her throat at the sight of his giant stone castle sprouting up out of the mountain, looking as if it had always been there. But what really caught her gaze was the sight of the huge formation of men and women lined up out front. They were at attention all along the drawbridge and in the cobblestone bailey out front. Her heart rate kicked up at the rows of men in kilts, of all his clanmates waiting for them, torches lighting the walls and turrets.

And…was that bagpipes?

On the wind she caught the sound of "Highland Cathedral" being played and it brought tears to her eyes as they flew down together, a unified front. She knew the show and bagpipes were for him, but she still loved everything about this proper greeting.

Moments after they landed, Lachlan shifted back to his human form and suddenly Cody was there with clothing, his demeanor respectful and serious. No longer was he the teasing younger brother as he handed Lachlan a kilt, sporran and other articles of clothing. He was a clansman giving his laird the respect he was due.

Her mate dressed quickly, with the efficiency of a male who'd done this many times before. A warrior returning home.

Star pulled her wings in and ordered her fire to die down as well. On the plane ride, Kartini had braided Star's hair in an intricate crown "fitting for a queen," and Star had opted to wear loose black pants and a flowy black top that had been created to fit with her wings in mind. Staring out at everyone, she was overwhelmed at all the curious faces in front of them, watching as if they were waiting for something.

Suddenly a female strode up to her, a genuine, if curious smile on her face as she bowed and handed Star a sash with Lachlan's clan colors on it. "My lady," she murmured.

The "lady" took Star off guard for a moment, but Lachlan simply thanked the female and placed the sash over Star's head and wrapped it around her shoulders before kissing her soundly for all to see.

A cheer went up around them as he deepened it, making her laugh against his mouth. Maybe that was all they'd been waiting for.

"Is it true that you don't wear anything under your kilt?" she murmured as they parted lips. She hadn't been paying attention to him getting dressed, she'd been too distracted by the clan and the gorgeous backdrop of the castle.

His grin was pure wicked. "You'll just have to find out, love."

Oh, she planned to. As soon as they were alone, she was going to have her wicked way with this male over and over. Hopefully on top of his pile of treasure.

Before she could respond, they were greeted by his clanmates, the males and females hugging her as if they'd known her their entire lives, completely welcoming her, this stranger, into their family as a long-lost friend.

In that moment she knew her fears had been for nothing—this was her home, and her place was with Lachlan.

As long as she had him, everything else would work itself out.

ACKNOWLEDGMENTS

First off, I owe a big thanks to Claire Robinson, Erin McRae, and Toni & Gary Anderson for reading over my Scottish phrases. Any and all mistakes are my own. I'm also incredibly thankful to Kaylea Cross who helped me plot out this book during our yearly plotting getaway and who has listened to me brainstorm random ideas for my Ancients Rising series for ages. I'm also grateful for such a thorough editor, Julia Ganis, who helps me keep everything on track. For Sarah, thank you for beta reading and all the other behind the scenes stuff that you do! Jaycee, once again, I love this cover AND the whole concept for the series. For my readers, who wanted more after the Darkness series, this is definitely for you guys! Thank you for all the encouraging emails and messages.

BOOKLIST

Ancients Rising Series
Ancient Protector
Ancient Enemy
Ancient Enforcer

Darkness Series
Darkness Awakened
Taste of Darkness
Beyond the Darkness
Hunted by Darkness
Into the Darkness
Saved by Darkness
Guardian of Darkness
Sentinel of Darkness
A Very Dragon Christmas
Darkness Rising

Deadly Ops Series
Targeted
Bound to Danger
Chasing Danger
Shattered Duty
Edge of Danger
A Covert Affair

Endgame Trilogy
Bishop's Knight
Bishop's Queen
Bishop's Endgame

ABOUT THE AUTHOR

Katie Reus is the *New York Times* and *USA Today* bestselling author of the Red Stone Security series, the Darkness series and the Deadly Ops series. She fell in love with romance at a young age thanks to books she pilfered from her mom's stash. Years later she loves reading romance almost as much as she loves writing it.

However, she didn't always know she wanted to be a writer. After changing majors many times, she finally graduated summa cum laude with a degree in psychology. Not long after that she discovered a new love. Writing. She now spends her days writing dark paranormal romance and sexy romantic suspense. For more information on Katie please visit her website: https://katiereus.com

Printed in Great Britain
by Amazon

47021365R00154